WITNESS

JEFFREY VANKE

AUTHOR OF
THE BERLIN DECEPTION

ISBN-13: 978-1484065785
ISBN-10: 1484065786

Cover design by Mark Ching.

for Rebecca Luttrell Vanke

Loving and Devoted Mother,
Model of Right from Wrong

Twenty years after the crucifixion of Joshua of Nazareth, known as Jesus to the Greeks, the people of Israel are bitterly divided. Aristocratic Sadducees control much of the country's wealth and religious power. Opposed to them, the Pharisees want to change Jewish doctrine to recognize an afterlife, but conservative Pharisees argue with progressive Pharisees about almost everything else. The followers of Joshua disagree about whether Joshua was the next Anointed One, a Messiah – and about which matters more, to serve the poor or to honor the late Joshua correctly. Above them all, Roman Emperor Claudius and his local deputy Felix will do anything to maintain their own control.

Palestine

Year 51, Current Era

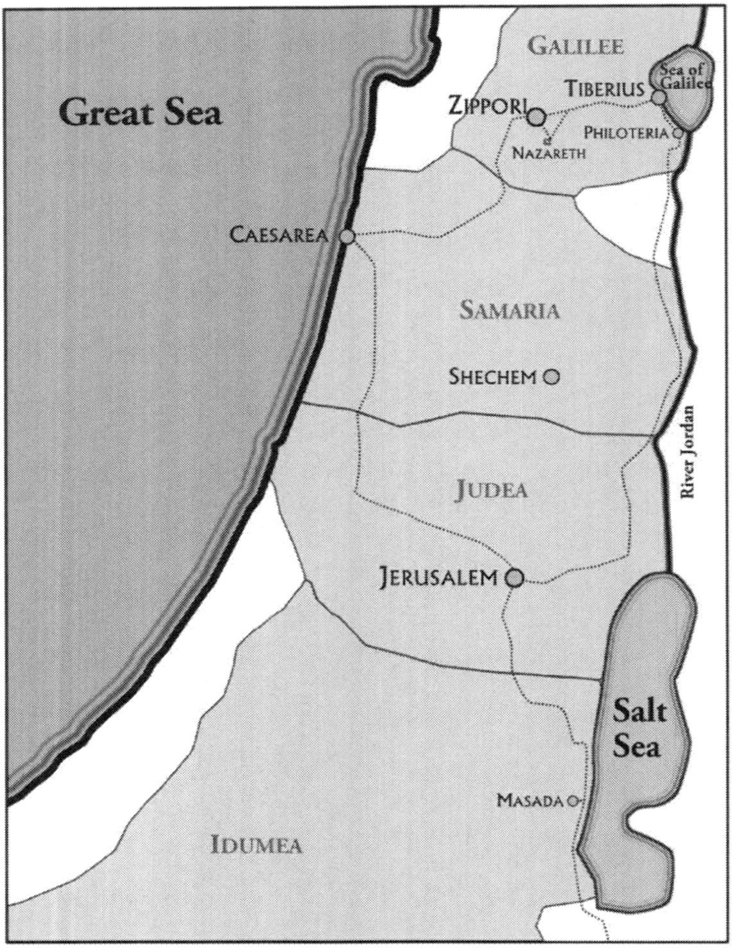

CHAPTER ONE

Late December, Year 51
Nazareth

"Burn!" In the black of midnight, a voice whispered through a wicked grin, under the makeshift hood of a gray woolen blanket. "Burn, Daniel! And your arrogance with you!"

One hand held the short handle of a small iron coal pan, while the other lifted the lid. Glowing orange coals burned brighter in the breeze, flickering dimly against the stone house wall just inches away. The hillside rose at the back of the house, bringing the roof within a man's reach. The flame keeper chuckled ominously yet softly and held the coal pan close, hiding its glow from any witnesses in the pitch-black cold. Most in Nazareth were already asleep under the cloudy sky, including Daniel and his family inside the house.

The flame keeper found the spot where mortar was missing around a rafter of the flat roof. Fingers filled the long thin crack with straw and then spooned in hot coals until the first straw burst into flame. "On the second try – burn this time!" the flame keeper whispered and frowned. The small coals from the previous night had gone cold without lighting the rafter. After briefly admiring the little fire, the keeper closed the coal pan lid and hurried away.

The Next Afternoon

"Papa Aaron, what if our enemies destroy the Nazareth Scroll before it can be copied?" thirteen-year-old Elisha asked after another long silence on their twenty-mile walk to Nazareth.

Aaron of Jerusalem knew that Elisha resented today's leg of their journey. The evening before, they had argued over Elisha's desire to stay behind in Tiberius until Aaron passed back through. Elisha had never seen so many stonemasons at work, and he wanted to stay and observe their trade. He still shared his adoptive father's interest in the Nazareth Scroll and what it could teach them about Joshua of Nazareth, known to the Greeks as Jesus. But Elisha was less optimistic that they could get access to the scroll or its author, Joshua's old disciple Daniel. And nothing fascinated Elisha like skilled trades, especially masonry. The entire walk today, Elisha had barely spoken to Aaron, and as usual, he called his adoptive father by his given name when he was upset with him.

"We'll do what we can," answered Aaron.

"Will you work less hard to protect the Scroll if you don't like how it answers the question?" asked Elisha.

"I have asked myself the same thing," Aaron replied. He knew what Elisha meant. Aaron was very friendly with Martha, a young widow who lived on their street in Jerusalem. He wanted to marry her, and Elisha kept repeating that he hoped she could become his new mother. Even though Aaron's sentiments toward Martha were less intense than those he'd felt for his first betrothed seven years earlier, he felt purer and more selfless in his affections for Martha.

But so far, they could not bring themselves to wed. Although they both admired Joshua of Nazareth, Martha went farther. She believed that Joshua was the next Anointed One, a Messiah, like King David and all the other ancient Jewish kings. Recently, Martha had even joined those who said that a resurrected Joshua controlled who could enter heaven. Her beliefs were too much for Aaron, and the difference was too great for Martha as well. So they remained kindly and even vaguely hopeful in their daily interactions, yet not too hopeful. As soon as Aaron heard about the Nazareth Scroll, written by Joshua's disciple Daniel, he raised his hopes that it would prove him correct and convince Martha to stop viewing Joshua as an

Anointed One. The Nazareth Gospel might remove the obstacles to his union with Martha.

Aaron kept walking and left Elisha's question unanswered. He was tall, with jet-black hair and eyes, and a tall, thin nose. In the style of Jews and gentiles alike, Aaron's hair was cut very short, and his face was shaved. His facial expressions were refined, and already in his late twenties, Aaron bore a look of patience. His posture was elegant and upright from his aristocratic upbringing. In recent years as a salt dealer, though, Aaron's fingers had widened with muscle and callus, and he had developed a slight slouch from lifting and carrying the heavy amphora vases. When he remembered this, Aaron pulled his shoulders back and stood taller as he walked.

Aaron had not yet told Elisha what he had learned the previous day in Tiberius from an old friend who worked for the Roman deputy procurator. After they reached Nazareth, they would stand in the path of immediate danger from one of the many enemies of the Nazareth Scroll. Some members of Joshua's churches did not like what they heard about the Scroll and its author Daniel. Beyond these were each of the groups responsible for Joshua's crucifixion twenty years ago – Sadducees, the conservative Pharisees, the royal Herod family, and even the Romans themselves. Now one of them had a plan to destroy the Nazareth Scroll – and more. Aaron needed to keep the secret after they entered Nazareth, which meant he needed to keep the secret from his impatient thirteen-year-old son Elisha.

Elisha's wisdom belied his boyish looks. At age thirteen, his short height and young voice had not yet grown into manhood, although his physical strength was impressive, by nature and by lifting in the salt trade. Strangers often underestimated Elisha, and Aaron had taught him to use that to his advantage. With impressive intuition, Elisha observed people's unspoken concerns, and he learned to ask childish questions to gain more help and information, whether in business, or in Aaron's work as the informal neighborhood judge, or in helping the poor. While Elisha played the child's part, he and Aaron would exchange knowing looks. Father and son were a great team. Aaron was thankful every day to have been the one who found Elisha and took him in.

Aaron and Elisha were latecomers to the six-week-old mass pilgrimage to Nazareth. Word had spread to Jerusalem and beyond: Back in Nazareth, an early disciple was telling and writing the life and teachings of Joshua of Nazareth, known to the Greeks as Jesus.

The man's name was Daniel, and he had been a childhood friend of Joshua and then his disciple. After Joshua's crucifixion by Pontius Pilate, Daniel returned to his wife and child in Nazareth, and there he lived for twenty years. This year, after the spring planting, Daniel began to write his account of Joshua of Nazareth. The locals were excited, and word spread to the next town, and then the next, throughout Galilee and Judea. From what Aaron had heard, after the autumn harvest and winter planting, many followers of Joshua had undertaken the trek to the tiny village of Nazareth, forming a spontaneous pilgrimage in tents. They wanted to learn from Daniel, and to hear stories of Joshua's childhood. Daniel had known Joshua even before Joshua's younger brothers and sisters were born of Miriam and Joseph. He would have much to reveal.

Above all, better than anyone in Jerusalem, Daniel could answer the question that divided Joshua's followers. Did Joshua of Nazareth claim himself to be the next Jewish Anointed One, a Messiah? The Jews were divided three ways over Joshua. First were those like the Sadducees who decried Joshua as a false prophet. Second were those who liked Joshua of Nazareth as a great teacher. Finally were the Jews who saw Joshua as the first Anointed One in centuries. Joshua's oppressors were murdering some of Joshua's followers. The Pharisees were divided against themselves. Fear and anger poisoned hearts on all sides.

Something had to give, Aaron knew. If the Lord had finally sent another Messiah and heir to King David in the person of Joshua of Nazareth, then the Jews who denied this were rejecting the Lord, or at the very least were blind to the truth. Yet if Joshua was merely a teacher, or worse a false prophet, then the

Jews who viewed him as an Anointed One were in serious error. At each year's Passover pilgrimage to Jerusalem, thousands and thousands of Jews debated this question more vigorously than the year before.

Suddenly, this man Daniel of Nazareth wanted to answer the question, on the oldest authority anyone would ever offer – his own experience of Joshua's entire lifetime and teaching. After two decades of near silence, finally someone from Joshua's earliest years was speaking up to the rest of Israel. At the very least, Daniel could testify whether Joshua had claimed himself to be an Anointed One, and Daniel had greater authority on this point than could be claimed by the younger disciples and siblings and scribes in Jerusalem and elsewhere.

As one of the golden-rule Pharisees, who were sympathetic to Joshua's teachings, Aaron was excited. For him, it went far beyond the Anointed question. As much as anyone, Aaron understood the power of the written word. Memories differed and witnesses died, but the word endured. How else but through their scripture had the Jews held together for centuries under the laws of Moses and the teachings of the prophets? Most of Joshua's disciples knew almost nothing of Joshua's life until his final year. This was true of the one account that Aaron had seen, written in Greek by someone named Mark. Now there would be a much more complete testimony from someone who had known the whole life of Joshua of Nazareth! It was supposedly being written in Aramaic, the native language of Joshua and most of his Jewish followers.

Aaron was also worried, even scared. From Jerusalem to Galilee, various authorities were upset that this Nazareth man Daniel might lay a written foundation and direction for Joshua's followers. Even within the fractured Pharisee movement, composed of part-time scholars and teachers of the law like Aaron, the conservative Pharisees, the ones who opposed Joshua's followers, were very agitated about the news from Nazareth.

Aaron and Elisha walked beside the three donkeys that carried their belongings. These were mostly sacks of rock salt from the Salt Sea cliffs, which Aaron had brought to sell along their journey. With thick cloud cover in the shortest days of winter, even the early afternoon sky was a dark shade of white. The low clouds looked full of snow, but none fell, and the road was dusty and dry, since the rains were late this year in the north. Occasional groves of trees broke the rocky landscape. Grasses and shrubs were dry, many of them stripped of all green by goats and sheep in their desperate search for food in the northern drought.

When Aaron and Elisha reached the side path to tiny Nazareth, they turned left. Aaron guessed they had about an hour or two to go. The donkeys managed the rocky path without much difficulty. Aaron glanced down the main road behind them and saw nothing.

"Look!" Elisha said, pointing in the same direction.

Aaron stopped and squinted, but still he saw nothing. Years of reading the scriptures had dimmed his once keen eyesight, already before age thirty. "What do you see?"

"Camel riders," said Elisha. "I think they are traveling toward us. Fast."

Aaron worried. He planned to tell Elisha tonight about the danger that would come down that road tomorrow, as Aaron had heard it described by his friend in Tiberius. The Roman Procurator Antonius Felix had decided to take action against the Nazareth Scroll. Felix wanted it destroyed. Not only that, he also wanted Nazareth's entire pilgrim encampment disbanded. In fact, Felix was planning to send a Roman cavalry to Nazareth, prepared to massacre the pilgrims if they did not obey – hundreds or thousands of them. The cavalry was due tomorrow, just one day after Aaron's arrival. He and Elisha had no time to waste in trying to save the Nazareth Scroll.

"How many camels?" Aaron asked.

"Three," Elisha said.

"Are you certain?"

The boy sensed more worry than his father was sharing, and he turned and looked over the donkeys at him.

Aaron could feel Elisha's gaze, but kept his own eyes on the horizon. The boy obviously felt that Aaron was keeping something from him.

Elisha looked back toward the road behind them. "Yes, only three camels."

"Good." Aaron relaxed, for now.

Father and son resumed their walk. The trotting camels would soon overtake them. Aaron anxiously waited for the pending encounter with whoever could afford three camels. Soon he too could see the camels and the cloud of dust around their trot.

The camel riders turned on the same side path to Nazareth behind Aaron and Elisha. As they approached, they made no indication of slowing down.

Father and son stepped off the path with their donkeys and waited for the camels to pass.

Without warning, the three camel riders halted their trot next to Aaron and Elisha and looked down at them.

Aaron looked up at the lead rider and couldn't believe his eyes. His jaw dropped.

Elisha did not recognize the camel rider, and he turned his head back and forth between the rider and Aaron.

The lead rider scowled at Aaron. Without a word, he clicked a command to his camel and led the other riders back into their trot toward Nazareth.

Aaron and Elisha stood silent for many breaths.

Elisha still moved his gaze between Aaron and the receding cloud of dust. Finally he asked his father, "Who was that?"

"That," replied Aaron, still gazing into the distance, "was my brother."

CHAPTER TWO

The Nazareth flame keeper walked among the hundreds of donkeys penned just downhill from the pilgrim camp. By the dim cloudy daylight of the winter afternoon, the figure found Daniel's donkey and reached to clutch the lead rope. The other hand grasped the donkey's mane, and the figure leaned down to the donkey's left eye.

"The third time will not fail," hissed the figure. "This time I will start with all your stable straw opposite the house. Tonight you burn with Daniel and his precious Nazareth Scroll!"

The donkey suddenly tried to pull away, braying its loudest.

"Hey, you!" called one of the men watching the animals. "Is that animal yours?"

The figure shook its hooded head and released the donkey.

"Get out of here!"

The flame keeper was already retreating up into the tent city.

"That was my little brother," the Pharisee Aaron mumbled again to his son Elisha. As they walked with their donkeys, they both watched the three camel riders disappear in a cloud of dust around a bend. "Benjamin. Ben. He was the next oldest, so he became heir when I left, and he quickly became a leading Sadducee and Temple priest."

After all these years, Ben still refused to speak to him. Aaron was surprised that his Sadducee brother had traveled to Nazareth. There could be only one reason – to control or destroy the Nazareth Scroll.

Elisha knew the basic story of his adopted father's rupture from his family, but he had never seen Ben to recognize him.

"Papa, tell me again about when you left the Temple priesthood."

With his body still facing forward as they walked, Aaron turned his head to his son. "I left for the sake of questions." Despite the recent drought, the cold winter air was moist from the clouds above, and Aaron's speech floated in wispy puffs from his mouth.

"The Sadducees of the old aristocratic families like mine are right about a lot of things. But they insist they're right about everything. And they think they're superior to all other Jews. This did not seem right to me, from a very early age," Aaron continued. "No man or woman knows everything, and many commoners are wiser than some Sadducees. Ethics and morality are for everyone to judge, not just the wealthy Sadducees. This is why the Nazareth Scroll is so important. Joshua of Nazareth was a great teacher. Already now, twenty years later, much is getting lost and confused when his followers argue with each other. In Jerusalem we have seen the great debates between Joshua's little brother, Jacob the Just, and Saul of Tarsus. Was Joshua the next Anointed One, and does it matter? During all this time, we have heard nothing from Joshua's very first followers here in the hills of Galilee, like this man Daniel who is writing the Nazareth Scroll.

"The wealthy Sadducees like my brother Ben refuse any debate. They say that the only authority is the Torah, the five books of Moses, and that only the Sadducees themselves have the authority to interpret it.

"We Pharisees say that everyone has the right to interpret the Torah. We cite the authority of the books of the prophets and other writings, too.

"It is true that some Pharisees insist on narrow readings of the later scriptures, and these conservative Pharisees are getting to be like the Sadducees. They think they are superior to other Jews, and they think there can be no debate about almost anything, since they have decided how everything should be.

"That's why I joined the golden-rule Pharisees. Like the others, we seek the truth and authoritative answers from the laws of Moses. But we will always give a respectful hearing to new questions and interpretations, however we may judge them. For guidance, we always return to the passage in Leviticus, '*You shall love your neighbor as yourself.*' Joshua of Nazareth taught in the same spirit, which is why my teacher's generation liked him. And it's why we golden-rule Pharisees are sympathetic to Joshua's teachings. We are less certain about whether he was an Anointed One, a Messiah. The time has come to push this question to its origins. It is time to seek answers in Nazareth."

As he continued walking in silence, Aaron remembered his rupture from his family and the Temple's chief priests seven years earlier. One consequence still troubled him, but he was at peace with the rest. He refocused his mind on the moist cold air of each inhalation as they walked uphill, and he knew they would feel the cold when they walked downhill again. During the occasional cold snaps of every winter, Aaron wished the Lord had given the Patriarchs and Moses balmy Egypt instead, far from the sometimes challenging winters of Canaan.

When they neared what looked like the final ridge before Nazareth, Aaron could make out a haze of smoke against the clouds ahead. From what he knew, Nazareth itself was tiny, just a few dozen families, if that. By the breadth of the haze from cooking fires, the pilgrim visitors might be every bit as numerous as Aaron had heard, as many as a thousand or more.

Aaron gasped when he reached the hilltop and paused. Beyond the ridge lay an entire tent city below, hundreds and hundreds of tents with people moving all around like ants under a rock. At first glance, the tent city seemed to be spread chaotically across the broad, gently sloped hillside below Nazareth's village center to the left. A dozen or more old stone village houses were in one cluster of shared walls. Scattered around the hillside and plateau were another dozen or so stone houses in ones and twos.

Then Aaron started to perceive some order in the sprawl of six weeks of pilgrim arrivals. Cutting through the middle was a wide ditch that started just below the village center and ran downhill. Aaron guessed this was a sewage ditch for the newly arrived masses. If Nazareth had a spring, it flowed there to wash it out. Then Aaron noticed that most people were walking on flat paths parallel to the main path through the village above them. Someone had been organizing the placement of tents from the beginning, to maintain parallel curved paths from one end of the tent city to the other. At the bottom edge of the tent city to the left were large animal pens, for a large herd of donkeys, dozens of camels, and three horses, all tended by a number of boys and men. Goats and sheep weaved freely between the tents.

"Elisha, can you see my brother's camels?" Aaron asked.

"Perhaps, Papa," the boy answered. "There are three camels outside a large tent on the opposite edge, not with the other animals."

"Ah, yes. Thank you."

Although Aaron felt a slight breeze crossing the rocky ridge where they stood, he observed no wind below, where thin streams of smoke rose slowly from small cooking fires between tents, emptying into the layer of haze above.

One detail emerged and sent a chill down Aaron's spine – the dark red flag of the Roman Empire flying over the first tent on this side of the camp. The tent was tall but small, and this made sense to Aaron. If Felix was sending a hundred-strong cavalry to break up the Nazareth pilgrimage, he would send a small team in advance to scout it out.

Beyond Felix's Roman guard, the field of hundreds of tents was colored like a tortoise shell – many shades of brown and gray, a few off-white, some black, most of woven goat hair, a few from camel hair. Many of the tents were very small, while others were large enough for two or three families. Some of the larger tents had more than one color, from patches or expansions. Aaron guessed that the larger tents must belong to some of the few wealthy converts to the teachings of Joshua of Nazareth.

When Aaron and Elisha began to descend the path from the ridge, they escaped the summit's breeze, and the sounds of some two thousand souls ahead became clearer. In the bowl-shaped plateau's cold air, Aaron heard more clearly than he ever had across a half-mile or more. Animals brayed and grunted, and their keepers shouted occasional orders. People called to each other across small distances. Hammers, picks, and shovels struck their targets and echoed up the hillside to Aaron and Elisha. Far to the left, almost a mile away across the hills, Aaron saw a small forest and heard the steady blows of axes. Several women and boys walked back and forth for a steady supply of firewood to the tent city.

"Are you ready?" Aaron smiled at Elisha as they walked downhill.

"Uh-huh," Elisha smiled back, both excited and nervous.

At the far side of camp, Ben and his two men climbed down from their panting camels, which had trotted the entire twenty-mile climb from the Sea of Galilee. A few days in advance of him, the aristocratic Sadducee Ben had sent several servants ahead to prepare his arrival in Nazareth.

"Take the camels to water," Ben ordered a boy servant by the tent.

Ben turned to his head servant. "How long have you been here?"

"Two days," answered the servant. "As you ordered, we raised your tent here on the far side and on higher ground. Everything is in place."

"Have there been any particular . . . developments since your arrival?"

"No, sir, I'm afraid not. We keep trying."

"Hmm," replied Ben. "And have you explored the path beyond Nazareth?"

"As you ordered, sir, yes. But that path is even more primitive than the one leading into Nazareth."

"Is it passable by our camels?" asked Ben.

"Certainly. In some places by walking rather than running, but passable, yes."

"Good." Ben hesitated. "You and the rest of the servants need to know something. The Jerusalem Pharisees have sent one of their own here."

"Yes, we know, sir," said the servant. "A man named Gad."

"Gad? From which faction of Pharisees?"

"The Shammai conservatives."

"Interesting," said Ben. "Actually, I was speaking of another Pharisee, a Hillel progressive. My brother Aaron."

The servant gasped, his eyes widened, and he almost dropped the camel's reins.

"We just passed Aaron on the path, walking with a young man and three asses." Ben looked across the tent city to the ridge above it. "That appears to be Aaron now," Ben pointed to the figures on the path on the far hillside, above Nazareth.

The servant looked in stunned silence.

"Tell the other servants, so they are not surprised when he arrives."

"Yes, sir. Why is he here?"

"I suppose the same thing led us both here. Have you met this Daniel yet?"

"We have seen him in a crowd, but we have not met him," said the servant.

"What do the people here think of him?" asked Ben.

"They are not disappointed. In fact, they love him. In two days, we have seen dozens of new arrivals, too – and no one has departed. The people come to see Daniel, to meet this childhood friend and adult disciple of Joshua of Nazareth. Almost no one here is interested in the scroll that Daniel is writing. It was news of the scroll that brought Daniel widespread attention, but the pilgrims are here to learn from his speech, not from his pen.

"However, there are a few here who do seem very interested in the scroll," continued the servant.

"What have you learned?" asked Ben.

"Almost everyone here is honest. Most of these people are simple, but some are village elders from across Galilee down to Judea, who have come here to learn more. These include some skeptics who dislike Joshua's followers, but who want to learn more from Daniel before passing verdicts back home. Finally, a few are well trained in the scriptures, and they can barely stand the wait for Daniel to complete his written story of Joshua.

"Then there are the others who want to destroy the Nazareth Scroll. None of us trusts the other. The conservative Pharisee Gad is full of hate for everyone, even his own younger traveling companions, it seems. He tolerates no dissent to his every tiny interpretation of the law. Among the two thousand people here, Gad spares no one from his furious lectures for lighting eight Hanukkah candles at the start tonight. It is as if he fears his spirit will be polluted for every nearby menorah that burns opposed to his will. His hatred for the followers of Joshua has actually convinced some of them to change old family traditions just to spite him. Tonight many of them will light just one candle instead of eight, with two lit candles the second night instead of seven, and so on to the eighth night. Gad is the most counter-productive preacher I've ever heard."

Ben and his servant laughed.

"Good work" replied Ben. "How many other enemies of the Nazareth Scroll are here?"

"We suspect several, but only one group is openly hostile to Daniel's Nazareth Scroll – Felix's three cavalrymen, who also arrived two days ago, just a few hours ahead of us. They raised their small tent at the entrance to the tent city. You passed it when you arrived. They do not act like they are prepared to stay here for the whole winter of this mass pilgrimage."

"They are not." Ben lowered his voice and whispered to his lead servant, "Whatever else happens today, prepare to depart at noon tomorrow, by the back path you found. But for today, do not tell the others more than you must. Procurator Antonius Felix is sending his cavalry tomorrow to break up the camp – or else destroy it."

CHAPTER THREE

The hooded figure clutched the cold iron circles of the coal pan hidden under a woolen blanket, and took measure of Nazareth's approaching new arrivals. The newcomers were a young man and a boy and their three donkeys, carrying a heavy load. Another merchant looking for profits from pilgrims, thought the flame keeper. However, the boy made the flame keeper wonder. Was this the merchant's son? Merchants did not require apprentices.

As the Pharisee Aaron walked down the path to Nazareth's tent city, his eyes kept returning to the Roman Empire's dark red flag, small yet ominous. As they drew nearer to the tent city, Aaron could make out the specific comings and goings in this giant ant maze of pilgrims. Most notable were the scores of men and women digging small trenches in the hard, dry dirt along the upslope edges of the tents. The diggers occasionally glanced to the thick clouds above. Aaron, too, could smell the imminent snow. No one could know whether the snow would fall precisely over Nazareth, or whether it might turn to rain before groundfall, but everyone seemed to believe it would fall somewhere.

When Aaron reached the tent of Felix's Roman cavalry, he expected a guard to question them as new arrivals. He tapped Elisha on the shoulder, nodded toward the tent, and immediately launched into a contrived conversation of the arguments about whether or not the laws of Moses allowed polygamy for any man who wanted it. The only soldier present showed no interest in them, as he stood wrapped in a woolen blanket staring across the field of tents, with his back to Aaron.

Just beyond the cavalry tent, a half-dozen men began to compete for Aaron's attention.

"Ample space for two in my family's tent!"

"Come see my very good bargain!"

"We can lodge you and tend your donkeys!"

They all shouted at the same time.

Aaron shook his head calmly. Tall and in controlled focus of himself, he held up both hands for them to stop, and they did. "One at a time."

Aaron turned to the one at the far right. "Where is your tent?" Aaron wanted to be as close to original stone houses as possible, near Daniel's house and the Nazareth Scroll.

"Not far from here, come and—"

"Point," Aaron instructed.

The man pointed toward the middle of the camp, and he was about to recommence singing his location's virtues, when Aaron cut him off with another hand gesture.

"And you?" Aaron asked the second man. "Point."

This one just pointed in his direction. The remaining men all pointed toward their own respective tents. Aaron considered all six locations and their distances from Nazareth's old village center. Two of the men pointed toward the highest part of the tent city, next Nazareth's stone houses.

"You two, how long have you been here?" asked Aaron.

"Four weeks," answered one.

"Five weeks," answered another.

"I will come and choose between you two," said Aaron. He turned to the others, allowing his eyes to soften with the hint of a smile. "Sorry, men."

"How long ago did the first pilgrims arrive?" Aaron asked the two final host candidates.

"Seven weeks, from what I understand," said one with the beard. Aaron wondered about the beard. It wasn't the longest he had ever seen, and it was cut evenly, but almost no one had a beard on purpose like that.

The other, younger man lifted the palms of his hands to gesture that he didn't know.

Since the earliest arrivals were encamped next to old Nazareth, they led Aaron down the path into the village center.

The tents they passed were all set close together except some regular intervals for shared cooking fires. Everywhere, occupants were either digging rain trenches or checking the ones they already had. Everyone naturally looked up to the new arrivals Aaron and Elisha.

One man asked, "Do you carry something for sale in your amphora vases?" He pointed at the traveling racks on the three donkeys.

"Rock salt, yes," Aaron replied.

Several others stopped their digging and rushed to join the conversation.

"What is your price?" they asked.

"Can you wait until the morning?" Aaron asked them. "No one needs salt right away?"

"We can wait," they agreed.

"But a little for tonight's dinner would help," added an older woman.

Aaron looked at the five men and two women before him. "Tomorrow morning, meet me at this spot, and I will sell you salt. Woman, can you keep accounts?"

The old woman lifted her chin a bit and scrutinized Aaron. "Yes."

"Do the rest of you trust her to gather orders?"

"Oh, yes," they replied without hesitation.

Aaron studied how well the others appeared to know the older woman, and she obviously commanded everyone's respect. He turned to her. "Then I will advance you one amphora of salt. Elisha, please unload it. This woman will dispense the salt in the quantities needed, for what you all decide is a fair price. We will settle those accounts in the morning when I return with more. Agreed?"

"Thank you," the woman said.

The others nodded vigorously. "Thank you! Thank you!"

Aaron's two prospective hosts widened their eyes at such trust in strangers.

Elisha smiled at the scene his father had created. Aaron knew very well how to make friends and how to deepen bonds of trust and mutual aid between near strangers.

Not much farther down the path they neared the old village center. In a single cluster of stone walls and flat roofs, more than a dozen separate homes were visible. Some were small, and one or two were larger than the rest, distinct by long uninterrupted walls and a palm tree growing from the courtyard of one of them.

On the far side of the village center was its central spring, carefully pooled in stone masonry. Women and children surrounded the pool with modest water vases, taking turns for their fill, arriving with light loads and departing under the water's weight. Everyone was careful not to spill a drop. Whenever someone scraped the bottom of the pool, everyone waited a few moments for the water to rise again, which happened quickly. The northern drought had not yet dried the spring's source.

From the left of the pool, the spring's stream bed ran downhill on the right side of the path that continued beyond Nazareth's center. The stream bed was moist but empty. The pilgrims took nearly all the water at its source. This explained the smell of sewage that was now apparent to Aaron and Elisha. The sewage ditch down the path was uncleansed, at least by day. Aaron hoped the spring might flow unimpeded each night to wash some of the sewage of two thousand pilgrims.

Aaron's first guide paused beside a very small tent.

"My name is Michael," said the prospective host. "Welcome to my humble home." Michael opened the worn, gray, goat-hair tent flap and invited Aaron to enter. Elisha stood by the donkeys in front, bored with Michael's tiny abode and looking around at all the different kinds of people who had journeyed to Nazareth.

Aaron had observed that Nazareth's tent city included dozens and dozens of this smallest, lowest rank of tent. On its shorter end, there was not even height for a man to sit. Nowhere in the tent could he come close to standing. In Judea and

Galilee, most tents had at least one central pole and four corner poles. But the poorest tents like this one lacked the central pole, and these poor tents were all over Nazareth. Without the higher central pole to create a top angle against collecting rain, this design relied instead on the difference between a higher pair of poles on one side than on the other. As with all tents, they were held up with ropes leading from the pole tops to the ground, about as far away from the tent as the poles were tall. In this tent city, each tent's guide ropes were staked very close to the base of the neighboring tent. The resulting criss-cross of angled ropes between tents was an obstacle course that most pilgrims avoided.

Concerned about the rain clouds overhead, Aaron rubbed the entry flap of Michael's tent between his fingers. Yes, he thought, it was thick enough to hold out the rain, especially with the normal swelling of goat-hair tent fabric when wet. The fabric's handspun threads were coarser than most, but they would do. Aaron glanced inside the tent, and it looked well kept. Before entering, he walked its short perimeter to inspect whether the flaps were buried sufficiently deep to deflect stormwater runoff. Aaron was careful not to trip on any of the guidelines to Michael's tent or his neighbors'. In two different tent corners, Aaron gently tugged the fabric upward from the ground. When this met stiff resistance, Aaron knew that the tent was properly secured. He came back to the open entry and squatted to waddle in.

"At the moment, my wife Naomi is tending to our two donkeys and our goat down the hill. She sleeps separately in that back corner, behind the curtain. We are poor, and we need a few coins for our food here, so two days ago I joined the group where the path meets the first tents, to offer lodging to new arrivals. You are my first prospect. To lodge the boy and you and your amphora vases of salt, it is one-quarter shekel per night. You will not pay less for lodging in Nazareth, I guarantee it."

"What about my three donkeys?" Aaron asked.

"The main herd keeper down the hill offers affordable boarding. There are also a few lesser herdsmen down there, if you want to compare offers."

Aaron decided that Michael's offer was sufficient for him and his son. But he had promised to consider the other man's tent, too.

"Your offer is very reasonable," he said, looking unwaveringly into Michael's eyes. "I will visit this man's lodging and then decide."

Michael smiled weakly and nodded, but he sighed and his shoulders sagged. He looked at his competitor, a young man in clothes that were basic but fairly new. Michael clearly expected rejection.

After standing silently, the young man waited for Aaron to give him the nod.

"Right this way, sir."

Just three tents away, directly opposite the village center, the young man stopped in front of one of the largest tents in Nazareth, with three center poles for three separate tent chambers, the middle one the tallest. The fabric was all camelhair. Even the corner poles were taller than Aaron, so that any man could stand straight anywhere in the tent. Aaron heard grown men laughing inside, adolescent boys arguing, and women and children in all manner of conversations. The wealthy man who presided over this tent and its company certainly did not need the meager income from two lodgers.

"Welcome to my master's tent," he said, opening a tall tent flap for Aaron to enter. "I can watch your donkeys," he continued and motioned for Elisha to enter as well.

Aaron wondered how much wealth this tent's master stood to lose if Antonius Felix's forces destroyed Nazareth's camp the next day.

After a quick glimpse to confirm the tent's strong construction and securely buried sides, Aaron and Elisha crossed the makeshift threshold, and their guide closed the flap behind them. "Please excuse me a moment while I adjust to the light," Aaron spoke to the yet unseen company before him. At first Aaron saw only a large number of oil lamps spread throughout the tent's central chamber, and a small fire in a bronze brazier in the middle. The smoke escaped through a hole where the central tent pole met the roof, covered after a gap on the outside to hold out any rain. Rather than wood smoke, though, Aaron smelled sweet incense. There was no trace of any unpleasant odors from outside. As Aaron's eyes adjusted to the dark, a figure seated on a cushion on the opposite side pulled a lamp closer to him so that Aaron could better see his face.

"Welcome to my quarters, strangers. My name is Seth. Sir, please join us. My servant tells me you are a man of much learning."

How could Seth know this about him, from a servant who still stood outside with his donkeys? Aaron's mind raced back to when they had first met the servant with the others selling lodging. Of course, Aaron realized, he and Elisha had been discussing Torah law to avoid conversation with the Roman guard. Seth must have given his servant instructions to seek out new pilgrims who seemed very learned. Or had he already known about Aaron and anticipated his arrival? Either way, Aaron now knew that he had been deliberately chosen to lodge with Seth. He found a cushion and sat in the circle of six or eight men and their host.

"Welcome to the encamped masses here to honor Joshua of Nazareth," Seth continued. "As a very young man on the Passover pilgrimage with my first wife, I happened to see Joshua as he was force-marched to his own crucifixion. Since that day, I have made eager association with all who knew him and all who follow his way. How did you come to follow Joshua? At your age, perhaps it started with your parents?"

Here was a man who knew what he was about, thought Aaron. A man who possessed an aura of command.

"Not my parents," answered Aaron. "I remember the day of the crucifixion, though I was only about seven years old. I came to Joshua's teachings slowly, you could say." Aaron felt not so much humbled as cautious, like he usually was in the face of power such as Seth's wealth. "My name is Aaron. I am a salt dealer and a Pharisee, and this is my son, Elisha."

Standing in back, Elisha bowed his head to their host.

Aaron's eyes were adjusting, and he could see his host Seth lift his chin and squint to inspect the unexpected Pharisee before him. Aaron was also getting a clearer picture of the tent's interior. Some half-dozen men sat in a circle with the host, all of them cross-legged on cushions. Another half-dozen or so men stood in the background, apparently servants, either to Seth or the guests in Seth's circle. This central chamber of the tent was partitioned from each of the side chambers by luxurious linen curtains hanging from lines tied across the tent to supporting side poles. Aaron could hear women and a number of children behind the curtain to the left. The curtain to the right hid occasional quiet teenage male voices in the men's chamber.

"Very interesting, Pharisee Aaron," Seth replied. "You are late to Nazareth. My family and I journeyed here as soon as we learned about this older disciple Daniel and his Nazareth Scroll, and we were among the first hundred pilgrims. Daniel has been my guest here several times, and I have had many fruitful conversations with him. He is every bit the saint you may have heard him to be," Seth continued. "Your accent is also from the south, like mine, no?"

"Yes," Aaron replied.

"In Caesarea where I have lived my adult life, we have heard practically nothing from these disciples of Joshua's younger years in Nazareth and Zippori. Can you believe that? Zippori, the second largest Jewish city after Jerusalem, just four miles from Nazareth, and its early followers of Joshua are completely unknown down in Judea."

Aaron knew that Daniel was not the only disciple from this region. He had long heard of Joshua's train of almost a hundred disciples, plus many more followers, to that fateful Passover in Jerusalem. But Aaron had never accounted for even half of them, despite his long efforts and questioning of older Joshua admirers in Jerusalem. How could Aaron have overlooked it? Nazareth was an outlying village to the large city of Zippori, where Nazareth farmers sold their produce and practiced their trades. Of course many of the other disciples must be from Zippori, a city so large that its inhabitants lived nearly in their own world, having rare contact with the outside world, including Joshua's later disciples and followers.

"I was surprised, too," said Seth. "But after I thought about it, it made sense. With some thirty thousand Jews to preach to in Zippori, why would Joshua's followers there need to go preach elsewhere? Their task in that great city is already immense. . . . But I digress. Please excuse my poor manners – your belongings are still unpacked outside! You are invited to join us here for as long as you stay in Nazareth."

Aaron knew this would be only one night, until Roman Procurator Felix's forces disbanded the whole thing the next day. Despite Seth's wealth, Aaron worried for him.

"I beg your pardon, Seth. My first offer was elsewhere, and I feel I must accept it. Also, that man could use the coin."

Standing behind Aaron, thirteen-year-old Elisha audibly gagged in surprise, and his mouth dropped open.

All the men in Seth's circle laughed.

"I see that your son is disappointed, Pharisee," Seth smiled.

Aaron smiled, too.

Elisha was suddenly embarrassed and stared at the ground.

"No matter," said Seth. "You are welcome here any time. You need only present yourself. Perhaps you can join us tonight for dinner and the first night of the Hanukkah menorah?"

"That is very gracious of you, Seth. I accept – if young Elisha here does?"

Elisha nodded his head vigorously.

All the men laughed a second time.

"May I ask one favor?" Aaron continued.

"Anything," said Seth.

"Perhaps you have space here for my amphora vases of salt?"

"Plenty, by all means, yes! My servant will be glad to help. How many amphoras?"

"Nine," Aaron replied.

"Let all here witness, the nine amphoras of salt in my tent are the property of Aaron of Jerusalem. Aaron, we will look forward to your company this evening!"

"Thank you." Aaron stood and took leave from the other men and stepped outside with Elisha.

"Couldn't we just give the first host the money and stay here?" Elisha half-joked.

"That would make him a beggar, or so he might feel. No, this way is better for him."

Aaron had another motivation, too. He had less than a day and a night to get to Daniel's Nazareth Scroll before Felix's Roman forces arrived. Accepting hospitality from Seth would have meant taking on social responsibilities of extended gratitude and conversation in return. No, it was better for Aaron to lay his head where he paid his obligation in coin and kept his time free for his purposes.

"All right, I get it," said Elisha. "But did you see that place?! At least we get to eat there."

"Calm down," said Aaron, getting annoyed at Elisha's protest.

Seth's servant removed all but one amphora of salt into Seth's tent. Then Aaron led the three donkeys a few tents uphill to Michael's small tent, whose flap was closed.

"Michael," Aaron called inside, "it is Aaron and Elisha. We're back, and we accept your offer, if your space is still available."

Michael opened the tent flap from inside and looked astonished. He glanced back and forth between Aaron and Elisha and down the path to Seth's tent. Finally he collected himself. "Of course, of course! Welcome. Please make yourself at home. I see you have found a place for most of your salt?"

"Yes, thank you" Aaron answered. "May I pay for four nights up front?" Aaron asked. He wanted Michael to be content, even though Felix's Roman forces would force them all to leave after just one night. It was never good to lodge with a resentful host.

"Certainly," Michael replied.

"In coin or in salt?" asked Aaron.

"Coin, if you don't mind."

Aaron counted out four quarter-shekels, and when he held them out to Michael, he noticed a thick scar across Michael's palm. "What line of work earned you that scar?" he asked.

"Carpentry, which I immediately quit." Michael laughed self-consciously.

Naomi gave Michael a quick glare.

Aaron then offered a small bag of salt from his donkey's saddlebag.

"You are a very generous guest," Michael answered. "Thank you. Rock salt – you are from near the Salt Sea?"

"Jerusalem, yes. You're welcome. Please tell me if you know of others who are low on salt and needing a good price."

"Yes, there are some others. I will send them to you."

"Thank you," Aaron replied. "Now I would please like to excuse myself to explore Nazareth."

"You want to meet Daniel?" Michael asked, his tone suddenly serious.

Aaron was caught off guard by the question and the abrupt way that Michael had asked it. "Of course," Aaron acknowledged. He felt desperately pressed for time, which he desperately wanted to hide.

"His old stone house stands alone, just a short way down the main path, around the bend."

"Thank you," said Aaron. He turned away and proceeded immediately to the house of Daniel, the old friend and disciple of Joshua of Nazareth.

The Pharisee Gad was engrossed in reading by an oil lamp when one of his young messengers entered the tent, flooding Gad with unwanted daylight. "What is it?" he bellowed without looking up.

"New arrivals, sir. I think I recognize the man, the Pharisee Aaron from Jerusalem."

Gad dropped his scroll to his lap, lifted his head, and darted his eyes around the tent's interior as his thoughts raced at this news.

The Sadducee Benjamin was settling in with the help of his lead servant when another servant arrived, out of breath. "Master Ben, sir, you won't believe it! While I was keeping watch, right after you, your brother Aaron has just arrived in Nazareth, with many laden amphoras and a young disciple!"

Ben and his lead servant nodded to each other. "Yes," said Ben, "I passed him on the road."

Roman Centurion Matthias returned to the animal paddock from a surveillance horse ride through the camp.

"Ah, there you are, sir," said one of his guardsmen, waiting for him. "Within the past hour, I spied some interesting new arrivals in Nazareth. A salt dealer and a boy were debating whether polygamy is just, in the manner of debate among the Pharisees. Our guard on duty didn't even pay attention to the conversation. You told me to watch for strange arrivals, sir."

CHAPTER FOUR

Aaron had no time to waste. It was already mid-afternoon, and Felix's Roman cavalry could arrive any time the next day. Even if the cavalry dispersed all the encamped pilgrims without violence, the Nazareth Scroll was in danger – as was Daniel himself. Aaron had to warn him. And he had to preserve what might be the only first-hand account of Joshua of Nazareth ever to be written.

Aaron had learned from his host which house was Daniel's. It was the one standing alone about one hundred paces down the main path from Michael's tent and the village center. This was also on the way to the herdsmen below where Elisha would take their donkeys. They walked together down the rocky and dusty path.

"When we reach Daniel's house," Aaron told Elisha, "stay outside awhile until I tell you to continue to the herdsmen. With the donkeys, it will be clear to Daniel that we are new arrivals come to see him. Do you have the next bag of gift salt ready?"

Elisha nodded.

When the front of the house came into view, Aaron took in the unusual sight. The small crowd of men was not surprising. But they were erecting the first of nine tall flag poles across the front of the house, and Aaron didn't see any flags around.

Aaron approached one of the men. "Is this the home of Daniel, disciple of Joshua of Nazareth?"

"You found it!" the man smiled. He noticed Elisha staring at the poles. "Does your youngster here like our giant menorah?"

Elisha nodded in wide-eyed awe.

Aaron tilted his head slightly to take in the fact behind what he observed. Of course – if two thousand pilgrims had come to

Daniel, he might honor them in return with a giant menorah for all to experience as one community. Aaron smiled at Daniel's thoughtfulness.

"You would like to meet Daniel?" the same man asked.

"If it is not inconvenient," Aaron answered.

"Not at all," answered another, older man. "*Shalom!* Welcome to Nazareth. I am Daniel, and this is my home. You have found lodgings?"

"Yes, up the path, with a man and wife, Michael and Naomi."

"If their tent is that close, they've been here longer than a month." Daniel looked like he was trying to remember them. "But I don't think I've met them. And you have boarding for your donkeys?"

"Not yet," said Aaron.

"Will you allow one of my friends here to arrange that downhill with all the other donkeys and camels? He will get you the best terms."

Aaron looked at Elisha, who shrugged. "Yes, thank you," Aaron replied.

"Now, please come in! The young man as well."

Daniel was shorter than average. His thick hair was nearly white, and his large face was wrinkled and dark from the sun, even in the winter season. The wrinkles were those of an easy-going, kind, and happy man, relaxed and often smiling. Daniel's posture was still straight, and he looked fit and muscular. His charcoal-black eyes beamed with youthful energy, as if they did not belong with the wrinkles and white hair.

"Aaron of Jerusalem," Aaron introduced himself.

"All the way from the holy city!" answered Daniel. "I am honored."

"Please accept this humble gift of salt from Judea."

"Oh, I couldn't," said Daniel.

"Please, I insist," Aaron answered, gently but firmly.

"To share with the others, then," said Daniel. "Thank you very much."

Daniel led them through the front door and onto a small patio, between a stable on the left and two doorways to the modest house on the right. Children's voices could be heard behind the first door. The house's stones and mortar looked worn and ancient, perhaps even older than most houses in the village center back up the path. After the stable on the left was the hearth, facing a covered open-air space to its left and a small walled kitchen on its right. The whole house looked large enough for comfortable living, even if it had less space than did several tents now in Nazareth. On the back end of the patio, workers were shoring up a large woodpile for the winter.

Daniel invited Aaron and Elisha into the main room behind the second door. They sat at his table, and his son-in-law served them hot water, so they could warm their hands around the simple ceramic cups and heat their insides when the water cooled enough to drink. The son-in-law also placed a simple lighted oil lamp in the middle of the table, and closed the door behind him. Even seated, Aaron still towered over Daniel across the table. Elisha sat next to Aaron, at Daniel's eye level. The fragrances of burning olive oil and a linen wick hovered over the table, and a slight draft kept the flame dancing. Aaron's eyes adjusted from daylight to Daniel's intimate reception by lamp light.

"What brings you to Nazareth?" Daniel asked, smiling, his eyes glistening in the reflection of the small flame. "You are a follower of Joshua's teachings? You are perhaps too young to have met him there in Jerusalem twenty years ago."

"I did not meet him," answered Aaron, "but I remember the news of his crucifixion."

Daniel's face fell at the reminder of that day.

"Many of us Jerusalem Pharisees admire Nazareth's native Joshua. Of course, I mean the golden-rule Pharisees of the Hillel tradition, not the conservative Pharisees. When we heard about you and the scroll they say you're writing, we decided that one of us would come to you. I have the good fortune to have been chosen for this journey, along with my son Elisha, who also studies the scriptures with me."

Daniel lifted his hands from his cup and folded them to his chin in reflection. "Another Pharisee. This one named Aaron like a priest. Hmm. . . ." Daniel's eyes inquired Aaron for more, and he let silence fill the room.

Aaron saw neither approval nor hostility in Daniel's eyes. Instead Daniel held his gaze gently, as if frozen in time. There was another Pharisee in Nazareth? Unlike Daniel, Aaron was now agitated.

"There are other Pharisees here?" Aaron asked, trying to mask his surprise.

"I know of one other, yes," said Daniel. "Perhaps you know him, as he is also a Jerusalemite, by the name of Gad."

Elisha gasped at the mention of Gad's name.

"He arrived about two weeks ago with three or four assistants." Daniel continued with the same uncommitted, calm gaze.

"I know only one Pharisee in Jerusalem named Gad," said Aaron. "He and his fellow conservative Pharisees scorn Joshua and his followers. Why did he come here, I wonder?"

"Good question," replied Daniel. "You were still explaining why you came here." Daniel raised his bushy white eyebrows and smiled.

"Yes, please forgive my rudeness," said Aaron. "You are correct, I belong to the family of priests, descended from the brother of Moses. Before I was a Pharisee, in fact, I was a regular Temple priest, and first-born heir in a wealthy family. In my father's family, for me to leave the Sadducees and become a Pharisee, I had no choice but to lose my rights of inheritance, and the prospect of marriage within the clan."

Elisha turned his head from Daniel to Aaron. Never had he heard Aaron mention marriage in this story. It must have been important to Aaron, held within him, yet a significant part of his story, drawn out by the strong gentleness of Daniel across the table.

Aaron felt Elisha's gaze and tried not to blush, thankful for the dim lamplight. He had no idea how Daniel had drawn that out of him.

"Because my father knew the high priest," said Aaron, "I expected to be dismissed from the Temple service as well, and I was."

"The high priest has changed recently," said Daniel.

"I would not go back," replied Aaron. "I feel the Lord has called me to serve in other ways."

"To change from Sadducee to Pharisee, you had to develop a new faith in resurrection after death. Which came first, your embrace of resurrection, or your rejection of the Sadducees?" Daniel asked.

"Rejection of Sadducee wealth and privilege, and of their closed-minded attempts to dictate the Lord's truth," replied Aaron.

Daniel leaned back a little and relaxed his face and jaw muscles even more. "I see."

"I might have left the Sadducees earlier, but I had to be sure I could believe in resurrection before asking to study with the Pharisees." In fact, Aaron had never embraced resurrection as enthusiastically as he sought justice for the poor, and as he advocated the right and even duty for all learned men, priest or no, both to study the certainties of the laws of Moses, yet also to deliberate the uncertainties with open minds. Before leaving the Sadducees, Aaron merely accepted the resurrection. He scarcely taught it, only when he had to, and he endured occasional taunts in the streets from former Sadducee colleagues about what they called superstitious resurrection. Even the Book of Mark that Aaron had seen mentioned nothing of a resurrection for Joshua of Nazareth, which Joshua's most radical followers had started talking about only recently.

"You asked a second question, why did I come to you," Aaron said.

"Indeed," Daniel smiled.

At that moment, the patio door opened behind Aaron and Elisha, and a new man appeared, much younger than fifty-something Daniel, perhaps a little older than twenty-seven-year-old Aaron.

"Simon, *Shalom*!" said Daniel. "Meet our latest arrivals, a Hillel golden-rule Pharisee from Jerusalem by the name of Aaron, and his son and disciple Elisha."

"*Shalom*," Simon greeted everyone. Peace.

"*Shalom*," Aaron and Elisha replied.

Aaron worried that this interruption might end the conservation before they could discuss the dangers to the Nazareth Scroll – this might be his only chance to help save it before it was too late.

"Aaron, this is Simon, the youngest son of Joseph and Miriam, and the little brother of Joshua of Nazareth."

This was a surprising and exciting development, Aaron thought.

"Before you ask, as most visitors, do," said Simon, "I did not know my eldest brother Joshua very well. The older generation knew him much better. Joshua was old enough to be my father, and I was still a boy when they crucified him. There's a reason that no pilgrim ever traveled to Nazareth to meet *me*!" Simon laughed. "Also, I am the last of our family still in Nazareth. Daniel is the man you seek, Joshua's best friend. The only other person here who knew Joshua even half as well was my family's servant, Miriam. She lives to this day in the village center, a very old woman, but she has not gone outside since the pilgrims started arriving. She tires easily of conversation, and she will no longer talk to outsiders. A wonderful woman, Miriam, like a second mother to all of my mother's children. Born and raised a Samaritan, she fled them before an arranged marriage to an old man. In my parents' household, she became a Jew, but she remembered her Samaritan mother and sisters fondly. I'm sorry, I am rambling now, as if you asked me what so many others ask. I am sorry to interrupt your visit with Daniel, Aaron of Jerusalem. I like you golden-rule Pharisees."

"Was there something you needed?" Daniel asked Simon.

"I just came to help Gabriel with the poles, and I wanted to say hello. Now I have! I'll get to helping him. It was a pleasure meeting you, Aaron, Elisha."

"Likewise," the two replied.

Simon exited and closed the door to the patio.

"I see you are familiar with us golden-rule Pharisees?" Aaron asked. He was concerned that people here in the north might assume that any Pharisee was the conservative sort.

"I have met one or two of you over in Zippori, a small minority of Pharisees there, yes," Daniel replied.

"We are a larger number in the south, still a minority, but substantial," Aaron said. "We thirst for knowledge and wisdom about the laws of Moses. We know that many of Joshua's disciples returned to their families and synagogues after the crucifixion, sharing Joshua's teaching in your own communities."

Daniel nodded his head slowly.

"We have heard from several of Joshua's younger disciples, and much from his younger brothers Jacob and Judah. We want to know more – what you learned from Joshua in earlier years, what you saw him do. The fisherman disciples met Joshua of Nazareth late in his life. And even during his last year, they did not accompany Joshua for all his journeys in Galilee.

"There's one more thing," continued Aaron. "We heard you are writing a scroll, a testimony of your experiences with Joshua. Everyone here in this tent city confirms this news. May I ask, is it true?"

"Nearly true," Daniel answered. "The later disciples came to know Joshua very well, and their authority is great. Perhaps you hear most from Simon Peter?" Daniel smiled. "He was always the most assertive. But he and the others from the Sea of Galilee did not always travel with Joshua, you are correct, even during that final year. When my friend Joshua came back upcountry to the great city of Zippori and tiny Nazareth out here, we natives were the ones who accompanied him. A few of us traveled back and forth across Galilee wherever Joshua went. Others rarely left Zippori, just like the disciples around the Sea of Galilee usually stayed there. In fact, I don't think any of them ever came to Zippori, where Joshua's teachings really got started. He had so many disciples in Zippori that he didn't need anyone else's help when he returned to these parts."

Aaron was fascinated by Daniel's knowledge of Joshua's life, which reached far beyond anything Aaron had learned in Jerusalem from Joshua's younger disciples and brothers.

"The Jerusalem disciples say almost nothing of this," said Aaron. "They mention just one brief trip that did not go well."

Daniel laughed. "Yes, the last time Joshua came to his home village of Nazareth, the elders of the time forced him to leave. Until that time, they were proud of him here in Nazareth. But Joshua brought it on himself, and that last visit ended badly. He came up here from the Sea of Galilee for a visit home, traveling with me and two of his Zippori disciples who had been down there with him. We were headed to Zippori to continue his longstanding teaching there, but Joshua first wanted to visit his family. Joseph and Miriam were healthy, and they had many children, most of whom still lived here at the time.

"After several days, on the morning of the Sabbath, we gathered for prayers in the courtyard of the big house in the village center. We are too few in Nazareth for a separate synagogue, at least as long as we are welcome in that house. All the men and older boys of the village, more than fifty, filled the courtyard and spilled onto the path outside. The strongest voice in the village read the Torah that day, so that those outside could hear over the courtyard walls.

"When the Torah reading was finished, Joshua came forward and read from the scroll of Isaiah, his favorite. Everyone there was awestruck by Joshua's command of Isaiah's voice of mercy for the poor and the oppressed.

"But then he did something I never saw him do before or after that day. He took a welcoming audience, including some skeptics, and he provoked them to reject him. It almost seemed deliberate. He told of when the prophet Elijah had rejected almost all of his homeland of Israel. The message was clear. Just moments after getting the Nazareth men to rejoice in his own teaching, Joshua rejected them, for no apparent reason, and then blamed *them* for rejecting *him*. The three of us disciples were stunned and perplexed. When we asked him later why he had done this, what it all meant, he answered only that it must remain hidden if we were too blind to see.

"Most of the Nazarene men and boys that day starting shouting at Joshua, even threatening him. Old Joseph looked worried. Many of the men told me later that they regretted how their momentary anger led them to behave that day. In their shouting, they slowly pressed forward, into a suffocating pack, so that even those outside entered the courtyard from the back of the congregation. Joshua was unusually calm at this point. Separated from him, I stood on a stool to see if he might be crushed up front. Instead, while speaking about Elijah, he had very cleverly maneuvered himself to the doorway on that end of the courtyard. When my eyes met his, he smiled at me and then ducked through the doorway to the hillside behind.

"Men and boys poured out of the courtyard by that back door, by the front door, and even over the walls. Joshua climbed straight up the steep hillside above the village. We all ran after him – the majority who were furious at Joshua, and the large minority trying to guard him. Joshua was fast! While the village elders led the angry ones, including most of their sons, most of the rest of the younger generation took Joshua's side, even as confused as we were by what he'd just said. As all of the men and boys of Nazareth ran up the jagged path, our ages separated us. The older men and the boys straggled. We younger men surged ahead, struggling on the steep incline. The two fastest young men reached Joshua first. One of them was his little brother, Joseph the younger, and the other was a young man who looked like he took Joshua's side.

"Joshua, his brother, and their ally stood there panting. Together they turned to face us young men just below them. Being evenly divided, we all paused and looked around us. The emotions of the synagogue courtyard were partially spent in the chase. Since most of my generation had enjoyed our time with Joshua that week, and since we'd gotten all mixed up running up the path, we realized he didn't know any more who was on what side! Some leaned on their knees out of breath, and a couple of us started laughing, while a couple of others resumed shouts of 'How dare you!'

"No one laughed among the elders downhill, and many of them were clearly exhausted by the brief chase. I could hear some of them mumbling, 'And on the Sabbath!' ashamed of their own violation of the commandment to rest. All of the oldest men and a few of the younger ones stood just outside the synagogue courtyard and swayed in fervent prayer at the sacrilege they were witnessing. Old Joseph's body and lips barely moved while he watched and rubbed his hands in anxiety for his sons, little Joseph as well as Joshua.

"Finally one of the regretful elders called up the hillside, 'Joshua son of Joseph, if you will promise to leave Nazareth at sunrise after the Sabbath, we will guarantee you no harm.'

"Joshua nodded his head and descended the path alone, walking past and between all his supporters and opponents who had followed the chase. After Joshua reached his father Joseph at the bottom, the two of them went into their family house, which is also in the village center, where Simon still lives. They remained inside until the next morning, when Joshua and we three disciples walked the four miles to Zippori. During the entire next month in Zippori, no one from Nazareth bothered us, and Joshua never gave us any more explanation for his provocation in Nazareth, except to call us blind for missing the point.

"Of course, even I did not accompany Joshua everywhere," Daniel said. "No one did, though I believe I did more than anyone, as his earliest childhood friend. Many men and women in the city of Zippori, Jews and Gentiles alike, still learn at the feet of Joshua's disciples there. We always tell our listeners in Zippori, we were not with Joshua everywhere, and more can be learned from the disciples down around the Sea of Galilee.

"For some reason," Daniel continued, "some of those disciples settled in Jerusalem after the crucifixion. Perhaps it is because most of them were ten or fifteen years younger than most of us up here. We had families and children. So we shared

Joshua's teachings with our neighbors around Zippori. With tens of thousands of Jews and Gentiles here, we have plenty to do.

"After twenty years of this, we have learned which of Joshua's tales obtain the quickest attention from people of all trades and classes, from countryside farm laborers to city tradesmen and their wives, and even the scribes. For those of us who knew Joshua his whole life, there is always something new to share even after years of telling."

"You ask about the scroll," said Daniel. "Yes, it is nearly complete. I do not read very well, and I do not know how to write. It is my son-in-law Gabriel who does the writing, in our native Aramaic, the language of Joshua's teachings. Gabriel and I discussed this project for years. Finally during last summer's farming lull, we began. I tell him the familiar stories, we discuss and improve the telling, and then he writes. After these many months, we expect to finish in the next evening or two."

Aaron was excited. So it was true – and nearly finished!

"Why now?" asked Aaron. "You might have written it earlier. Or you might have waited longer. Why is this the year you have written your testimony of Joshua of Nazareth?"

"Of all who have traveled to Nazareth these many weeks," answered Daniel, "you are the first to task this question." Daniel took a long pause for reflection. "Writing the scroll was always important to us. It became more important when we heard that the great debate among Joshua's followers was starting to dominate his congregations, drowning out the rest. Was he the next Anointed One, a Messiah, or was he not? What did Joshua himself have to say about it? This question needs to be answered, and correctly."

"And what did he say?" asked Aaron, on the edge of his seat.

"Much," replied Daniel. "It all fits together. You will soon see."

"This is why your scroll is important to so many, Teacher Daniel. We need to hear Joshua's teachings from the beginning. With your permission, we golden-rule Pharisees would like to help make copies of your scroll.

"You propose to tell Joshua's whole story in good time," said Aaron. "That is just it – time is much shorter than you probably know. You need to know something I learned from an old friend back by the Sea of Galilee. Elisha, son, forgive me that I have not told you this before now, but I thought it was better that way. Teacher Daniel, Procurator Antonius Felix has decided to end this pilgrimage encampment in Nazareth."

Suddenly, Elisha slammed his hands on the table and stood up. "What?" he shouted.

"Not now, son." Aaron wasn't sure if Elisha was angrier at Felix or at him for withholding the news.

Elisha seethed, panting loudly through his nostrils. Then suddenly he stood and stormed out the patio door behind him.

Aaron raced to catch Elisha on Daniel's patio, before he ran farther away, and he snagged Elisha's arm.

"Let go of me!" Elisha shouted. "You lied to me, to get me to come on this trip!"

The men working on the menorah poles paused their work and watched.

Aaron replied firmly but in a whisper, "Elisha, I only learned last night at the Sea of Galilee, long after we left Jerusalem. Please calm down or you'll endanger everyone here, especially Daniel."

"Oh, so it's my fault," Elisha smiled wryly and angrily. He darted his gaze back and forth at all the workers staring at him. Two little girls peered out from the other main room in Daniel's house, probably his granddaughters. At the sight of them, Elisha relaxed his anger a bit.

"Come back in," Aaron insisted.

"I'm staying here." Elisha stepped to the back corner of the patio and sat there cross-legged.

"Very well." Aaron returned to his conversation with Daniel and shut the door.

"I'm sorry," he told his host.

"His reaction is understandable." Daniel's voice and body shook, and he looked all around him, disoriented by Aaron's shocking news that Procurator Felix was targeting the Nazareth pilgrimage, and presumably Daniel and the Nazareth Scroll. "When? . . ."

"Tomorrow before noon," answered Aaron. "A hundred of Felix's cavalrymen will arrive to disband Nazareth's tent city, by force if necessary."

CHAPTER FIVE

Tiberius City

Procurator Antonius Felix sat with several advisors standing around him, when the cavalry commander entered the room and stood as casually as he could get away with.

"Tribune Philip," Felix said coolly, "is everything in place?"

"Yes, sir," replied the tribune. "We depart at dawn. In these short days of winter, we should reach Nazareth before noon. By mid-afternoon, the tents of Nazareth will be coming down – one way or the other. The message from Centurion Matthias promises that one hundred cavalrymen are more than enough to do the job, even if the pilgrims will not break camp voluntarily."

Tribune Philip was hoping they would not. He hated Joshua and his followers. Late in Philip's childhood, his father Thomas had abandoned their family in order to follow Joshua. Even after the crucifixion, Philip's father wandered preaching for the rest of his life. Philip was left to provide for his mother and younger brothers and sisters. He joined the Roman army for income and to learn the arts of fighting. Philip was so angry at being abandoned and so frustrated by his burdens that he decided to kill Thomas if he ever saw him again. In the army, after every arrest and every skirmish, Philip's love of fighting grew. He could barely contain it any more. It had been too long since he had seen battle, even a one-sided slaughter. He was still angry that he'd missed the massacre of hundreds of zealot heretics in the Jordan Valley a few years earlier. He was eager for action.

"What does Centurion Matthias expect the pilgrims will do?" asked Felix.

"He expects some families to leave voluntarily, but he is not sure of the rest," said Tribune Philip. "They follow the local elder Daniel, who lives in his own house, not one of the tents. They will probably do what he says."

Felix reflected in silence, while his advisors waited.

Finally he spoke to all around him. "I serve by the grace of the emperor, and the emperor does not like trouble. He could remove me – or promote me – following tomorrow's events. We must be patient."

"Tribune Philip," Felix continued.

"Yes, sir."

"There need be no fighting in Nazareth tomorrow."

"Yes, sir," Tribune Philip frowned.

Felix continued, "If anyone is so foolish as to draw weapons against your forces, you may deal with those men as you wish. When you reach the camp's borders, stop your advance and send for this Daniel. Demand that he order the pilgrims to depart Nazareth by sunset. If he refuses – or if any of them refuse – take Daniel as your prisoner and bring him here. The pilgrims will not remain long in Nazareth without him. And you will undoubtedly ensure that they do not. Inform them that any tents still standing at nightfall will be burned to the ground." Felix smiled. "They will fight each other to ensure compliance."

"Yes, sir. Is there anything else, sir?"

"One last thing. Councilor Marcus will ride with you, to help with your report upon your return." Felix knew that Tribune Philip understood his intent. He did not trust Philip to employ restraint, so he was sending an advisor as political control, to report the truth afterward.

"Yes, sir," Tribune Philip bowed and departed the throne room. He was furious. Marcus was Felix's lifelong best friend. At last Philip had a chance for action, but the Roman procurator was tying his hands! If Felix did not want people hurt, why send the cavalry at all? Philip felt misled. He had been so hopeful. He reassured him, though, that he could provoke a fight and unleash the violence he wanted. He smiled wickedly as he returned to the cavalry stables.

Nazareth

The flame keeper sat in a tent doorway, hand in a satchel, stroking the edges of the hidden coal iron coal pan. When a herdsman led Daniel's donkey back to his house stable for the night, the flame keeper's lips stretched into a twisted grin.

Daniel's eyes widened and stared blankly at the table before him, in the flickering light of the oil lamp. He lifted his hands together in reflection, fingertips at his sealed lips. This new arrival, Pharisee Aaron, had just informed Daniel that the Roman forces would arrive in Nazareth tomorrow, to disperse the two thousand camping pilgrims, and possibly to claim the Nazareth Scroll. Daniel could not imagine rewriting the scroll if it were lost. It was the fruit of years and years of discussions, and of the past eight months of intense labor with Gabriel, choosing the ideal episodes and forms and words to tell the story and teachings of Joshua of Nazareth. It would be impossible to repeat such perfection, Daniel knew. He lifted his gaze from the table, stared blankly at the wall, and combed his fingers through his thick white hair, deep in thought. Then he began to punctuate the silence with sharp inhalations and sighs while he rubbed his head.

Daniel looked across his table. His guest Aaron watched him in respectful silence.

"Procurator Felix's forces are due to arrive before noon tomorrow, you say?" Daniel asked Aaron.

"That's right," Aaron replied.

"Will your son Elisha tell others?

"Probably not. I don't think so."

Daniel reflected further. "Have you shared this news with anyone else?"

"I have not," said Aaron, "but another man here might know of it. This afternoon on the road to Nazareth, we were passed by camels carrying a Temple Sadducee by the name of

Benjamin. He almost certainly stopped in Tiberias on the way here. He is probably obtained news from the lower-ranking Roman officials and soldiers there. Ben's father taught his sons that trick, which I know because Ben is my younger brother and my father's heir. For seven years he has refused to speak to me."

Daniel tilted his head and furrowed his brow at this surprising twist in the unfolding news. The Pharisee Aaron's story was almost incredible. But it was all possible. And this story about Aaron's Sadducee past and brother – Aaron had not volunteered any of that. Rather, it had come in answers to Daniel's questions, and it was all consistent.

"Your words, Aaron, are like a rainstorm on dusty soil after a drought – so much startling news at once that I struggle to capture it all. We must consult my daughter Rebecca and her husband Gabriel. Excuse me a moment." Daniel exited to the patio and left the door open.

Aaron followed him outside, where he saw Elisha still brooding in the corner of the patio. He approached his son and squatted to whisper to him.

"Their whole family is about to decide what to do. We did it, Elisha, we got to them in time. You are welcome to join us again inside."

Elisha kept his head turned away and his lips sealed, but he watched Aaron from the corner of his eye.

Aaron rose and stood still a moment, and then returned to Daniel's table inside.

Daniel returned with Gabriel and Rebecca behind him. As Rebecca began to close the door, Elisha's hand stopped it. He entered silently, closed the door behind him, and sat next to Daniel on the opposite side of the table from his father Aaron.

Rebecca sat next to her father, opposite Gabriel and Aaron. She stared at Aaron in silence, her eyes slightly squinting in severe curiosity at this unusual interruption. Not only did her husband Gabriel not object to her behavior – he seemed to await his wife's verdict on their visitor.

"Rebecca, will you please hand me a second oil lamp?"

Rebecca walked to a shelf, found a lamp brimming with olive oil, and carefully handed it to her father.

Daniel lit the second lamp by kissing its nozzle to the first, and then spread the two lamps a forearm's length apart on the table. No one spoke, and they all looked each other, while they could hear the others working outside on the poles and torches for Hanukkah.

"Aaron and Elisha, I believe you met my son-in-law Gabriel when you arrived. This is his wife, my daughter Rebecca, my only child. Her mother departed this world long ago, may the Lord rest her soul. Rebecca has helped with the scroll all along, and she has found just the right words for many, many passages."

"Rebecca is such a rare name these days, and a beautiful one," said Aaron.

Daniel smiled. "Thank you. I named her for my cousin, an innocent girl who died far too young." He sighed wistfully.

"That was—" started Gabriel.

"Not now," Daniel told his son-in-law.

Rebecca continued to study Aaron. He was used to incisive interviews and discussions, but he had never experienced such intense silent attention before.

"Do you know any Greek plays?" Rebecca asked him.

Daniel and Gabriel nodded their heads and smiled, clearly aware of where this was headed, while Aaron was not.

Aaron smiled. "It has been a very long time since I thought much about Greek drama, but yes, my family used to go to the theater, and we liked to act out the plays and create our own adaptations for months afterward."

Rebecca raised her eyebrows in surprise and finally cracked a smile. "You have a favorite playwright?"

Aaron wasn't sure he did. He wondered if Rebecca was seeking a particular answer. Of course, the only right answer was an honest answer, and perhaps how he provided it. "I'm not sure. Maybe Sophocles."

Rebecca rolled her eyes.

"Oh no!" Gabriel laughed.

"She'll make you answer for that!" Daniel smiled.

"Aaron of Jerusalem, you need a lesson in good taste," said Rebecca. "Sophocles is great – that's true – but he's so serious. *Oedipus Rex*? How can that be anyone's favorite? A favorite should bring human happiness rather than trample the entrails of suffering."

"You've seen a Sophocles play, then?" Aaron pushed back.

"Of course not," Rebecca replied. "We don't speak Greek. Well, Gabriel does. No, we know the playwrights from Gabriel's retelling in Aramaic. Before we started writing the Nazareth Scroll, we spent most evenings listening to his tellings, and then we all reenacted parts, changing many of them."

"So you have a favorite playwright?" Aaron asked.

"Menander, and his play *Dyskolos* above all," Rebecca replied.

"So you do like at least a little seriousness? The rich heir pleads with his father to allow his marriage to a poor woman, to share their riches rather than hording them in a wealthy match."

"Of course," replied Rebecca. "The good lessons are much better with comedy than with unrealistic torments. What is it with you men and your dry, dark tastes? Comedy is supreme. The philosophers and the tragic poets, they are mere building blocks."

"Don't let my daughter fool you," said Daniel. "As she learned the philosophers from Gabriel, she took apart their arguments and rebuilt them. Gabriel was always running back to our friend's library in Zippori just to keep up with her questions."

"And what I learned," said Rebecca, "is that none of their learning is as good as the examples of good life on earth and in good, realistic stories. Protagoras is interesting, but Menander is real."

"All right, Rebecca, Hanukkah's first dusk is sneaking up on us. Hear what Aaron tells." Daniel asked Aaron to repeat everything to Rebecca and Gabriel. Aaron explained his Pharisee faction's interest the scroll and Procurator Felix's looming disbandment of the Nazareth encampment. When

Daniel prompted him, Aaron told his background, including the switch from Sadducee to debate-friendly Pharisee.

"Thank you, Aaron," said Daniel. "You seem to be an honest man. We all believe you. Whether you were told the truth from Antonius Felix's soldiers is a different matter, but I believe that you heard and believe what you say you heard. And I believe your sincerity about my scroll. But we have just met you. You will have to leave us to decide how to protect the scroll from Felix. If you and the other pilgrims are forced to leave Nazareth tomorrow, know that you and your son are always welcome to return after things calm down and to stay in Nazareth as our guest. We will be more than glad to allow you and your golden-rule Pharisees one of the very first copies of my testimony of Joshua of Nazareth."

"But first," continued Daniel, "we need some salt! Not just for ourselves, but to share with the poorest villagers and pilgrims. Would you be willing to sell us one of your amphora vases full?"

"I can think of no better use for it. Yes, of course," replied Aaron.

Aaron and Elisha stood up to leave. Daniel, Gabriel, and Rebecca then rose as well. Aaron started to bow in respect, but the much shorter Daniel grabbed his shoulders and embraced Aaron good-bye.

"Until next time," said Daniel.

"Until next time," replied Aaron. He and Elisha closed the door gently on their way out to the dusk's darkening white clouds and moist freezing cold air.

"Now what?" Daniel asked his daughter Rebecca and her husband Gabriel, all seated back at the table.

"We need to get the secret second copy away from Nazareth," said Gabriel. "What about your old friend in Zippori, Isaac the Samaritan?"

"Yes, Papa," said Rebecca. "No one has been more interested in the scroll than he has. And he even added a few things about Joshua that you did not remember at first."

"The problem is, so many people know about his interest in our scroll," said Daniel. "He is the next Joshua disciple that Felix's forces would look for, after me."

"Not if they don't know about the second scroll," said Gabriel. "Felix's men might take the first scroll from us and be satisfied with that."

"Don't you think they will ask if copies have been made?" asked Daniel.

"If they are clever, yes," said Gabriel.

Both men looked at Rebecca. They knew she could not get away with answering dishonestly, even if she wanted to.

"This Centurion Matthias is clever enough," said Daniel.

"Isaac can keep it hidden with one of his many friends in Zippori," said Gabriel. "He won't even need to know exactly where it would be, just to know which person to ask when he needed to retrieve it."

"When?" asked Rebecca. "With these clouds, night will come soon. There isn't time for the eight-mile walk to Zippori and back, even if the messenger found Isaac instantly. By the time of delivering the scroll, Isaac would surely be presiding over his great household's Hanukkah gathering. Many would notice the scroll. And if it finally rains or snows, that could ruin the scroll parchment before arrival."

"True," said Gabriel. "If the skies are clear enough, I will deliver it at the first light tomorrow. Surely I can return before Felix's cavalry will have had enough daylight for the twenty miles from the Sea of Galilee."

"All right, Gabriel," Daniel spoke. "If we have no rain, you will depart at first light, deliver the scroll to Isaac, and return immediately to Nazareth. Your wife and two daughters need you for whatever faces us from Antonius Felix tomorrow."

"That sounds best," Gabriel agreed.

"And if it *is* raining?" asked Rebecca. "How do we preserve the scrolls before Felix's men come?"

"Perhaps we could hide it here in our house," said Daniel.

"But Daniel," said Gabriel, "you know that your daughter, my wife, will not be able to hide her worry from Felix's men, if we pretend that we have only one copy."

Daniel nodded. "All right, even if it is raining in the morning, we need to risk transport. We have good amphora vases. We probably need to get some grain or flour to fill around the scroll and hide it."

One of the workmen from the Hanukkah poles opened the door. "Daniel, it turns out we do not have enough pitch for lighting all nine torches on the first night. What should we do?"

Daniel came to doorway. "Should we ask for a repeat Hanukkah miracle – that enough pitch for one or two torches somehow multiplies for all nine?" Daniel laughed. "No, that is asking too much of the Lord for such a trivial cause. . . . Is there enough pitch for two torches tonight?"

"Yes," answered the worker.

"Then we will light the candles the other way instead. It never much mattered to me which way to do it. Gad's conservative Pharisees say to light all candles the first night and subtract one each successive night. Aaron's golden-rule Pharisees say to start with one candle the first night and to add one each successive night. We'll have to change to Aaron's way for this year.

"Oh, how this will anger the Pharisee Gad! It will be as if we're choosing sides with Aaron's opposing faction of Pharisees." Daniel laughed again. "Gad will just have to live with it. Frankly, I think his way makes more sense for honoring the original miracle of one night's lamp oil lasting for seven days and eight nights. But observing Hanukkah is recent, just two centuries old, not a matter of the ancient law of Moses or the old Hebrew prophets."

"That is certainly fine with us," said the worker. "We had already discussed the possibility. And we will be happy to stir up the false righteousness of Pharisee Gad," laughed the worker.

"We do not need to provoke for the sake of provocation, all right?" said Daniel. "Tomorrow morning, Gabriel will buy some more pitch in Zippori."

As Aaron and Elisha walked from Daniel's house up to Seth's tent, Elisha blurted out, "Do you know what's going on in Zippori?"

"You mean that all these pilgrims will have to go to the big city as their first refuge from the Roman cavalry?"

"Not that. I mean day-to-day, year in and year out. I heard those menorah workers talking about it – construction! They're still building and rebuilding that huge city like crazy! Lots of woodworking – and lots and lots of masonry! Papa, it's just like the new city of Tiberias where we visited yesterday. The whole north is growing, bustling with commerce and interesting gentiles and foreigners. It's not like stodgy Jerusalem with all its scripture debates, and life centered around the three big annual pilgrimages. I mean, sorry, I like learning the Torah and everything. I love studying with you. But there are Pharisees up here in Galilee, too, and so much more happening than in Jerusalem. Papa, I don't think I want to go back. I want to try life in Zippori. For two years I've wanted to apprentice as a stone mason. Now that I've heard about the work in Zippori, I'm sure this is what I want to do. I am *supposed* to learn masonry in Zippori, Papa. I just know it! I'm sorry."

Hidden at some distance between the tents, the hooded flame keeper watched Aaron and Elisha emerge from Daniel's house. The Pharisee Aaron was carrying an amphora vase. Why? Daniel had nothing to sell. And from the looks of the easy transport, the amphora was empty. Unless – could it be the scroll? No, Daniel would not part with it that easily, would he? The flame keeper frowned at the thought that the scroll might be leaving Daniel's house. There was consolation in the new pitch pot for the Hanukkah torches to burn above Daniel's house. Pitch would come in handy tonight, the flame keeper realized. The third attempt would burn Daniel's roof and entire house to houses, and Daniel too.

CHAPTER SIX

At the guard tent in Nazareth, the cavalry's Centurion Matthias summoned his trusted soldier to follow him. They left the young guard at their small tent by the edge of Nazareth's tent city, and they walked many paces up the path away from Nazareth, well out of earshot.

Matthias stopped to turn around and survey the sprawling tent city just below. "It is time for me to tell you about tomorrow," he told his soldier. "Tribune Philip is coming with a hundred cavalrymen."

The soldier's eyes widened with surprise, while his lips pursed with resolve to play his part, whatever that would be.

"The cavalry arrives before noon. Their orders were not final before we left the Sea of Galilee two days ago, but the main point is to terminate this mass pilgrimage to Nazareth. Tribune Philip is aching for bloodshed, whatever his orders from above. We will obey him. You see now why I ordered you to have minimal conversation with the pilgrims here. We must not make friends, for we must be prepared to follow any order."

The soldier nodded, without hesitation but without enthusiasm.

"The Procurator Antonius Felix is interested in this man Daniel and his scroll. I expect we will see some activity about that as well. Tribune Philip will want another scouting report before they arrive," Matthias continued. "Tomorrow at dawn, you will collect your horse and travel this path away from Nazareth. Ride back toward Tiberius, but at a slow pace. The cavalry will be riding much faster this way, I expect, so you should meet them no farther than halfway back. Unless you are given new orders, you will return to Nazareth with them after you have told them everything you know about Nazareth and all these pilgrims. Is everything clear?"

"Yes, centurion."

"Good."

Aaron carried Daniel's empty amphora to his salt stores in the rich man Seth's tent just a short walk back uphill from Daniel's house. Elisha's desire to move to Zippori weighed heavily on Aaron, but neither of them spoke more of it. When they arrived at Seth's tent, they were greeted by the same servant who had first guided them into the tent city offering lodging.

"Is your master Seth still here?" asked Aaron.

The young servant nodded, without expression, and pulled back the tent flap for them to enter.

The same circle of men was still gathered with Seth. Although Aaron's eyes needed a few moments to adjust from the outside light, his memory of the space and the people guided him from the start.

"Back so soon, Aaron!" Seth called out.

"We have another salt customer," said Aaron.

"You need one of your amphoras?"

"Thank you, yes please, Seth."

Seth motioned for one of his servants to retrieve an amphora from the men's quarters behind the large curtain to the right.

"Not many in Nazareth have such large capacity for salt as this amphora you carry," said Seth. "Besides the native Nazarenes, of course, here in their own homes. Does this mean you have already met Daniel?"

"That's right," said Aaron.

"Isn't he a wonderful man? It is easy to see why Joshua took Daniel as one of his disciples, all the way from Nazareth to Jerusalem. Ah, here is your salt."

With Elisha's help, Aaron put on his amphora back harness and lifted the heavy vase full of salt.

Two men from Seth's circle helped Aaron stand from his awkward position on the tent floor.

"Thank you," Aaron nodded to them and was about to turn to leave.

"We'll see you soon for dinner?" Seth asked.

"Of course – gladly and gratefully!" answered Aaron.

"Excellent!" said Seth. "My friends here are staying until then. You are welcome to arrive any time."

"Thank you," said Aaron. Even under the weight of the salt, Aaron bowed slightly to Seth in departure, and he and Elisha exited Seth's tent.

"After all these years, soon you'll be big enough to do the heavy lifting," Aaron half-joked to Elisha on the path outside Seth's tent.

"Enough, Papa. Masonry, Papa, masonry."

Aaron reflected on the years with his adopted son Elisha. Six years earlier, at age seven, Elisha had been his family's sole survivor from a midnight fire that tore through several homes in the poorest district of Jerusalem where Aaron lived. Even many of the stone walls collapsed. Elisha had escaped to the roof and then jumped to the street just before his roof collapsed. Few survived the fire, and no one ever learned what had caused it. That winter night had been cold, with oil lamps and fireplaces and bed warmer coal pans in ample use.

As the youngest child of youngest children, Elisha had no living uncles or aunts to take him in. He did not know any of his older cousins or even where they lived – which was mostly in Galilee, his parents had mentioned. He was completely orphaned.

This was during Aaron's first year with the Pharisees, working long and hard to establish customers around Jerusalem for the salt he hauled back and forth from the Salt Sea area. With no money at the start, Aaron obtained lodgings in the poor district in exchange for performing as a scribe for simple documents for the family and friends of his landlord. The barter arrangement worked for lodging and a little food, but there were too many scribes in holy Jerusalem for Aaron to earn enough cash. He did not possess any other trade skills.

At the same time, Aaron's thoughts often turned to the Great Sea, where his family had an estate that they had often visited during his childhood. That seashore was Aaron's favorite place in the world, especially its stormy winds and smells of winter. One day, Aaron's two sets of thoughts collided – his reverie of the sea and his need for income – and this is when he decided to try dealing in salt. And since he was getting established among the poorest city dwellers, he focused on the cheaper rock salt from the Salt Sea cliffs. Little did he know then that over the next seven years, he still would not see the Great Sea again. It was the happy place where his dreams often retreated but his daytime life never approached.

The night of the Jerusalem fire, Aaron was home asleep, in a room shared with another boarder. The screams awoke him. From his bed, he perceived the dim orange glow immediately and rushed outside, one of the first in the street. As he ran toward the fire, he watched a child jump from the roof and crumple onto the street below. Aaron made a beeline for the child.

The very thin boy was balled up in fear, with only slight injuries. As the boy's eyes looked into Aaron's by the fire's light, Aaron heard the fire's roar behind him, sucking in wind and forcing it upward through the burning houses. The sound was not violent like a storm, but steady and mesmerizing, like a giant blacksmith's bellows. It was a sound that could have been soothing by itself. Then the roof collapsed, and the boy stared in wide-eyed shock with a cobblestone as his pillow, expressionless except the stream of tears from his eyes. Aaron lifted the boy, who still clutched his knees into a ball, and carried him home.

It was days before Elisha uttered the simplest words, and weeks before Aaron's thousandth effort finally drew out a short-lived smile. But Aaron was patient, and the family that lodged Aaron helped with the boy during Aaron's frequent trips to the salt cliffs. As soon as he could, Aaron borrowed money to buy a second donkey for carrying more salt, and the donkey more than paid for itself. The added income allowed Aaron to buy what food and clothes Elisha needed, and by the end of that first summer, Elisha had gained a little weight, and he looked healthier and less impoverished.

When he was in Jerusalem, Aaron taught the boy the Torah in the early evening by lamplight, and he studied the prophets by himself while the boy slept at night. He always had two scrolls at a time, one book of Moses and one prophet, borrowed from his fellow Pharisees. The writings of the prophets had been less familiar to Aaron, since his Sadducee family upbringing taught that there was little worth in any writings beyond the five books of Moses.

Over the years, Aaron taught Elisha to read and write. As Elisha grew, he accompanied Aaron on more and more of his trips to the salt cliffs. Aaron's Pharisee friends encouraged Elisha's learning, and just a few months before this trip to Nazareth, they had started calling Elisha the disciple of Aaron, his years-long student, not just his son. They did not know that Elisha had started threatening to quit his studies, if that was what it took to become an apprentice stonemason.

Elisha had nearly refused this trip, which he saw as an opportunity to seek and obtain an apprenticeship while Aaron was traveling. But Elisha was perhaps even more interested in Daniel and the Nazareth Scroll than Aaron was, so here he was.

As Aaron carried the salt to Daniel's house, Elisha said, "You know, Papa, you do not have to hide dangers from me anymore." For the first time ever, Elisha's voice cracked and fell, briefly, to the lower voice of a man.

He and Aaron both laughed as Elisha's voice reinforced the point that he was no longer a child.

"You're right. I'm sorry. You can obviously handle the news from Procurator Felix's headquarters."

"Thank you," Elisha smiled in pride and sighed in hard-earned satisfaction.

Rebecca worried as she watched her own two young daughters play in their little courtyard. The scroll meant so much to her father Daniel, to her husband Gabriel, and to herself as well. It was not just what Joshua had said about predictions of an Anointed One, the next Messiah leader like Abraham and David. After twenty years of sharing the stories and lessons of Joshua of Nazareth, her father Daniel had written them through her husband Gabriel's hand, for a much wider audience. The followers of Joshua were eager for a book of Joshua of Nazareth, like the scrolls of the old prophets.

Rebecca did not remember her mother, who died the year after her birth. Her father raised her with the help of his sister. Rebecca knew that the father she adored played an important role as the leading elder of Nazareth. Daniel led Nazareth's families through their hard times and conflicts. A few words from Daniel carried great moral weight, and he often resolved problems before they had to be taken to Zippori for a scholar's rulings. Nazareth was too small to have its own hereditary priest, so the male villagers led themselves in their weekly Sabbath worship together, usually in the courtyard of the big house. Daniel could barely read, so others did the readings. But Daniel had memorized much, and he was the villager's best cantor, singing ancient hymns as well as new ones that he improvised for the scriptures he had memorized.

From the earliest Rebecca could remember, strangers from miles around sometimes showed up to meet her father and to hear from him about Joshua of Nazareth. No one had known Joshua of Nazareth as well as Daniel had, from Joshua's childhood, to Daniel's time as one of Joshua's many disciples, to Joshua's crucifixion. After Daniel settled back in Nazareth, whenever he had business in the big city of Zippori, four miles away, he attracted people yearning to learn from him what he had learned from Joshua.

Occasionally, men traveled from farther away to visit Rebecca's father Daniel in Nazareth. A scribe named Gabriel had been one of these men, from the Sea of Galilee region. As a follower of Joshua's teachings, Gabriel was concerned and confused about divisions and conflicts over Joshua's actual teachings and their meanings. Gabriel wanted to know: Did Joshua ever claim to be an Anointed One, the next Messiah leader for Jewish unity and peace? So Gabriel traveled to

Nazareth to learn more. He, too, came knocking at Daniel's door, and as usual, Daniel offered his hospitality while Gabriel stayed in Nazareth.

Rebecca still remembered those hours and days well. When Gabriel realized how important Daniel was for his witness of Joshua's teachings, Gabriel offered to write Daniel's testament of Joshua. There was none other like it, Gabriel claimed, and Joshua's teachings deserved to outlive their generation. Gabriel honestly warned that writing this testament could create enemies of men and forces far beyond Nazareth. Daniel declined. He had been with Joshua in the last, dark days in Jerusalem, and he knew full well the truth of Gabriel's warning. But Daniel's refusal was not from fear. Rather, he thought it would be too prideful to lift himself as the chronicler of the great Joshua of Nazareth, even as his best friend. Daniel saw himself as an illiterate Jew and a small village elder, not as an author of Jewish scripture for the ages.

Rebecca smiled as she remembered Gabriel's repeated pleading with her father to write his account. Day after day, Gabriel failed to convince Daniel. By now, Gabriel had learned enough from Daniel to write an unauthorized testament according to Daniel. But he would not write Daniel's tales without Daniel's blessing. So Gabriel turned to Daniel's daughter Rebecca for help.

Rebecca felt the setting like it was yesterday. Her widowed father Daniel had raised his girl as Joshua had taught, to be seen as valuable as any son. Daniel showed Rebecca how to think and how to understand the world well enough to make her own way in it. So when Daniel offered room to travelers, as he often did, Rebecca struck a middle ground. She neither showed too much interest in the guests nor faded into the background like many women did. She shared the table and sometimes joined their conversations.

The third night in a row when Daniel refused Gabriel's offer to write his testament, Gabriel turned to Rebecca at the table and asked her to try to convince her father. Rebecca looked to her father for guidance. But all he offered was a raised eyebrow and a slight grin – an invitation for Rebecca to decide her own response to Gabriel's request. Rebecca was already convinced that the proposed scroll was a good idea, but she asked to be excused for the evening for further reflection.

The next morning, in a sunlit thin fog, she took the goats and sheep to graze where spring greens sprouted from Nazareth's rocky soil. Gabriel followed not long after her.

"You don't come with advice on shepherding, do you, Gabriel the scribe?" Rebecca smiled.

Gabriel returned her smile and shook his head. "You want him to write his testament with me, don't you?"

"You make a persuasive case to him. I know little of the world beyond Nazareth, but I am concerned by your description of the confusion among Joshua's followers. Papa is the wisest man in Nazareth and well beyond, they say. He knew Joshua from childhood until his death. If anyone can help, my father can."

"He will do whatever you ask, won't he?" asked Gabriel.

Rebecca's light brown eyes sparkled as she smiled, full of her father's love and suddenly alight as the sunlight finally burned through the last morning fog. She nodded.

"You understand I would have to stay many months under your roof?"

Rebecca nodded again.

"Rebecca, daughter of Daniel, would you object if I had an entirely different conversation with your father, on my own?"

Rebecca looked Gabriel straight in the eyes and continued her smile. She shook her head gently – she had no objection.

Gabriel smiled in return. Then he bowed his face and eyes to the ground before her, and quietly returned to the house up the hill.

That evening's supper brought the fourth long conversation about Gabriel's offer and desire to write down Daniel's account of Joshua of Nazareth. Daniel repeated that he felt too lowly to send forth his testament for reading and copying among all the Jews.

Then Gabriel repeated last night's question to Rebecca – would she please try to convince her father?

Rebecca gave her father a long, silent smile. Then she began, "Papa, I believe that Gabriel speaks the truth about confusion among the Jews regarding Joshua. There is this growing disagreement about how Joshua viewed the line of Biblical Anointed Ones, the Messiahs from Abraham to Cyrus and all the priests. Joshua's followers are arguing over what Joshua said about this, and what Joshua meant by what he said. While most of the debaters are surely honest, it seems that some are not, that they stand by different accounts of Joshua in order to gain power over his followers.

"Papa, you are an honest man. You will tell the truth as you remember it. I trust that Gabriel will write it honestly, and so do you, I can see this in your spirit. What harm can come of spreading the truth about Joshua, Papa? Your testament will not claim to be the final authority. You are the first to acknowledge that no one is the final authority, that only the conversation of men and women can come closer to full truths, and not always certainly. Give Gabriel the fruits of your years with Joshua, Papa, so that he may share the bounty abundantly. I think this is what Joshua would want, and I think you know that."

Daniel smiled as his daughter spoke so eloquently. "It is decided. Gabriel may write my testament of Joshua." He smiled even more broadly and put his strong hands one each on the younger shoulders beside him, Gabriel on the left and Rebecca on the right. They smiled too, and laughed.

"And now, Rebecca," Daniel continued, "will you please excuse your father and our visitor?"

Rebecca stood and bowed her head respectfully to a nervous Gabriel. All three were quiet enough to hear a burning log fall into two pieces in the hearth across the patio. Rebecca lit a second oil lamp from the one on the table, and exited the house's main room.

She went to their animals in the stable, set the lamp on a ledge, and sat on the straw beside the donkeys, the sheep, and the goats. From where they rested, all the animals shifted to encircle

Rebecca where she sat, and a lamb climbed into her lap. Rebecca took a long, deep breath of the straw, the clean animals, and the traces of sheep's milk still on the corners of the month-old lambs' mouths. She waited for her Papa to come to her after his conversation with Gabriel.

Half an hour later, Daniel entered and sat cross-legged on the straw beside his daughter and their animals, beneath the steady glow of the oil lamp on this pleasant evening of no breeze and mild temperatures. The animals shifted to include Daniel within their circle. A goat rested its head on his lap, and Daniel began gently scratching its scalp and neck.

"You know why I come to you?"

"Gabriel has asked to marry me?"

Daniel nodded, focusing intently on his daughter's expressions.

Rebecca responded with a small, serious smile, lips unparted. Finally she spoke, "Gabriel is a kind and determined man. He will be a good husband and provider. What will he do when his work with you is done?"

"I told him what he already saw. All that is mine is yours – the house, the animals, the fields down in the valley. I told him that if you agreed, he will have my blessing to marry you, even if he wanted to return to the Sea of Galilee. He explained that he is the fourth son, with no property, and that he would be happy to make Nazareth his home."

Now Rebecca's entire face smiled, and she leapt into her father's arms. She wept into her father's shoulders, "Oh Papa, I was afraid of losing you if he took me away. Oh Papa, I am so happy!" She cried and cried for the joy having both Gabriel and her father together in the same home.

This Hanukkah evening seven years later, Rebecca remembered how swiftly the next months and years had gone – the wedding at Sabbath services, the spring planting, the summer weeding, the fall harvest, and a first baby in late winter, just when the year's new lambs were born. Daniel graciously ceded the marital sleeping chamber and moved to the tiniest room, scarcely more than an attic cubby, with barely enough height to sit up. In the next years, more farming and pasturing and parenting followed, and then another child. Daniel and Gabriel spoke diligently about Daniel's testament, what to include and what trivia to leave aside. Six years came and went, and the writing project was discussed, and organized in their minds, and partially composed in stories told by Daniel, rephrased together, and memorized by Gabriel until the day when he would start writing it all.

The seventh spring, word came of bitter debates all the way in Jerusalem. Was Joshua of Nazareth the predicted next Anointed One, a leader to bring all of Israel together as had successive Messiah prophets and kings centuries ago? Joshua's followers were beginning to focus on this question more than on Joshua's main teachings of neighborly love and charity. Finally, when Daniel saw a new letter from Jerusalem, he and Rebecca and Gabriel decided that they must begin writing Daniel's testimony even while they still collaborated orally on the final parts. The world of Joshua's followers needed the structure and direction of an eyewitness testimony that was well composed for the present and future generations, like some of the Jewish books of prophets and histories, and like some of the Greek books that Gabriel had read in the library in Tiberius.

So Daniel bought a blank parchment scroll in Zippori, and Gabriel began to write. As they had long composed it by memory, Gabriel wrote Daniel's narrative in the best version of Nazareth's poetic, accented Aramaic, as Joshua had spoken it. Whenever they wrote the words of Joshua himself, Daniel revisited various possible phrasings each time aloud, until he chose which sounded most like Joshua had spoken. They all knew that Daniel did not remember every word perfectly, but the phrasings were generally accurate, as only Joshua's lifelong best friend could recall them. After Daniel was satisfied with each sentence, whether quoting Joshua or just telling the story, Gabriel put ink to parchment. Then they repeated the process for the next sentence. All summer long they continued, after the day's shepherding and the occasional trip to oversee their grain fields in the valley below.

By the autumn harvest, Gabriel had written most of Daniel's testimony. Even during the harvest, almost every night, the two men forged ahead until sleep caught up with one or both of them.

Then after the winter planting, pilgrims suddenly began arriving in Nazareth, far more than Daniel had ever received in twenty years since the crucifixion. The pilgrims soon exceeded tiny Nazareth's native population of about a hundred. The pilgrims came to visit the home of Joshua of Nazareth, to learn from Joshua's fellow villagers like Daniel, and to congregate with other followers of Joshua. Some of them spoke of the "Nazareth Scroll," and word was traveling fast about Daniel's and Gabriel's progress. As Daniel and Gabriel offered their hospitality to the pilgrims, who raised their own tents just downhill from the village center, the two men paused their writing for several days. But when the swelling pilgrimage seemed endless, they found a new rhythm and forged ahead. Finally the Nazareth Scroll was done, or nearly. Tonight after the Hanukkah meal, Gabriel and Daniel expected to write the final sentence or two. They had all been very excited until the news they had just received –Felix's Roman forces were coming to end it all. Rebecca was still in shock.

CHAPTER SEVEN

Rebecca was jolted from her thoughts by the shrill, high-pitched voice of the conservative Pharisee Gad. Rebecca's two little girls scurried across the patio to clutch their mother in fear of the angry man outside the open patio door to the village path.

"Get Daniel out here, I demand it!" shouted Gad. "I don't care if you don't have enough pitch for nine torches. You are supposed to light all eight lights the first night of Hanukkah, not just one! It's bad enough when people make the error in their own homes. You want to display it over your rooftop to corrupt all two thousand of us here?"

A crowd was beginning to gather on the path outside Daniel's house. Almost all the tenting pilgrims revered Daniel, and most of them feared Gad. On the other hand, most of them were accustomed to lighting the Hanukkah candles Gad's way. Daniel was breaking that rule, which made many in the crowd uncomfortable, even upset. After all, Daniel was not even switching out of conviction, to join the minority who followed the opposite rule, with one light the first night. Instead, Daniel was suddenly reversing his practice for convenience.

Among the crowd were Elisha and Aaron, carrying the amphora heavy with salt in its shoulder harness. Elisha looked to his adopted father for his reaction. Aaron thought it was Daniel's place to answer Gad, and he did not think Daniel would need any help.

Daniel emerged from inside his house, walked across his patio, and stepped onto the path to meet Gad and the silent, anxious crowd.

"How dare—"

"I heard you the first time, Gad," said Daniel. "We all heard you the first time."

Several people in the crowd chuckled. Most of the pilgrims had been in the Nazareth camp long enough to know about Gad's hectoring, from personal experience or someone else's.

"Where is it written how many Hanukkah lights for each night?" asked Daniel.

"It is written by the great Teacher Shammai and many others," answered Gad.

"But isn't the opposite written by the great Teacher Hillel, his archrival?" asked Daniel.

"That woodcutter? Hillel was a fraud, an imposter," said Gad.

"Some say the same of Shammai," said Daniel.

"Are you slandering the late great Teacher Shammai?"

"I am suggesting that neither man had the right to impose his will on the other." Keeping his voice calm, Daniel raised it to be heard up and down the path and into many rows of tents. "It is well and good that we continue their disagreements on questions unanswered in the books of Moses. This can make us all better Jews."

"Nonsense!" screamed Gad, his facing turning red even in the waning daylight. "Everything – I mean everything – has a right way and a wrong way. Once we find the right way, we must practice it. We must ensure that others practice it. To miss this point is to lead others astray, to risk their very salvation in the hereafter."

Daniel sighed. It was hopeless to sway Gad from his self-righteousness. Instead, it was for the hundred or more listening in the crowd that Daniel pleaded his case, and to the many hundreds they would tell in the next hour back with their families and friends.

Suddenly a voice from the crowd took Gad's side. "Gad is right. It is obvious from the Hanukkah story that we must commemorate the miracle of the Temple light as it happened, starting with more candles and ending with the last, single light."

Daniel recognized the voice of Nathan, a thirty-year-old native of Nazareth. He had also been the first, and failed, suitor of Daniel's daughter Rebecca. From that day to this, Nathan was the only Nazareth native who disliked Daniel. Nathan's hostility had seethed and deepened with each passing year of his half-hearted and failed efforts to find a bride. He never got over Rebecca. He had no property or skills, just basic farm labor to offer. Daniel had suggested that Nathan move to Zippori for a better job and more chances at finding a wife. But Nathan would not so much as make the one-hour walk to Zippori except when absolutely necessary, and then only briefly.

Why was Nathan speaking out now on Gad's side about the Hanukkah lights? Daniel knew that Nathan resented the pilgrims, and the filth they brought to the sewage ditch through the middle of their encampment, and especially their risk to Nazareth's water supplies. By the second week of more and more pilgrims arriving after harvest time, Nathan kept pleading with Daniel to send them all away, before they might drink Nazareth's wells dry during this drought. Nathan got angrier with each passing week of their burgeoning encampment. But he had never expressed much opinion on religious matters. Daniel understood Nathan's current outburst as an attempt to join any rare opponent of Daniel, no matter the cause.

"Nathan and Gad, no one will force you or anyone else to look at our menorah tonight." Daniel continued in his commanding yet reassuring voice. "If you wish, turn your heads away. Go light your own menorahs how you want. I will not threaten you with hellfire for it. I even encourage you to do it your way. But many of the poor souls encamped in Nazareth this Hanukkah cannot afford a menorah or even slight candles to set in the dirt. To them we offer this menorah. I will lead the Hanukkah prayer here in one hour."

Before Gad could repeat his objections, Daniel turned his back and re-entered his front door.

Gad stood fuming for several breaths, opening and closing his mouths in search of the right words. Finally he stormed off, and most in the crowd returned to their tents for preparation of the evening meal.

For a moment, Aaron and Elisha remained on the path to watch Daniel's son-in-law Gabriel and the other men continue their work with the nine menorah poles. The first fifteen-foot end pole was already lashed to supporting poles angled along the two sides from the left corner of the house.

Suddenly, Aaron noticed a young man pull one of the workers away from the right end pole as they put it into place. As this young man sprinted to disappear between the tents across the path, the workers lost control of the pole. Instead of resting along the side of the house, the top of the pole continued moving past its new upright position. Just longer than twice the height of the house, the pole pivoted on the roof's front edge, with the top plunging toward the flat roof. The bottom of the pole kicked out dangerously into the path. Before anyone could react, the pole smacked one man to the ground, and he cried out in pain. That wasn't enough to stop the pole, which slammed into the roof. For a brief moment, all stood silent, and Aaron watched a few small pieces of mortar fall from the side of the house, crumbling audibly onto the ground below.

Then a commotion arose as some people helped lever the pole off the roof, while others ranted about the man who had sabotaged the effort before running off. A couple of other young men briefly darted after him, but they were too late and too slow.

"It's broken," said two men at once as they looked at the man on the ground whose right forearm was bent outward. The victim winced while the two men helped him to his feet and led him to a nearby tent where a woman offered help.

No one seemed to have recognized the culprit. Everyone assumed his motive was an excess of piety, in line with Gad's opposition to lighting only one menorah candle-torch the first night. The workers proceeded to erect the rest of the menorah, more solemnly than before, braced for opposition and constantly checking over their shoulders.

Gabriel recognized Aaron and motioned him and Elisha through the front door, where Rebecca then escorted them back into the small house's main room.

"Ah yes, the amphora of salt," said Daniel. "Could you please place it in the corner there? Your strength is surely greater than mine."

Elisha helped Aaron remove the tall amphora vase from the shoulder harness and put it in the corner.

"How much?" asked Daniel.

"I don't know," said Aaron. "Whatever the market price is here for rock salt."

Daniel handed Aaron two shekels.

"For cheap rock salt?" Aaron protested.

"My friend Isaac will pay at least that much for it," said Daniel.

"I am in your debt," said Aaron.

"Not in the slightest."

"I thought you responded very well to Gad about the menorah," said Aaron. "I watched faces of doubt in the crowd sway to your position with just a few words from you."

"Gad made it easy!" Daniel laughed, and Elisha and Aaron laughed with him.

"Good luck tomorrow," said Aaron. He knew he might not be able to speak with Daniel before Felix's Roman cavalry arrived.

"Even more so to you," answered Daniel.

Aaron turned and began to leave when Daniel stopped him.

"I never fully answered your question, what moved us to write the scroll this year, not to wait any longer. Please, come back in for a moment."

Aaron and Elisha followed him back inside the house's main room. On the table, next to the oil lamp, was a folded sheet of parchment. Daniel closed the door behind them.

"Last spring," Daniel started, "my friend Isaac received this letter." The folded parchment remained untouched on the table between Daniel on one side and Aaron and Elisha on the other. "It is written in Greek, by a Greek Jew from far away. Isaac added the Aramaic translation at the bottom, because he didn't know that Gabriel can read Greek."

"We knew we had to write the scroll to answer questions about whether Joshua of Nazareth was the next Anointed leader of the Jews, and to tell the whole of Joshua's message. This man Saul presents a more urgent problem. He never knew our friend

Joshua of Nazareth, but now Saul is pretending the authority to denounce what others teach about Joshua. Read the letter. You'll see."

Aaron gently lifted the parchment and unfolded it before him. He pulled the oil lamp a little closer on the table. He saw the Aramaic translation at the bottom, but focused on the original Greek. He furrowed his brow at what he read, and then invited Elisha to look as well. "This is why you ought to learn to speak and read Greek. The affairs of the world outside are reaching deeper and deeper into the world of the Jews."

Aaron folded the Aramaic section closed, to reinforce the point to Elisha, who understood very little Greek and did not know the Greek letters on the page:

> Παῦλος ἀπόστολος . . . . Ἰησοῦ Χριστοῦ . . . .
> Εἴ τις ὑμᾶς εὐαγγελίζεται παρ' ὃ παρελάβετε,
> ἀνάθεμα ἔστω!

Even when Aaron read the passage aloud in Greek, Elisha still could not understand. Then Aaron unfolded the parchment.

"Now listen to the Aramaic translation, Elisha, and understand why it is important to know Greek," said Aaron. Then he read aloud:

> Saul an apostle, to Isaac of Zippori: Many years ago, after the crucifixion of Joshua of Nazareth under Pontius Pilate, you knew me as the oppressor of Joshua's disciples in Jerusalem. Since that time, you have heard of my conversion and my good news for the gentiles, which I will soon bring to the city of Zippori. I received the good news through a direct revelation from Joshua the Anointed, on the road to Damascus. For years thereafter, I did not confer about it with the apostles who knew Joshua of Nazareth during his life. Joshua's revelation to me is the final and definitive authority. If anyone

> proclaims news contrary to what I proclaim, let that one be accursed!

"Did Saul ever come to Zippori?" asked Aaron.

"Not yet," Daniel answered.

"This is one reason why the disciples in Jerusalem still dislike Saul," said Aaron. "Saul never even met Joshua of Nazareth, unlike Joshua's brothers or you, Daniel, who knew Joshua from childhood all the way until the crucifixion. When Saul stopped killing Joshua's followers, he suddenly insisted that he had greater authority from his claims of visions of Joshua than the authority of those who had followed Joshua during his life. Yet for a long time, Saul refused even to meet those who were closest to Joshua of Nazareth. Saul was careful to work far from Jerusalem and Galilee, where no one could contradict him. Years later, by the time Saul finally conferred with the main disciples in Jerusalem, he had established his own congregations abroad. And I see now how clearly they are *his* churches. Saul threatens a curse on anyone who dares to contradict him!"

Even in the shadows of the oil lamp, Daniel's face was visibly angry, his lips pursed. "No man has the right to curse another, especially not in the name of Joshua or the Lord. Even here in Nazareth, we saw the problem. In the zeal of his conversion, in opening the window to Joshua's teachings that he once slammed shut, Saul is shuttering other windows. For years he built this network of Jews and gentiles in Assyria and Greece. Now through the life of the written word" – Daniel slammed his palm onto Saul's letter – "Saul's stature is growing, with deep roots, also here in ancient Israel."

Daniel leaned back and calmed himself slightly. His hand remained on Saul's letter. "Let Saul preach and write what he wants. We friends and followers of Joshua of Nazareth are mostly too poor and illiterate to respond in kind. But with effort, my son-in-law scribe Gabriel and I can manage writing. When we read about Saul closing windows and doors on Joshua's teachings, we knew we had to offer the truth in writing, not just in local storytelling and preaching. Someone has to do it, and so far, none of Joshua's other disciples have."

"Never until this moment did I fully understand Saul's power," said Aaron. "In Jerusalem, he seems secondary among Joshua's followers, even among the annual Passover pilgrims from far away. But farther from the Temple, Saul's authority grows and grows. He would no doubt find something in your scroll as grounds for cursing you, too."

"For eight months, we have labored under this maddening fact," said Daniel. "This all is sad, too, since Paul also preaches love in the name of my friend Joshua."

"Daniel, your scroll is critical." Aaron placed his hands on Daniel's hand on the table. "You must get it out of Nazareth before Antonius Felix's forces arrive tomorrow!"

CHAPTER EIGHT

Aaron and Elisha walked back up the path to the small, short tent where they were staying. Their host Michael was talking with another man in front of his tent.

"Aaron, Elisha, this is my wife Naomi," said Michael.

At a small fire pit shared between several tents, a woman squatted over a pan she had removed from the fire. Naomi made brief eye contact with her husband's lodgers, bowed her head, and continued her work at the fire and her conversation with the man squatting next to her. She kept nodding her head while the man talked, and encouraging him with pats on the back.

"Also, please meet Sol." Michael motioned to the man next to Naomi and whispered, "He reminds us of Naomi's little brother, who just died three months ago. Sol has lived his whole life in Nazareth and likes to make sure everyone feels welcome here."

"Michael." Naomi didn't like something about her husband's conversation.

Michael turned back toward the cooking fire. "Sol, this is Aaron, along with his son Elisha."

"Wel-come t' – t' – to Nazareth," Sol stammered.

Aaron smiled at Sol and bowed his head slightly. "Thank you."

Michael and Aaron exchanged looks and smiles of sympathy. Solomon was the village's special case, with the mind of a young child, in a short, thin adult's body, about thirty years old. His hair was some of the longest that Aaron had seen on a man, almost down to his shoulders. Aaron lived among poor men in Jerusalem, who often had very uneven haircuts. But even among the poor, all of them had short hair, exposing some or all of the ears and most of the neck. No man in his right mind had hair anything like a woman's.

"We were just discussing Sol's new haircut," said Michael. "How do you like it, Aaron?"

"You like your hair long?" asked Aaron.

"Longer than yours, yes," answered Sol. "But past the shoulders was t' – t' – too much."

"How is your mother this evening, Sol?" Michael asked.

"All right. Thank . . . you," replied Sol. "I'm going t' – t' – to see her now. Good-bye."

"Good-bye," Michael and Aaron replied, and Sol left them.

"You didn't have to make him leave," said Naomi.

Michael turned to Aaron. "Sol's head works better than his tongue, but even there he has limitations. He observes quite a bit, and he can tell you a lot about Nazareth's families, including Joshua's parents Miriam and Joseph along with his brothers and sisters – if you make the time to listen at his speed. You're most likely to get his attention at night. They say he barely sleeps, and he walks around like a night watchman, lonely for company."

"Is he honest?" asked Aaron.

"He seems so, yes," replied Michael. "In that regard, he deserves the name Solomon. By the way, he says the loud accident down at Daniel's house turned out all right. Were you there?"

"Yes," said Aaron, "that's right. Those menorah poles are ambitiously tall and top-heavy. I think Daniel's crew will manage the rest fine, though, with extra men on them now."

"It's nice that Daniel is doing that menorah for people like us," said Michael. "My wife and I do not have our own, and I assume you traveled here without one yourself?"

"That's right," replied Aaron.

"Oh, you don't know yet," started Michael. "We are invited to the same Hanukkah meal this evening at Seth's big tent over there. Naomi and I will join you and Elisha there. She had already begun cooking when we were invited, so she is putting away tonight's meal for tomorrow."

"It will be nice to make better acquaintance with you this evening," said Aaron.

"Let me tell you a few things first," said Michael. He looked down the path at Seth's tall tent and lowered his voice.

"Naomi and I come from Caesarea on the Great Sea," said Michael. "So does this rich man Seth, although he does not know or recognize my humble wife and myself," said Michael. "For his part, he is very well known there."

"And respected?" asked Aaron.

"Michael!" his wife beseeched him in a low, stern voice, and glared up from her place by the fire. Now she looked scared as well as displeased.

"Um . . . he is well known," said Michael.

Aaron could see that Michael, too, feared this man Seth from Caesarea.

"If you do not mind, please do not tell Seth where we come from," Michael requested.

"Understood," said Aaron.

Young Elisha nodded to Michael that he understood as well.

Michael elaborated, "I started life in Zippori, actually, so I do not speak with the accents of the coast. When I was ten years old, I once even saw Joshua of Nazareth preach in my synagogue. Soon after that, my father got into some trouble, and we moved to be near his family by the Great Sea. I never got to see Joshua again.

"A few years ago, Naomi and I made the Passover pilgrimage to Jerusalem, and I heard some of the same teachings again, by men claiming to be disciples of Joshua of Nazareth. After that, back home in Caesarea, we joined the congregation of Joshua followers there. Our numbers are substantial, including many who work for Seth. In fact, Seth acts as our sponsor. He controls much of the port trade, and when those who work for him get sick or hurt, he helps them and their families. Well, some of them."

"Michael!" Naomi nodded in the direction of Seth's big tent.

"My wife and I usually work at the palace of the Roman procurator," continued Michael. "But we are often without work in the cold months. So when we heard about the new following of Daniel in Nazareth, we came."

Naomi covered the pan of cooling food and put it in their tent. When she emerged, she was bundled in a clean, blue headscarf that barely revealed her eyes.

Aaron was impressed that Naomi seemed to be wearing her best possession to honor their wealthy dinner host.

"Should we walk over to Seth's tent together?" asked Aaron. "It is nearly nightfall."

"Gladly," replied Michael. "Are we ready, Naomi?"

Naomi nodded.

Aaron and Elisha and their two hosts walked the length of a few tents to Seth's large tent across the path from Nazareth's main cluster of stone houses. Seth's young servant greeted their arrival with a nod, and he pulled open the large tent flap for them to enter.

"Are you Naomi?" asked a woman.

Naomi took a deep breath and held it. Moments passed, and the conversation paused. Finally Naomi exhaled. "Yes," she replied from behind her scarf.

"I am Rachel, Seth's second of three wives." As she spoke, she looked briefly at Michael and Aaron, too, with melancholic eyes above the gentle smile that welcomed Naomi. "Please come with me and join the women." Rachel led Naomi behind the large partition curtain and into the large women's and children's tent chamber on the left.

This time, Aaron's eyes needed no adjusting from nightfall outside to the abundance of oil lamps inside Seth's tent. He savored the smell of lamb and lentils and fresh bread. The same men still sat in their circle with Seth, which they widened to make space for the newcomers. Aaron, Elisha, and Michael sat on cushions like the other men. On a small table behind Seth rested two Hanukkah menorahs full of nine unlit candles each.

"Aaron, welcome!" said Seth, sitting somewhat higher than the others on a larger cushion. "I see you have already spotted our menorah compromise! Some want the Hanukkah candles one way, some want it the other way. So why not both ways?" he laughed.

Seth rose to light the menorahs. "Ladies and children, other servants, will you please join us now?" he called to their tent sections beyond the curtains on opposite sides of the central chamber.

The women's conversation quickly lowered to whispers as they spoke to the three younger children and two babies, who still chattered and garbled as they all entered the left side of the central tent chamber. Except for Seth's three wives who had cushions like the men, the female servants, the children, and the male servants entering from the right all sat on the floor rug.

"Everyone, please blow out all the lamps except mine," Seth said.

Some of the older children clamored back to their compartment behind the curtain to be the first to blow out the lights there, and the small assembly in the center room sounded more than a dozen quick puffs, leaving the sight and scent of wisps of smoke across the darkened tent interior.

Everyone resumed their places, and all eyes and ears focused on Seth up front. He started with the menorah on his right. He took the taller, middle candle and lit it at the oil lamp on the same table. From that he lit the eight candles. Even the babies became quiet. Neighboring tents, too, fell mostly quiet, as everyone marked sundown with the same ceremony, either inside their tents, or watching Daniel's giant outdoor menorah.

After lighting the full menorah, before turning to the second one, Seth paused for the prayers. The company in his tent could already hear the same prayers being chanted here and there in Nazareth's tent city. For the past three hundred years or so, the Jews no longer spoke Hebrew, which they had dropped for the similar Aramaic of the kingdoms around them. But the Jews still understood much of the Hebrew of the scriptures and prayers, especially the Hanukkah prayers, which were only two centuries old. Seth began, in a sonorous, hypnotizing, baritenor voice that flowed clearly from his beardless face:

> *Baruch atah Adonai, Eloheinu Melech Ha-Olam, asher kiddeshanu b'mitzvotav, vitzivanu, lehadlik ner shel Hanukkah.*
>
> Blessed are You, Lord our God, Ruler of the universe, who has sanctified us with Your commandments, and has commanded us to kindle the lights of Hanukkah.

Seth chanted the second and third prayers after this, to the silent reverence of everyone present.

Next he lit the second menorah, but only the center candle and the first one on his right. Then he sat back down on his tall cushion.

Conversation quickly resumed as everyone looked from the candles on the table up front to the faces next to them.

After several minutes, Seth's first wife motioned to him that it was time for the meal.

Seth acknowledged this with a nod. "Which menorah would the ladies prefer?"

"Easy," answered his first wife, who came forward and lifted the fully lit menorah and removed it to the women's and children's tent chamber on the side. The rest of the women and children followed. The main tent chamber was now barely lighted by the two candles from the second menorah.

"Servants, relight the lamps." Seth looked toward the male servants.

Four male servants collected the lamps, brought them to the one lighted lamp up front, and lighted the others, before sitting in the back corner of the main tent chamber.

Seth's wives and female servants began serving large, communal platters of food – wheat bread, barley bread, lentils and garlic, and roasted lamb. The lamb platter came straight to Aaron and Elisha, and Aaron could see Elisha's mouth agape, ready for the delicacy after the day's twenty-mile walk from the Sea of Galilee.

It was the second wife Rachel who bore the lamb platter to Aaron and Elisha. Without a word, she made the same gentle, melancholic smile as earlier. Old enough to have borne Seth several children, she was still pretty, with some of the palest, smoothest skin Aaron had ever seen, against her black eyes and black hair with its few strands of white. Then she quickly retreated to the women's tent chamber behind the curtain.

Aaron was curious about Rachel's sadness, and he glanced at Seth, who was glaring at Aaron. It lasted only a moment, but it was unmistakable, until Seth transformed his face into a softer expression, but still intimidating.

Then Seth spoke to Aaron across the circle of other seated guests. "Aaron of Jerusalem, before you arrived for dinner, we were discussing what the wealthy should do with their riches, according to the prophets and according to Joshua of Nazareth."

Seth turned his gaze to Elisha. "What do you think, Elisha?" Then Seth grinned mischievously at Aaron, for the challenge he had just presented the thirteen-year-old.

Elisha squirmed and looked to Aaron for guidance. Aaron nodded his confidence in Elisha.

"It is not really my place to say," replied Elisha.

"Please," insisted Seth.

"How do you approach this question, sir?" Elisha continued to evade the question himself.

"With great difficulty, every day," said Seth, "which is precisely why I seek as many opinions on the matter as I can obtain. It helps my own thinking. So, please."

"Do you know the parable of the widow's pennies?"

"Of course," answered Seth.

Elisha continued, "Joshua of Nazareth taught that no action is as good as the sacrifice of one's last possessions, like the widow's two pennies for the Temple treasury. But who will feed the widow her next meal? Someone who has not spent all their money. Is the widow more righteous than her benefactor?"

"That *is* one way of looking at it." Seth spoke in a neutral voice, encouraging the young Elisha to continue.

Aaron smiled at Elisha's cleverness. The rich and powerful Seth of Caesarea was inviting Elisha – almost forcing him – either to condemn the accumulation of wealth or to defend it. Elisha was engaging the question without answering it.

"Then there is the difference between regular poverty versus poverty by choice," Elisha continued. "Some followers of Joshua of Nazareth say that we must give up all our possessions, teach kindness and faith, and live from the charity of others. But how kind is it to accept from others what you could have earned for yourself?

"Those who do this reply that the resurrected Joshua of Nazareth will soon return, that it is only a question of a short time. But it's now been twenty years. The first generation has already started to die, without seeing the promised return. It seems there must always be some men with more than others. It becomes a question of what they do with their riches."

"Has your Papa Aaron taught you to reason like this?" Seth asked the question with calm intensity, revealing neither approval nor disapproval.

Aaron did not like Seth's cold approach to the interrogation of Elisha.

Elisha looked at Aaron, who could offer no guidance. "Like what, sir?" Elisha asked Seth.

"With such pragmatism."

"Even the high priests have been known to decrease required gifts to the Temple, sir, in order to meet the needs of the poor."

"I see," Seth answered coolly. "No straight answer. But what about my question – is it, or is it not, harder for a rich man to enter the kingdom of heaven than for a poor one?"

By now, all the men had stopped eating the steaming hot food in front of them. The tension of Seth's persistence was overpowering the moment. Everyone held their breath during Seth's questions and again during Elisha's responses.

"I suppose it depends, sir."

"Joshua of Nazareth answered the same question with authority," Seth insisted.

Elisha had no response.

"Aaron, what do you say about the rich's chances for the kingdom of heaven?" Seth persisted.

"Seth, I was a young boy, and I never saw Joshua until they carried him away from the cross. And my impressions of heaven were long directed by my Sadducee upbringing, specifically, that there is no afterlife of the soul. Before the Jews went to Babylon six centuries ago, there was none of this talk about heaven or hell after death. That came from the Babylonians, and the priestly Sadducees of the ancient aristocratic families never accepted the change. Even though I left for the Pharisees, frankly, I remain unconvinced of immortality of the soul. I suppose I'll never make a good Pharisee, although I was an even worse Sadducee. So, to answer your question narrowly, about a rich man's chances for heaven – it does not concern me.

"More broadly, though, I do think that greater wealth creates greater problems for observing the commandment to love your neighbor as yourself. If a man has much more than most of his neighbors, how can he offer everyone else what he has? It is a numerical impossibility. The greater the riches, the harder the golden rule."

Seth's silence commanded everyone else's. He turned his head for a moment toward the curtain separating the women's compartment.

Aaron followed his gaze in the same direction. There was the second wife Rachel again, watching her husband Seth interrogate his guests. Aaron shifted his eyes immediately back to Seth, who was already glaring at him again.

"What does Daniel say about the rich, Master Seth?" Michael suddenly asked.

"I've never asked him or heard him say," said Seth. "Perhaps I should."

"That sounds like a good idea," said Michael.

Aaron was relieved for the solution. The surrounding guests exhaled their tension and resumed eating from the shared platters. Aaron, Elisha, and Michael all took huge bites of lamb as swiftly as possible. Aaron and Elisha exchanged looks over their stuffed mouths, and shared a smile. They were both anxious for a mouthful as an excuse not to answer any more questions from Seth.

Several of the women came back out to serve wine. Aaron kept his eyes on the food and on Elisha beside him. He would not risk eye contact again with Rachel. When he was growing up, Aaron learned the stereotype of the second wife of a rich man. She was happy only until the third wife came to displace her as the newest wife, and ever after she was frustrated by the lack of rank, either as the preferred newest wife, or as the authoritative first wife. No matter how many wives a man might take, the second wife usually seemed most disgruntled with her polygamous marriage. But this one, Rachel, seemed beyond struggling for position, and just sad. Aaron was quickly observing that life with Seth might be very difficult for just about anyone.

The circle of men began to pass the platters around, so that each might try the other dishes. They began to settle into small talk in twos and threes.

Suddenly they all heard a shout not too far away. "Fire!"

CHAPTER NINE

"Fire!" Many more shouts echoed the cry up the path from Seth's tent.

The men in Seth's tent stopped their meal and raced outside. As the last to arrive for dinner, Aaron, Elisha, and Michael were the first out onto the night path.

Aaron glanced down the path at Daniel's giant menorah with its two torches in the air above the lines of tent tops. But everyone down the path was looking back up past Aaron.

"Naomi!" shouted Michael to his wife, who was still inside Seth's tent. "It's us!"

Michael and his two lodgers ran to what was left of his short, small tent. A dozen men were gathered to stop the fire. But the tent was so small that it was already burning into ashes before anyone could extinguish the flames.

Naomi arrived just behind them. She screamed. "We sold everything we had for the tent for this trip. No! Michael, what will we do?"

Michael embraced his wife. "We'll get through it, Naomi. We'll get by on the charity of others until we get home for the spring hiring by the Roman procurator."

Sparks and burning goat hair fibers floated into the night sky and tinted the burgeoning snow clouds orange. The air was moist, but the ground and surrounding tents were dusty and dry from the long northern drought. Aaron looked at the surrounding tents. Dozens and dozens of men and women stood ready to brush off any ember that landed on a tent. Occasionally one did, and each was quickly smothered by blankets.

A distant slam startled all the onlookers who quickly looked toward Daniel's giant burning menorah torches. Another one of

Daniel's menorah poles had fallen, one that was not burning this first night. Unlike the earlier fallen pole, this one fell away from the house, smacking a very small tent across from it

A man screamed. "My wife! It hit my wife!"

Dozens ran back down the path from Michael's tent fire to the crushed tent. Aaron guessed the screams came from inside that tent. With enough people to help there, he stayed by Michael's tent to survey the damage, especially to Michael's and Naomi's property.

Elisha looked toward the menorah pole collapse. "I was sure they were even more careful with lashing those things after the first pole was so easily pulled down. I saw them double-lashing them all afterward. It doesn't make sense that another one fell."

"Hmm," Aaron pondered the possibilities.

Naomi sobbed into her husband's chest. "You saw me put everything away, Michael. I didn't miss any cinders, did I?"

"No, Naomi, not at all. And we've never had such an accident. It wasn't from us."

"She's knocked out!" screamed the man down the path. "Help! My wife is knocked out!"

"Look! Someone cut the lashing!" another voice shouted from the path, around the bend toward Daniel's house.

Aaron looked down the path. Oil lamp flames flickered up and down in the night as their owners darted between Michael's tent fire and Daniel's sabotaged menorah.

Michael looked toward the shared fire pit where Naomi had been cooking, and Aaron looked, too. It looked safe, and its smoke was drifting gently away from Michael's tent, not toward it. That wasn't the source of the tent fire.

"What could have started it?" Michael asked himself out loud.

From down the path, the Pharisee Gad watched the figures gathered around the waning fire of Michael's tent. He saw them talking but couldn't hear them. When he saw Aaron, he smiled in selfish satisfaction.

In his own sprawling tent, Seth paced while two women servants awaited instructions. "Someone will need a place to sleep." Seth looked at the half-full platters of food before him, now encircled by empty cushions. "How much space remains on the women's and children's side?"

"Enough for several more, sir."

Seth nodded but did not reply. A young male servant stood by the tent entrance, and at Seth's nod, he left the tent.

Just a few moments later, Seth's servant was back. "A surprising development, sir. The fire was at the tent of the same four people who were just with us – the married couple and their two lodgers, Aaron and Elisha."

"Go ahead and invite them to stay," Seth ordered matter-of-factly.

The servant continued, "The crashing pole appears to have hurt one woman in a tent across from Daniel's house. She and her husband will spend the night with family in another tent."

"They sound fine," said Seth.

The servant left the tent again and approached Michael's burnt-out tent. "Ma'am, sirs, my master Seth has learned of your misfortune, and he would like to offer you shelter for the night."

In the dim flickering of the remaining flames, Michael and Naomi looked at each other and hesitated. Michael silently pointed his head toward some place in the tent city behind them. Naomi nodded slightly in agreement.

"That is most generous, thank you," said Michael. "We have many friends here now, and I know just the ones to stay with. Please tell your master Seth that Naomi and I are very grateful for his offer of hospitality. And please excuse us for missing the rest of the meal. We must tend to our belongings and the night ahead."

Aaron and Elisha looked at each other and hesitated as well. After the rich man Seth's hostile interrogation about whether a man can be wealthy and righteous at the same time, Aaron was not eager to subject Elisha to further antagonism.

"My son and I accept your offer," said Aaron. He didn't like it, but he didn't see a choice, not at this late hour, in the dark without even a lamp, knowing almost no one in Nazareth's tent city. Besides, he had already accepted Seth's offer to store most of his amphora vases of salt in Seth's sprawling tent. "Thank you. It will take a short while to gather our belongings here, and to help Michael and Naomi do the same. Please tell your master that we will be there shortly."

"We can manage fine," Michael told Aaron. "But thank you for offering to help."

"Are you sure?" Aaron asked.

"Yes, thanks."

"A lamp, sir?" Seth's servant offered Aaron his oil lamp for Aaron and Elisha to search for their belongings.

"Thank you."

Aaron and Elisha borrowed a neighboring man's walking stick to sift through the ashes for any remaining possessions. Their woolen blankets were burned up, along with their dates and bread and other food for their travels.

"Papa, we can look again by daylight, don't you think?" asked Elisha.

"Of course," said Aaron. "It's not like I expect to find anything."

Aaron turned one last time to Michael and Naomi. "You'll manage all right?"

"We're fine, yes. We traveled here with some friends, and we have made many more friends during our weeks here. I'm sorry we no longer have the honor of lodging you, and I apologize for your inconvenience."

"Not at all!" said Aaron. "I'm glad to hear you'll be all right. We'll look forward to seeing you around Nazareth while we're here."

"Likewise," said Michael. He reached into his pocket and pulled out the shekel that Aaron had paid in advance for four nights' lodging. "Here is—"

"I will not take it, Michael. You must keep it. This is not your fault."

"Thank you," he whispered past surging tears.

"You're welcome."

"Thank you," he stammered again.

"Until next time," said Aaron.

Aaron handed the oil lamp back to Seth's servant. "We'll follow you." The three of them walked back down toward Seth's tent, guided by Daniel's two Hanukkah torches well past that.

"What do you think started the fire?" Elisha asked Aaron as they walked.

"I've been asking myself the same thing," said Aaron. "Something feels strange about it."

"And all that business when they were erecting Daniel's menorah," said Elisha. "First Pharisee Gad's tirade, then that man who pushed the workers and ran off while the tall torch pole fell."

Aaron, too, sensed the swirling intrigue in Nazareth. This place was dangerous enough without tomorrow's arrival of Antonius Felix's cavalry.

When they reentered Seth's tent, all the other dinner guests had also returned, but the platters were gone.

"My maid servants are heating the food on the fire in back," Seth said. "Please forgive the delay. . . . Aaron, have you accepted our invitation?"

"Very gratefully, Seth. Thank you. It will be our pleasure to rest our heads under your tent's roof tonight."

"You did not lose too much in the fire, I hope?" Seth asked.

"Not much, no. We didn't bring much to lose!" Aaron chuckled. "Poor Michael and Naomi, though. They've lost that little tent they had invested in."

"Have they found somewhere to stay?" Seth asked.

"They said they had friends, yes," said Aaron.

"Good, I'm glad. Any idea what started the fire?"

"None at all. Michael and his wife seemed just as puzzled as I was. The nearest cooking fire was tiny with no sparks to be seen, and the breeze was blowing its smoke away from the tent anyway."

"No one is hurt?" asked Seth.

"Thankfully, no," said Aaron.

"All right then, we may resume our dinner without any disrespect." Seth gave one look to the closest maid servant, who immediately stepped out a back door tent flap to retrieve the reheated platters from their cooking fire outside.

"What was this you were saying about resurrection, Aaron? You're still like the Sadducees, not believing in life after death of the body?"

"That's right. What about you?" Aaron tried for once to seize the initiative in conversation with this man.

"Of course the soul is immortal," said Seth. "Our people have always believed this."

"Not always," said Aaron. "There is nothing of it in the five books of Moses."

"The books of Moses are the laws for earthly life, not for our eternity with the Lord," said Seth. "Of course Moses did not write of the immortality of the soul. It's so obvious, he didn't need to include it."

"I might remind you, Seth, that the priestly families, all of us Cohens, including many Sadducees, are the direct descendants of the brother of Moses," said Aaron. "For more than one thousand years, we have led the religious affairs of the nation of Israel under this authority. And almost none of us nephews of Moses have ever swayed on this question of immortality. Should human souls live forever, as angels in heaven or demons below? The Lord told Moses, You shall have no other gods before me. Are we to start worshipping ancestral spirits as immortal gods?"

"But Papa," interjected Elisha, "don't you always tell me that the true way must be found in the free deliberations of men, not in the pronouncements of any special living authority? If we are all children of Israel, why should you Cohens have greater authority?"

"We should not, Elisha. But thank you, I got a little carried away there. I beg your pardon, Seth. My point was to subject this belief in immortality to the deliberation of men, as Elisha reminds me."

Seth lifted his chin in mild surprise. "Elisha is not a Cohen? He is not your son?"

"He was orphaned at age seven, and I adopted him," said Aaron.

"I see," Seth reflected.

Elisha was accustomed to answering questions about how Aaron had adopted him. But it meant telling of the night fire that had killed the rest of his first family, which always pained Elisha in the retelling.

The lamb platter had made its way to Seth, and he removed the largest piece from the center, still attached to the bone, which none of his guests had seen fit to take. He took a large bite and chewed it slowly in silence, while the ten or so guests resumed their smaller conversations.

Aaron and Elisha ate little during this second part of dinner after the fire. They barely sipped their small cups of wine, to avoid the constant refilling by Seth's wives and maid servants. Aaron and Elisha had pleasant conversations with the other guests.

Among Seth's guests as elsewhere, both Aaron and Elisha spoke eagerly about the salt trade that occupied most of their time, journeying down to the Salt Sea salt cliffs, spending the night, and making the arduous, daylong climb back to Jerusalem, sometimes twice a week. Of course, they admitted, it was harder on the donkeys than on them. They had steady customers, but they occasionally lost some and constantly had to seek new ones. Even during their evening studies with other Pharisees, Aaron and Elisha were always alert to a potential new customer. And during their daytime travels and salt deliveries, they were always eager for conversations about the law and justice and the teachings of recent authorities of scripture, including Joshua of Nazareth.

During all this dinner conversation, for the rest of the meal, Seth ate in silence, except for the occasional understated order for servants to replenish food platters and wine cups.

When the Hanukkah candles were about one-third burned, Seth's other dinner guests all parted for the night, as soon as the first of them took the initiative. Seth motioned for one of the male servants to snuff out the Hanukkah candles, and he then spoke to Aaron and Elisha.

"I hope you enjoyed the meal and company this evening," he said.

"Very much, thank you," said Aaron. "We did nothing to deserve such a lavish feast. You are a very generous man, Seth."

"Not at all. You're most welcome. It will not be the last, I hope, during your stay in Nazareth. And should your travels ever take you to Caesarea by the Great Sea, you are welcome to stay in my home, both of you. I think you will find our sea salt to be of exceptional quality."

"Thank you, sir," said Elisha.

"Thank you," said Aaron. "No salt is better than the fine, fresh grains of the evaporation beds by your home port city of Caesarea. If I ever find customers who can afford to subsidize the journey, you can be assured I will pay you a visit. For now, we deal exclusively in the roughest rock salt from the Salt Sea salt cliffs, not even the better salt from that sea. Our customers do not have much money."

"I certainly understand," said Seth. "Servants," he called to the male servants behind them, "please make our guests comfortable for the night. After the losses they just suffered in the fire, we want to do everything we can for them."

"Yes, master Seth," the lead servant replied. "Right this way, sir," he said to Aaron as he pulled back the flap to the tent's side chamber.

The male quarters were almost as large as the central tent chamber, except for a side section curtained off again for Seth himself. Provisions for travel and tenting were stored at the back end, next to Aaron's amphoras of salt. The floor was the native dirt and rock, unlike the carpeted central chamber of Seth's tent. In one section were very nice cushions, pillows, and other bedding, apparently for Seth's older sons. The rest was for daytime sitting and nighttime sleeping. The servants began preparing their humble beds for the cold night, all right next to each other for a little warmth, more like one large bed on the floor. This was where Aaron and Elisha would join them.

Four servants made way for Aaron and Elisha to sleep on and under the shared blankets in the middle of them, for maximum warmth for the guests.

The youngest servant excused himself with a lamp, and spoke to another servant. "I will come get you when it's time for your watch."

The other servant nodded and took his place in the blankets.

One servant blew out the lamp, and all of them lay down their heads. Beyond Seth's tent walls, the tent city of Nazareth was mostly quiet except a few muted conversations and occasional protests of young children. Many of the two thousand souls in Nazareth were already asleep, as the remainder soon would be.

From the distance, a loud, insistent call interrupted Aaron's passage into sleep.

"Centurion Matthias of Procurator Antonius Felix's cavalry seeks Aaron of Jerusalem, the Pharisee. Aaron of Jerusalem – present yourself immediately!"

CHAPTER TEN

"Aaron of Jerusalem, present yourself immediately!" cried Procurator Felix's cavalryman a second time. In the cold night air under snow-laden clouds, with the entire tent city drifting to sleep, the cry carried far and clear.

Aaron's mind was whirring. He knew that Felix's cavalry was arriving tomorrow to break up Nazareth's tent city. Felix's Centurion Matthias, already in Nazareth, probably knew the same thing. Could Matthias know that Aaron possessed this dangerous knowledge? Aaron climbed out from the shared blankets, trying to spare Elisha and the other men too much cold air. It was almost completely dark, with very dim light from the watchman's lamp seeping in through the crack where the divider curtain drooped from the tent ceiling.

"Elisha, I don't know when I'll be back," Aaron whispered. Elisha lay between three of Seth's servants. They had all just lain down in their tight space sharing blankets and warmth in the cold. In fact, Aaron didn't know *if* he would be back, and he expected that Elisha understood this as well. But he didn't want to phrase it that way in front of Seth's servants. "Sleep well, like I would."

"Of course, Papa," said Elisha.

"They're calling for you, Aaron," said Seth from his private sleeping compartment behind its own curtain.

"Yes, I'll answer as soon as I'm a few more steps away from your sleeping children," Aaron answered, as he pulled on his boots.

"That is courteous, thank you," said Seth.

"Aaron of Jerusalem, answer Procurator Felix's guard! Report to Centurion Matthias – now!"

This third time, the shout was followed by murmuring of fear and curiosity audible from inside dwellings throughout the nighttime tent city.

Now in the central chamber of Seth's tent with the first watchman, Aaron took a woolen blanket for warmth, and he lit one of Seth's oil lamps from the one held by the watchman. Then Aaron exited the tent and walked several paces away before he finally shouted a response. "This is Aaron of Jerusalem, on the way!"

"Now!" shouted the guard in response.

In the cold, dark night, Aaron walked quickly up the path to the edge of Nazareth's sloping tent city, where he and Elisha had passed Felix's Roman guard in the afternoon. Aaron's small lamp flame reflected many shining eyes peering out of tents at this unknown wanted man, Aaron of Jerusalem.

At the end of the pilgrim tents, Aaron approached the modest tent of Procurator Felix's Centurion Matthias. The guard held his own lamp, and opened the tent flap as soon as Aaron reached it. Aaron tried not to be too afraid of arrest. He was more worried about Elisha than himself.

There was Ben! Aaron was shocked to see his brother by the light of three small oil lamp flames. Benjamin the Sadducee looked both angry and worried. Next to him was a young servant, with his hands in iron shackles before him. Centurion Matthias, still in the day's uniform, sat in a chair, and his two soldier guards stood to the side.

"Aaron, I—" started Ben.

"Silent!" Matthias spoke firmly but not loudly.

For seven years in Jerusalem, Ben had refused to speak to his brother. Suddenly, at this moment in distant Nazareth, he seemed to need Aaron.

Centurion Matthias and Pharisee Aaron sized each other up. By the looks of Matthias' wrinkled face and gray hair, he was about fifty years old. But his shoulders were upright, his posture was fit and firm, and his eyes burned with ambitious energy, like a much younger man's.

"State your name, including your father's," ordered Matthias.

"I am Aaron of Jerusalem, son of Jesse."

"When did you arrive in Nazareth?"

"This afternoon," Aaron replied.

Matthias jerked his head slightly in surprise. Then he looked at the younger soldier.

The soldier nodded, as if he remembered Aaron's arrival that day.

Aaron tried not to smile, remembering the negligent guard when Aaron and Elisha had passed.

"Why did you come here?" asked Matthias.

That was the question. What did Centurion Matthias already know, Aaron wondered. There stood Aaron's estranged brother Ben with his servant in chains. It must have been Ben who told Matthias about him. But why? Did this have anything to do with tomorrow's planned raid on the Nazareth pilgrims by Felix's cavalry? Surely Matthias knew that was coming. But he wouldn't think Aaron knew about it, would he? Should Aaron mention only the standard pilgrim's interest in Daniel, or should be confess his primary interest in the Nazareth Scroll? Aaron looked into Ben's eyes and saw more worry than anger. Ben must have come to Nazareth because of the scroll, and Ben knew his brother Aaron well enough to know that would be his reason as well.

"I came to Nazareth to learn from Daniel, the old friend and disciple of Joshua of Nazareth."

"You are a Joshua follower?" asked Matthias.

"In my own way, yes. I am one of the Pharisees who thinks that Joshua brought valuable teaching about the law."

"A Pharisee, yes, that is what this man told us. You know him?" Matthias pointed to Ben, not the chained servant.

"Yes," replied Aaron.

"How?"

"He is my younger brother, Benjamin son of Jesse, Sadducee and Temple priest, and heir to our father's lands and fortune."

"Younger brother? The younger brother is the heir? Did he do you wrong?"

"He did not," said Aaron. "My own actions made him the heir."

"Then he is who he claims to be. Ben here told me that he had a brother visiting Nazareth who could testify to his character." Matthias paused and looked at Aaron.

"Is there a problem?" Aaron asked.

"There most certainly is," said Matthias. "Would you consider your brother Ben capable of criminality?"

"Criminality?"

"That's right," said Matthias. "Thievery, dishonesty, adultery, . . . murder."

"Until this moment, my brother has not spoken to me for seven years. I no longer know him. But when I did, yes, he could be dishonest. So could I. The rest I would not have guessed. Adultery? Ben, you didn't?" Aaron was furious at the idea that Ben might have cheated on his wife Ruth, or even that Ben might cheapen Ruth by taking more wives.

"No," insisted Matthias. "Do not speak to the detainee. You are only to answer my questions until I allow otherwise, Pharisee Aaron. So you cannot rule out that your brother might be capable of ordering murder?"

"I find it very hard to imagine," said Aaron.

"Yes or no, is it within your brother to order murder?" asked Matthias.

"I don't know," Aaron finally answered directly.

Ben glared at Aaron.

"But I doubt it," Aaron added.

"Here is my problem, Aaron," said Centurion Matthias. "While the recent small tent fire burned near Nazareth's old village center, this servant was caught running from the scene. He denies involvement. Naturally, we interrogated him and discovered that he is a servant of your brother Ben. So we brought Ben here as well. He, too, denies involvement, although we have not questioned him as forcefully as we could. Not yet."

Aaron couldn't believe this. His brother Ben was under arrest as a suspect in a fire that could have killed Aaron.

"What about the tent that burned?" asked Aaron. "What motive would they have?"

"We haven't made any progress on that, I'm afraid," said Centurion Matthias. "By the time we started, the tent's remains were abandoned. We learned from its neighbors that its owners were named Michael and Naomi from Caesarea. They didn't have much money or anything else remarkable about them."

"So why would anyone attack them?" Ben asked.

Centurion Matthias glared at Ben to be quiet.

"I did a little investigating about that fire myself, actually," said Aaron.

"And what did you learn?" asked Matthias.

"Did you know that this Michael had just taken two paying lodgers into his tent?" asked Aaron.

"No one told us that," said Matthias.

"In fact," Aaron smiled, "those two were my son and I."

Ben's jaw dropped.

Aaron saw it, but Centurion Matthias missed it while he stared, surprised at Aaron's news himself. Whether or not Ben was involved in the fire, Aaron was now certain that Ben had not targeted *him*. That was a relief.

"Where were you when the fire started?" Matthias asked.

"All four of us were dinner guests in a nearby large tent owned by one Seth of Caesarea, of no relation to Michael or Naomi, as I understand it."

"Did you learn the fire's cause?"

"We did not," replied Aaron. "Michael and Naomi discussed several possibilities and ruled them all out. And the breeze was blowing the wrong direction for the cause to have been the nearest cooking fire."

"Do you know any reason why your brother Ben would want to target Michael and Naomi?" asked Centurion Matthias.

"No."

"Or you and your son?"

"Elisha. No, not us, either."

Aaron had decided to omit any mention of Daniel and his Nazareth Scroll, if he could help it. Then he remembered – many people had seen him carrying the amphora vase of salt to Daniel's house. His new connection could have drawn the attention of anyone wishing to destroy the Nazareth Scroll. Like Ben.

Aaron tried to read Ben's face, but Ben's anger could have been about his arrest alone, not anything else. What did Ben know?

"You suspect that I targeted my own brother? My father will have your head!" Ben blurted at Centurion Matthias.

"Your father has no business here in the province of Galilee," Matthias calmly replied. "This is Procurator Felix's domain. What's more, I suspect your father will not like much about tonight's news, including your own behavior with me, Benjamin. Nor will Felix, if it comes to that."

"If I may, Centurion?" asked Aaron.

"Go ahead," said Matthias.

"I have no grudge against my brother." Aaron tried to lie to himself, as well as to Centurion Matthias. He was ashamed, but he did begrudge Ben the marriage to Ruth. "Ben does have a grudge against me, from when I became a Pharisee reformer and turned against my family's traditions. But that is purely a matter of honor as he sees it. He gained everything from my break with my family, including his inheritance." And Ben gained a wife, Aaron kept to himself. "I see no reason to suspect him of an attempt on my life."

This was a half-truth. Aaron did harbor doubt about whether his brother was behind the tent fire that could have killed him. He didn't think so, but he wasn't certain. Especially if it had something to do with Daniel's scroll. Aaron had no doubt that Ben wanted the scroll destroyed, and he knew that Ben would suspect Aaron of attempting to preserve it. In fact, Aaron was all but certain that Ben saw Aaron as an enemy in the battle over the scroll – to preserve it and publish copies, or to destroy it, as Ben and many others wanted.

Aaron second-guessed his testimony to Centurion Matthias about Ben's character. He had long since forgiven Ben for ignoring him and even for speaking ill of him. But he did not fully know his younger brother. When Aaron left the family, Ben was young and still working out what he stood for. Here in Nazareth, Aaron stood in Ben's way. But if Ben was anything, he was loyal to family and the Temple, as well as to his own self-interest. He was not an executioner of religious heretics. Although Aaron stood in Ben's way to the Nazareth Scroll, he thought Ben was probably not capable of murder on this count.

"Sadducee Ben, do you agree that your brother Aaron bears you no grudge?" asked Centurion Matthias.

"That is not true," answered Ben.

Matthias gestured for Ben to continue.

"You still think her father cancelled the wedding with you, don't you?" Ben was looking confident for the first time this evening.

"What does Ruth have to do with this?" Aaron asked.

"Ruth has nothing to do with you, and that's just the point," said Ben. "Seven years ago, you had it all planned out. When our father and his kinsman arranged for you and Ruth to marry, you were already thinking of leaving the family and the Temple, as it later became clear to us. Then you got lucky with the betrothal to Ruth – I don't think our fathers knew how much you two played together as children. I don't think you knew that I noticed. Am I right so far?"

Aaron barely nodded, half-entranced by this resurrection of his past.

"As is our family's custom," continued Ben, "before marriage, she was allowed to have visits with you along with her maidservant. That's when you told Ruth your desire to join the Pharisees."

"What?" Aaron exclaimed. He had never imagined that Ruth or her devoted maidservant would share Aaron's planning with anyone.

"Ruth told you that if you really wanted to, she would still marry you as a poor Pharisee. This emboldened you."

Aaron could not believe that Ruth had ever shared this secret with Ben. It must have been Ruth's maidservant.

"That very evening at our home," continued Ben, "in front of our father and mother, our little brother and sisters, and all the servants, you stood before our father, you ripped your cloak in half, and you renounced your birthright and your Sadducee priesthood. Mother asked, what about Ruth? You answered that she was marrying you anyway, already promised by her father. But you never saw Ruth again. Do you know why the marriage was cancelled?"

Aaron knew in his heart that Ruth had loved him but that her father had obstructed the marriage after Aaron had renounced his aristocratic succession. "Her father, of course."

"No, Aaron. Ruth's father told her that she could still marry you, since he and she had both already agreed. But he also told her that she did not have to marry you. She thought about it for a day and the whole night, awake, and the next morning.

"The next day, our father and mother paid Ruth's family a visit. Our father spoke with Ruth's father and offered that she could still marry the heir of our family – me – as you know I became after you left.

"At the same time, our mother went to Ruth's room and apologized for how you renounced everything after the betrothal. She told Ruth the whole story of your drama, down to ripping your cloak in half. Ruth was humiliated to learn of your behavior.

"After mother and father left Ruth's family, her father told her the news. Our father had offered his new heir, me, in your place as her groom. Do you know how long Ruth troubled herself over that decision?"

Aaron's eyes bulged at the story. He kept holding his breath without realizing it, taking sudden breaths, and holding it again. He did not answer.

Centurion Matthias sat back and let Ben continue his tale.

"She didn't wait the length of ten breaths before telling her father she accepted me as her husband. And before we married, when it was my turn to sit with Ruth and her maidservant, she told me your story, including how she had promised to go with you into your new Pharisee life."

Aaron was staring so hard that his eyes dried until they hurt.

"But your arrogant display of self-righteousness to our family changed her mind. When her father allowed her to marry you anyway, she declined. When her father gave her a choice to marry me, she accepted. From that day to this, never has she regretted her decision. Humble yourself, Aaron. Perhaps you are more mature now. I hope so. I am."

"You call maturity walking past me in the streets as if you didn't know me?" shouted Aaron. He was beside himself with rage at the story Ben had just told. Angry at himself, mostly, for ruining his near marriage with Ruth. His mind sought some way to discredit Ben's account. But it made sense. It was too detailed to be a lie. It must be true. Seven years of regretting Ruth, and all his own doing.

"That's enough, you two," ordered Centurion Matthias. "Pharisee Aaron, you say you don't suspect Sadducee Benjamin in the tent fire that his servant was caught fleeing. Well, I still do. But Aaron, your testimony will help your brother sleep better tonight. We will not intensify his interrogation tonight. And I will decide what to do about that in the morning."

Matthias then turned to Ben. "However, Ben, you will have to stay with us for the night, along with your servant who fled the scene of the tent fire."

"You are detaining me for the entire night?" shouted Ben.

"I suggest you lower your voice, Ben," said Matthias. "In respect for your aristocratic birth, I was planning to offer you my own bed for the night. Do not tempt me to leave you sleeping on soil and rocks, or worse."

Ben held still and silent.

Aaron thought Ben started to look less angry and more resigned and confounded, like he was wondering what he could do tomorrow, since tonight was lost.

"Thank you, Aaron, for responding to our call and coming here to testify," said Matthias.

"You're welcome."

"Yes, thank you," said Ben.

Aaron could scarcely believe Ben's expression of gratitude.

"Good night," Aaron said to Procurator Felix's forces, and to Ben and his servant.

"Good night," they all responded.

What a bunch of half-truths that was, Aaron thought to himself as he walked back down the path to Seth's tent for the night. There had been no discussion of the Nazareth Scroll, and no mention of tomorrow's arrival of the Roman cavalry. Yet they all knew about the scroll. And if Aaron knew about the cavalry's plans, surely so did Centurion Matthias, and probably Ben as well, with the Sadducee connections among the Romans.

Tomorrow, Nazareth's tent city was coming down, one way or another. Antonius Felix was having no more of it. Over the years, Aaron had trained himself to sleep past troubling thoughts. But tonight would strain his sleeping discipline as it had never been tested.

CHAPTER ELEVEN

The first watchman was still on guard in the main chamber of Seth's tent when Aaron entered and blew out his lamp. They greeted each other with silent nods. Most of the men and women and children of Seth's household were already asleep. Aaron proceeded in the near darkness behind the separation curtain to the bedding and blankets he shared with Elisha and Seth's male servants for warmth on this snow-cold night.

Elisha was still awake and welcomed his adopted father back by lifting the blankets just enough for Aaron to climb back in. "So?" asked Elisha.

"Nothing important," whispered Aaron. "I'll tell you in the morning."

Elisha closed his tired eyes and rolled to his other side for sleeping. The three servants barely moved. If Aaron's return had awakened them, it wasn't for long.

Aaron closed his eyes and thought about his brother for a long time. That had been their first conversation in seven years. Hearing Ben's aged voice and looking into his eyes was even more of a shock than had been their initial rupture. Aaron's mind repeated their conversation over and over and over. Ben was older, wiser, cleverer. What else? Aaron wondered.

His thoughts turned to Ruth, Aaron's former betrothed and now Ben's wife. They had three children, Aaron had learned. News like aristocratic births traveled fast in Jerusalem. Unlike the men of Aaron's family, whom he sometimes spotted in public near the Temple, the women were rarely seen in the streets of Jerusalem, at least in the city center. Aaron almost never ventured to their part of the city. He had never seen Ruth again, perhaps because she spent most of her time with Ben's children at the family estate near the River Jordan.

Aaron had often imagined what he would say if he ever came across her. Now he had to re-imagine it. He had always imagined Ruth crying because her father forced her to marry the resentful second son Ben, suddenly the family heir. But if Ben's story tonight was true, as Aaron guessed it mostly was, passing Ruth on the streets of Jerusalem would not be the delicate matter of old feelings versus new realities. Or at least it wouldn't be the old feelings as Aaron had imagined them. No, instead Ruth had gotten angry at him, Ben said. She had broken from him on her own accord.

The imaginary conversation in the street would be different, Aaron realized. How might it unfold? It would take Aaron a while to settle into a new imagining of it. Before tonight, Aaron's musings had been self-assured. He would play the noble role, forgiving and sympathetic for the marriage that Ruth's father had forced on her. But that was not how it had happened, according to Ben. Ruth was the decision-maker, not the victim. If anyone was the victim, it was Aaron – a victim of his own youthful arrogance.

If Aaron ever spoke with Ruth again, perhaps she would scold him for the rude manner of his departure from his family. Perhaps she would ignore him, giving him just enough of a glance for him to know that he was being ignored. Or perhaps Ruth would be friendly and smile and talk, and try to understand what kind of man Aaron had become as a self-providing Pharisee, outside the comforts of his family's rent collections. She might have her children with her and introduce them to their Uncle Aaron. Then she would send them home with a maidservant while she lingered in conversation with Aaron. The passersby on the street would fade away, and the two childhood playmates and adolescent flirts would be left alone. The buildings would fade away and the streets would transform into golden fields of wheat in the valley. In the cool morning breeze, under the sun and blues skies, Ruth would take Aaron's hand into one of hers, and she would pull his head down where she could kiss him, and—

Suddenly, a donkey brayed wildly, and a sheep screamed, and a wooden door crashed.

Aaron was jolted upright from his dream. The livestock's mortal screams in the distance chilled him to the bone and nearly made him vomit. He sat panting and violently shook his head to clear it from his dream. The one scream was like a sheep from the mouth of a wolf. But the donkeys? And the loud thump?

The screams were becoming only slightly less desperate – and they were coming closer, as donkey hooves pounded the ground.

"Papa! Papaaaaa!" a woman shrieked. "Papaaaa! Gabriel!"

Elisha still slept, and Aaron jostled him awake.

"Wha– What is it?" Elisha struggled from his deep sleep.

"Papaaaaa!" screamed the woman again.

Aaron was already standing in the men's bed, wearing the boots he'd slept in. "It's Daniel's daughter," he told Elisha. "Meet me there!" He dashed past Seth's watchman, who stood in the tent entry looking down the path.

Aaron almost stepped in front of a galloping donkey in the path. Not far behind followed a bolting sheep, half of its wool in flames. Aaron braced himself and tackled the sheep as it ran past. He pulled the sheep close to him and smothered its flames against his own chest. Then he slowly released the sheep to be sure it was safe. Strands of wool still glowed.

Somewhere behind him, a large fire burned and lit up Nazareth under the clouded night sky.

"Douse it with water!" Aaron ordered Seth's watchman as he grabbed the watchman's hand and guided it to the scruff of the sheep's neck. When he saw the grip was tight enough, he patted at the flame some more. Then he turned around to the fire down the path.

Daniel's entire house was in the flames. Aaron could only see the top of it, but it was unmistakable with the lengths of the towering menorah poles aflame themselves, like some heathen ceremony. Aaron dashed down the path, passing more sheep and goats as he went. As he rounded a curve to the left, the terrible scene came into view.

Rebecca and her two girls kneeled and swayed on the path in front of Daniel's house, looking into the flaming front doorway.

"Gabriel! My Gabriel! No!"

The girls were screaming, and their mother was collapsed into heaving sobs, unable to hold her girls, though she kept trying.

Onlookers were already gathered from the tents opposite Daniel's house, and others kept arriving. A couple of the women tried to comfort Rebecca and her girls.

The livestock in Daniel's stable must have been trapped in the fire, but from the thunderous smack he had heard, Aaron guessed that the donkey had kicked the side door open. He could hear goats on the hillside behind Daniel's house. Not far down the path, one sheep ran in frenzied circles.

Rebecca's heaving sobs were punctuated by painful wailing. From this close, Aaron saw that her hair was singed into a blackened tangle in the back.

The house's entry door and doorway were aflame. So was every part of the house that was not made of stone.

At the far end of the patio, a man lay sprawled and motionless across the threshold to the home's main room. Too tall for Daniel, the body was Gabriel.

Despite the victim it had claimed, the fire sounded as harmless as an ironworker's bellows. If not for the sobs of Rebecca and her girls, it could even have been peaceful. Aaron remembered the Jerusalem fire that had orphaned Elisha. This fire pulled in air from all sides and created the sound of a steady, giant breath into the hypnotizing firelight of broad flames pouring upward from doors and windows.

Crack! Crack! Whoosh! The stable roof cracked and collapsed. The animals had escaped none too soon.

Seconds after Aaron arrived, he knew what he needed to do. He thought he remembered where Daniel's tiny alcove was, above the main room, and he sought Daniel first. Aaron saw the nearest tent's water basin, covered by a thin film of ice, and without hesitation, he lifted it with both hands and dumped it on himself. Soaking and freezing, and he ran through Daniel's front doorway.

Rebecca screamed again at the sight.

Aaron paused on the patio between the house on the right and the kitchen and stable on the left. The kitchen was the only place where the fire had not yet burned through the roof. Normally, the kitchen was the first place a house fire would start, but it was the last place where this fire could have.

More than ten feet in front of him, Aaron saw Gabriel's body lying at the entrance to the main room of the house, right in front of the large burning wood pile. His head was surrounded by several large rocks that had fallen from the top of the doorframe. His body was completely aflame, not just his clothes, but his entire being caught in the inferno. It reminded Aaron of the Temple sacrifices he used to perform.

The narrow patio where Aaron stood felt like a furnace. Aaron felt his skin start chafing and his eyebrows getting singed. He looked down and saw his woolen cloak sprout glowing orange embers, as if it were about to erupt in flame. Aaron was going to be burned alive. He had no choice but to dash back out the front doorway to the path outside.

More men were now gathered on the path in front, and they helped Aaron stagger away from the fire.

Without warning, a coat was pressed around his head. He was being smothered! He tried to escape, but many hands gripped his upper arms and more pressed the coat against his face and skull. The coat twisted and turned, and Aaron could not pull his arms free from the men who gripped them. He couldn't breathe!

Then just as suddenly, the coat was lifted. The unknown faces that watched him were concerned, not hostile.

"Your hair was on fire," said one man. "It looks all right now." The man turned Aaron around, and his eyes darted around Aaron's head, trying to make sure the little fires were out.

Aaron looked around and saw Elisha staring at him in shock.

By now, flaming pieces of Daniel's roof were falling from the eaves to the outside base of the stone walls. They lay burning harmlessly on the ground until one of the tall Hanukkah poles whipped loose from its burned-through lashing. The pole's bottom kicked out and uppercut Aaron's ribs, throwing him to the ground, while the pole's top slammed down through Daniel's roof, breaking the burning beams that were bone dry and older than anyone knew.

"Noooo!" cried Rebecca. "Papa's room! Papaaaa!"

Moments later, a dark silhouette staggered out the front doorway and crumpled forward to the ground.

"Papa!" shouted Rebecca. "You're alive! You're alive!"

As Rebecca stood up, several men restrained her from leaping toward her father at the edge of the flames. Her two daughters clutched each other in paralyzed terror and needed no restraint.

Other men moved forward, wincing in the searing heat, and pulled Daniel from the fire's edge. They all threw their coats onto Daniel, but there was little fire to douse. His clothes and hair were burnt to a crisp. By the bright, yellow-orange light of the house fire, everyone could see that Daniel's skin was charred black here and bloody red there. He breathed in short and shallow breaths.

"Oh, Papa!" Rebecca started to throw herself on him, but she stopped and kneeled by his side, fidgeting with her own hands, afraid to hurt him further.

Daniel slowly turned his head and looked at Rebecca. He attempted a slight smile, and then closed his eyes and exhaled after the effort.

"Water!" cried Rebecca. "Get him water!"

Elisha stood at Aaron's side. The thirteen-year-old's face stared paralyzed at the blowing, cracking, and snapping house fire.

"Let's cut the other poles loose before they go wild and hurt someone else," Aaron said to Elisha and a few other men nearby. Aaron held his side where the Hanukkah pole had strafed his ribs. He moved forward and started cutting the lashings of the pole on the far left. "All right, Elisha, slow—"

Aaron stared into the faces of helpful strangers, but no Elisha. He looked behind him by Rebecca and the men who held her away from her smoking father. There stood Elisha, wide-eyed like a small child, entranced by the flames pouring out of the roof, paralyzed by the scene of the burning house.

Of course, realized Aaron. This was like the night when he had rescued Elisha, when his family had died in that awful fire in Jerusalem. Daniel's house fire must be horrific for him.

"Do the two of you have it?" Aaron asked the two men who eased the pole's bottom up and its top down, on the edge of the top of the stone wall of the house. He recognized them both as having helped erect the poles that afternoon.

The three of them lowered the remaining Hanukkah poles over onto the house, one by one, until none remained standing. Aaron winced at the bruises on his legs and the scrapes and bruises on his torso, but he did everything he could to hide his facial contortions and his pained inhalations from the others. Somehow he would get through this night and worry about the rest tomorrow.

Just as they finished the last pole, Aaron saw it – the pot of pitch was empty. Although the pitch had not been enough for nine Hanukkah torches, it had been more than enough for two. A third of a pot of pitch had remained, Aaron had noticed that evening. Now all the pitch was gone.

Rebecca's daughters continued sobbing in the arms of village women, while Rebecca wailed over her burnt father Daniel as he barely clung to life.

"Don't leave us, Papa! Don't leave me! Stay alive! Stay alive!"

Aaron turned to tell Elisha about the missing pitch. The poor boy still stood paralyzed by the inferno before him. Aaron walked to Elisha and stood beside him. He eased in front of

Elisha, blocking his son's view of the fire, and then held him tight. Elisha began to sob and fell to his knees.

"This one was arson, Elisha, not like the other."

Elisha lifted his head and looked quizzically at Aaron.

"The pitch they used for Daniel's torches – it's gone," said Aaron.

Elisha shifted his gaze to the house fire. His expressions of sorrow and confusion transformed into anger. He pursed his lips and clenched his fists.

Aaron thought Elisha might scream.

"Someone did this on purpose?" Elisha's voice shook, and anger flooded his tear-filled eyes. "Someone did this on purpose?"

"Careful, Elisha, we don't know any more than that. If you say too much too soon, not only will the culprit evade us, but we might also increase the danger ourselves."

Another loud crack pierced through the fire's howling wind, and another section of the burning roof collapsed. The fire-wind blew louder through its new vents.

"Remember the mortar that fell loose when the pole slammed on the roof this evening?" asked Aaron.

"Yes," Elisha whispered.

"We need to look for marks of pitch on the surrounding wall. It would be less conspicuous if you did it. Will you?"

"Yes." Elisha still stared in anger at the flames. Then he looked around him and meandered to the side of Daniel's house.

Aaron discreetly shifted his eyes around to look whether anyone took much note of Elisha's approach to side of the burning house. A few noticed, but no one seemed to care very much. Curiosity of the disaster seemed natural. Elisha was playing covert inspector very well.

A few moments later Elisha reappeared beyond the right corner of the house. He ambled back to Aaron, and his eyes showed more aim than his gait.

"All burned up," said Elisha. "But yes, the remains of pitch are smeared all around the broken masonry where Daniel's bedroom is . . . or was. I didn't see anything else remarkable."

"Good work, Elisha," said Aaron.

Then father and son heard a man shouting down the path to their left, and they turned to see what the commotion was about.

"This afternoon my wife was knocked out – and now this!" A man ran up the hill shouting. It was the man from the afternoon's menorah pole crash. "Who did this? Who did this? Who did this?!" He pounded his fist into the air.

Behind him ran others.

"We want answers!" shouted a man.

"We must have answers! For my sister!" shouted a woman.

"Who could have done this?" added another man.

The gathering crowd grew louder.

Daniel's daughter Rebecca barely noticed, from her vigil next to him on the path.

But Daniel himself seemed to be aware. His charred face grimaced, and he arched his head backward in pain. He opened his mouth to talk, but no words came out.

The crowd started to notice Daniel moving.

"He's trying to talk! Quiet everyone! Elder Daniel, tell us – who do you think did this to you?"

The crowd fell quiet.

Several times, Daniel began to open his mouth but failed to speak and closed it again.

"Who did it?"

Daniel closed his eyes in exhaustion and panted in quick shallow breaths. Then he opened his eyes again and rotated them toward the most insistent man in the crowd. With his arm down to the wrist still resting on his daughter Rebecca's lap, Daniel lifted the fingers and palm of his hand and sliced a short space of air. Enough of that, he seemed to say. A second and a third time he repeated the gesture before he let his hand fall and closed his eyes.

"Who disliked Daniel?" shouted the crowd's leader. "We know who! It was Nathan of Nazareth. Nathan has hated Daniel for years. Nathan did it! Find Nathan! Get Nathan!"

CHAPTER TWELVE

"Get Nathan!" echoed the cry across the growing crowd. The men farther from the fire could see their own shouts, as fire-orange breath vapors punched into the freezing cold air.

"Murderer!" called one man. "Nathan's the one who burned Daniel's house!"

"He lives up there!" shouted the leader.

Most of the crowd started running up the path and around the bend to Nazareth's village center.

Lying on the path in front of his burning house, Daniel finally managed to speak a word. "No," he whispered. "No." But the crowd was gone.

Aaron watched Daniel's rejection of mob justice. Did Daniel know who did it? Or did he just dislike everyone jumping to conclusions about Nathan's guilt?

Rebecca noticed Aaron standing there and looked up from where she sat on the path between other village women. "Help us. Help us, Aaron." Her voice wavered, and then she clutched the neck of an older woman and wept.

Aaron looked back up. Elisha was watching him, ready for Aaron to take the lead. Aaron stepped where no one could hear them and spoke to Elisha.

"Daniel will die," Aaron whispered in great agitation. "Another martyr witness to the life of Joshua of Nazareth. What is wrong with this world?" He kicked the path in frustration, and then kicked it twice again.

"No scroll could survive that fire," he continued. "Now is not the time to bring that up with Rebecca. Tomorrow, before—" Aaron looked around them and whispered even more softly, "before Procurator Felix's cavalry arrives, we'll see what we can do. At least I know who did not do it."

"What do you mean?" asked Elisha.

"When Felix's guard called out for me earlier tonight, it was about the first fire, at the tent we were going to share with Michael and Naomi. They caught someone running away from that fire. It was a servant of my brother Benjamin."

"What?" Elisha was shocked.

"I didn't think Ben was involved, which is what I told Centurion Matthias. Since Ben had seen me in the afternoon, in his own defense he asked Felix's centurion to summon me as a character witness."

"Did it work?" Elisha asked.

"Not entirely," said Aaron. "They kept him and his guard detained for the night."

"In that little guard tent?"

Aaron smiled. "Yes. But the centurion honored my brother's aristocratic rank and ceded his bed. I'm sure they'll let him go now, but I want to go up there and be sure of it. You can go back to sleep."

"I'll come with you, if you'll permit it," said Elisha. "I'm wide awake."

Through some combination of fatigue and shock, Elisha suddenly looked several years older to Aaron.

"Come on," replied Aaron.

"Nathan! Come out here! Nathan! Murderer!" The mob's leader pounded on the door.

Angry men and women shouted and threw their own fists at the door. If anyone in the dozen conjoined stone houses had slept through Daniel's fire, they were awake now.

Aaron and Elisha were still many paces away, with a view of the houses' rooftops that could not be shared by the mob in front.

"Papa, look!" Elisha whispered.

Aaron turned to Elisha and saw his eyes directed above the crowd and to the left. He followed his son's gaze and saw it. A crouching figure scrambled across the back of the roof, and then he dropped out of sight into the courtyard of Nazareth's big house.

"Say nothing, and don't look there," Aaron whispered as they continued walking. "We'll come back to this soon enough."

Father and son stepped off the path to the right to get around the crowd, and kept walking.

"Why are you leaving?" one man challenged them. "Justice must be served!"

"We'll be right back," Aaron spoke calmly, without pausing his pace.

When they passed Seth's tent, Aaron briefly entered to borrow an oil lamp again, as the light from Daniel's house fire waned with time and distance across the tent city. Continuing the walk up the path to the guard tent, they came across two figures coming toward them.

"Aaron son of Jesse." It was Ben and his servant.

Aaron and Elisha stopped. "Benjamin son of Jesse. Brother."

"Aaron, I am grateful for your testimony to Procurator Felix's centurion tonight. You might have refused, after these seven years. Thank you. I would do the same for you."

"I think you would, Ben. I actually think you would."

"Any news from the new fire?" asked Ben.

"Bad news, yes," Aaron replied. "Daniel will not survive his burns, and his son-in-law Gabriel is dead. The daughter Rebecca and her two girls escaped mostly unscathed."

"What about the house?" Ben asked.

Aaron thought that Ben might as well have asked directly, What about the scroll? There was no other reason for Ben to ask about the house. And Ben seemed little interested in the welfare of the two poor men from Nazareth. For a moment, Aaron wondered whether Ben was behind the fire – both fires – after all. He had other servants here in Nazareth who could carry out an order even while Ben was detained. No, Aaron decided, almost certainly not. Still, he wished he could be sure.

"The house is destroyed on both sides of the patio, the living quarters as well as the kitchen and stable," Aaron answered.

"Really?" Ben asked, not disappointed, and almost eager.

Aaron paused and stared at Ben long enough to make him self-conscious of his transparent antagonism to the Nazareth Scroll. He kept staring in silence, to increase Ben's discomfort. Finally Ben averted his eyes, and looked above the tents behind Aaron at the lingering orange glow on the clouds.

"Really," Aaron finally replied.

"Listen, Aaron, I know we have shunned you these seven years. I regret none of it, in fact. And despite it all, tonight with Centurion Matthias, you were loyal and true. If you would like to share time tomorrow, as you have sometimes sought in the past, you are invited to visit my quarters on the far side of the tent city. Just follow the path past Daniel's house, and continue downhill even when it becomes a mere goat path, now widened by all these people. Mine is the larger tent among modest ones down at the end."

"Thank you, brother. Perhaps we will come." Aaron turned halfway to Elisha. "In your years ignoring me, Ben, you have never met my adopted son. Meet Elisha, your nephew."

Ben was at a loss for words. Finally he managed, "Did you need an assistant for income?"

"Don't be so crude, Ben." Aaron thought that Ben meant his question seriously, not trying to offend. But he wanted to defend Elisha from possible offense taken. "No. Elisha was an orphan who needed shelter. I had it to offer, and he is very likable, and I made him my son."

After another moment of shock, Ben held out both hands to Elisha, palms up. "Nephew Elisha, I am honored to meet you. You are welcome to visit with your, uh, father tomorrow."

Elisha placed his hesitating hands into Ben's, and Ben pulled him into a brief, awkward embrace.

Aaron's eyes widened at Ben's surprising kindness to Elisha. The over-proud Sadducee, heir to centuries-old aristocracy, embraced the poor child from the slums of

Jerusalem. Aaron would not have guessed Ben capable of such kindness. Seven years of marriage and fatherhood seemed to have softened him up a little.

"I hope you will excuse us," Ben said. "I did not rest well while with Centurion Matthias, and I am eager to sleep before my first full day in Nazareth."

"Aren't we all," Aaron smiled. He and Elisha stepped aside while Ben and his servant continued down the path.

When Ben was out of earshot, Aaron whispered to Elisha, "He will stop at Daniel's house and try to find out about the scroll. While it's still too hot to dig around, there's nothing to worry about. But in another hour or two, I will worry. And Ben might not be the only vulture clawing after the Nazareth Scroll before the night is through."

"Should we go there, too?" asked Elisha.

"Not yet. First there's the matter of this man Nathan. He didn't care about the scroll itself, I'm sure of that, except that it was important to Daniel's family. Why would Nathan enter the huge commotion this afternoon with Pharisee Gad, if he intended to return for arson and murder tonight? It doesn't make sense. This mob chasing him is scary and unjust. I want to try to get Centurion Matthias to protect him."

"Why would the centurion do that?"

"He wouldn't. But he might arrest him. That would be effective for keeping Nathan from a stoning mob, at least for the night."

They continued up the path to the tent of Centurion Matthias. When they were nearly there, the slight sound of their feet on the dirt and rocks alerted one of the guards.

"Who goes there?" called a young voice as the guard stepped out and held out his oil lamp to see. "You again? What do you want?"

"A word with Centurion Matthias, if at all possible," replied Aaron.

"I released your brother," Matthias shouted through the tent wall. "He obviously didn't start the second fire. Now go away!"

"It's not about my brother, Centurion, though I'm glad for his release," said Aaron.

"Kronos be damned!" Matthias shouted a Greek curse. "Won't Nazareth ever get to sleep tonight? It's cold out there, guard. Bring them in and shut the damn flap."

Aaron observed that without high-ranking aristocrat Benjamin the Sadducee around, Centurion Matthias observed many fewer formalities.

Inside the tent, Centurion Matthias lay on his bed, with his upper body propped up on his elbow. "What in Hades' name do you want? Make it quick. We can't stay up all night here."

"I thought perhaps someone should tell you, in case they haven't already—" started Aaron.

"Out with it already!"

"They have a suspect for the second fire."

"What?"

"Well, they don't have him," said Aaron. "They're looking for him. But I think I know where he might be."

Matthias threw off his covers and stood up, fully clothed and ready to go. "If it will put a finish to this endless night of fire and intrigue, let's have done with it." He walked through the tent flaps and started down the path into the tent city. "Is this man near Daniel's house?"

"That's where I think he is, yes, in the village center," said Aaron. "Only, he's not at his own house, where they're looking for him."

They could already hear the angry crowd down the hill.

"Do I hear the name Nathan?" asked Centurion Matthias.

"Yes, sir," answered Aaron.

"Do you know anything about him?" Matthias walked quickly and impatiently.

"Nathan is one of the native Nazarenes, sir, not a pilgrim. Late this afternoon, he joined a big argument with Daniel."

"With Daniel? I haven't been here that long, but I thought everyone liked Daniel."

"Not the Pharisee Gad," said Aaron.

"No, not him," said Matthias.

"Gad started the argument. Nathan just jumped in, like he'd take any chance to oppose Daniel."

"There's a bitter one in every village, isn't there?" said Matthias.

They were almost around the curve in the path where they could see the mob.

"There's one more thing," said Aaron.

"What?" asked Matthias.

"I don't see why this Nathan would have joined a big argument with Daniel just hours before trying to kill him," said Aaron.

"I see your point. But the crowd thinks he did it?"

"Right."

"I see," said Matthias.

As they came around the curve to the left, the crowd came into view by several oil lamps in their midst. They were no longer pounding on Nathan's door, which was now open. While Nathan's old, shivering, angry mother stood outside, the crowd threw one object after another out the front door, scouring the little house for the missing Nathan.

"You people have no right! No right! My baby!" Nathan's old mother shouted at the top of her lungs as she rocked back and forth in worry for the life of her only child. "All you people come here to Nazareth, drink our wells dry, and soil our paths till everything stinks of sewage. And now you attack us? You have no right, no right at all!"

Matthias spoke softly before they were in earshot. "Where is he, Aaron?"

"I would try the courtyard of the big house, the last one on the far side of the complex," said Aaron.

Centurion Matthias and his young guard approached the crowd while Aaron and Elisha stood back.

"Make way, make way, everyone." Matthias walked right past Nathan's door to the big house at the edge of the block. The crowd quieted down, and half of them followed Antonius Felix's officer and soldier to the door to the big house.

"Soldier, put down the lamp."

The young guard did as he was told.

Matthias then knelt in front of the soldier and folded his hands, palms upward, on his thigh. The soldier understood. He placed one foot into his officer's hands, and Matthias then stood and raised the soldier the top of the house's courtyard wall. The soldier grabbed the top with both hands, pulled one leg over and then the other, and dropped into the courtyard. The next moment, he was unbarring and opening the front door. Matthias lifted the oil lamp from the ground and stepped into the doorway.

"No one follows," he ordered.

By now, the second half of the crowd had followed from Nathan's door to this one, including Nathan's mother. Aaron and Elisha trailed them. Everyone stood silent outside.

Moments later, they heard the sounds of a scuffle.

"Don't try it!" Matthias' voice ordered. "You're much better off with me than with them out there, at least for now."

This was followed by the sound of manacles locking around Nathan's hands and feet.

The young guard led Nathan out the front doorway.

Before they could start shouting again, Nathan yelled, "I didn't do it!" His voice broke as he did, and he began to sob.

His mother rushed forward to embrace him.

For a moment, Centurion Matthias stood aside and said nothing. Then he continued the arrest. "Stand back, woman!"

The prisoner and his captors stood still for a moment.

"Listen, all you blind followers of that criminal Joshua of Nazareth," Matthias spoke. "This man Nathan is coming with us, and he will spend the night in chains. You will have no further worries from him. Now get out of the way and leave us alone. Good night!"

Matthias ignored Aaron as he walked back up the path, speaking to his prisoner: "You will spend the night warm with blankets in our tent. In chains and on the ground, but warm. Sleep if you can. But you damn well better let us sleep. If you give us any trouble, I'll be glad to release you back to that mob and be done with the whole affair. I need some sleep for tomorrow."

"Yes, sir." Nathan's voice still cracked through tears as he walked up the path to his nighttime tent prison. "And thank you, sir."

Then they were out of Aaron's earshot. Centurion Matthias' last audible words reminded Aaron that after everything tonight, they still faced Procurator Felix's cavalry tomorrow and the end of Nazareth's pilgrimage tent city.

While Aaron and Elisha watched Matthias lead Nathan away, a single clump of snowflakes fell between them.

"Papa, look! It's been years since we've seen snow."

"And by the looks of that, we might see more rain tonight than snow."

Aaron's mind was on Daniel's scroll. "Elisha, I'm certain that my brother Ben has someone watching Daniel's house until it's cool enough to search for the scroll," Aaron whispered. "And not just Ben. There might be others, like the Pharisee Gad. With all these tents so close, we can never know who might be watching from inside one. Let's go see Daniel's house, and think about where he kept the scroll."

As they turned back toward the old village center, they were stunned by what they saw. Every member of the angry mob was quietly entering Seth's tent – Aaron's and Elisha's own lodgings – and Seth himself stood at the entry to welcome them.

CHAPTER THIRTEEN

Aaron and Elisha halted in their tracks.

As Seth of Caesarea welcomed the last of the angry mob into his sprawling tent about thirty yards down the path, he looked toward Aaron. The light from Daniel's house fire was still bright enough for Aaron to recognize outlines and shadows. Seth motioned an invitation for Aaron and Elisha to join the midnight meeting.

Aaron nodded and lifted the palm of his hand to gesture delayed acceptance of the invitation.

Seth nodded his acknowledgement and entered his tent to join the stewing mob.

"Elisha, I must accept Seth's invitation." Aaron held the shorter Elisha's shoulders and whispered into his left ear, so that even eavesdroppers from the nearest tents could not understand. "Also, I want to be there to see what he intends to do with that crowd. It cannot be good. An angry mob should be dispersed, not coached."

Aaron pulled back for a moment to make sure Elisha understood.

Elisha looked back into Aaron's eyes and nodded.

Aaron bent over again and whispered further. "We also need to see if anything can be salvaged of Daniel's scroll. Who's there to defend it? Probably no one. You heard the conversation this afternoon about moving it – they named no one in Nazareth but their family members. Now Gabriel is dead. Daniel is about to die. And Rebecca is in no condition to worry about the scroll."

"I understand," Elisha whispered into Aaron's ear. "I'll go stand guard at Daniel's house until I think any of it is cooled off enough to explore."

"Exactly. When it is, come get me immediately. Do not enter Seth's tent. Just call 'Papa Aaron' from outside. That will make it easier for me to leave right away. No other words. Just 'Papa Aaron.'"

"Understood," said Elisha.

"Good," said Aaron.

Father and son walked down the path to Seth's tent. Aaron entered the tent while Elisha continued toward Daniel's house.

Elisha followed the path to Daniel's collapsed front doorway. A few other onlookers lingered. The roofs on both sides of the patio were gone, collapsed or burned or both. Parts of the walls were collapsed, especially at joists on the tops where rafters had burned and fallen.

Elisha was able to get his head inside the front doorway. For the first time, he saw Gabriel's burned body sprawled across the far end of the narrow patio. Elisha tried to pass through the doorway to the patio, but it was still too hot. The burning rooms, the stable, and especially the store of winter wood had heated the stone walls until the patio between them was like an oven. Elisha stepped back out to the path before his hair might catch fire. He checked his clothes and felt his hair to make sure no sparks had caught flame.

Then Elisha backed farther from the house and sat on the far side of the path to watch the fire, alongside the few others who stood or sat in silence as well. Most of Nazareth's onlookers had either returned to bed or joined the mob against Nathan and now conspired in Seth's tent. Elisha looked at each of his fellow observers. They all looked into the flames, and none returned the thirteen-year-old's gaze. Whether they were merely sleepless and curious, or ready to scavenge the household's remains, Elisha didn't know.

Then one of his fellow onlookers lowered the blanket from her head and looked at Elisha. "You're the boy with Pharisee Aaron, aren't you?"

Elisha recognized Naomi, Michael's wife, of the couple that was going to host him and Aaron until their tent burned. "That's right. I hope you and your husband have found comfortable lodging?"

"Thank you, yes, with friends from home," said Naomi.

"Is Michael here with you?" asked Elisha, looking among the other onlookers.

"He was. I'm afraid he got caught up in the fury against this Nathan man. Now Michael is with the others in Seth's tent, plotting who knows what. Michael is very angry about the loss of our tent and belongings this afternoon. He is eager for justice. Too eager."

"I see," said Elisha, not sure what else to say.

"Where is your father Aaron?" asked Naomi.

"In the meeting with Seth," said Elisha.

"I see."

For several minutes, the onlookers watched the mesmerizing flames and coals, and listened to the fire breathe in air from the still night, punctuated by occasional cracks and crashes of what solid wood and roofing remained. So far, no further snow or rain fell.

"That's enough for me," said Naomi. "Good night."

"Good night," said Elisha.

Naomi walked down the path. Only a handful of silent men remained to watch the fire. Elisha wondered which of them were interested in the Nazareth Scroll, but he didn't dare look too long at any of them.

"Welcome, Aaron!" said the meeting's host and leader Seth as Aaron entered the tent. "Fellow pilgrims: Aaron has honored me by agreeing to be my guest in this tent while he stays in Nazareth. He arrived here just today, and he is still learning about Daniel's long-time enemy, Nathan."

"We should've expelled Nathan from the village years ago!" interjected one native Nazarene. "Elder Daniel would not allow it. A lot of good that did him, keeping Nathan here."

"After Rebecca rejected Nathan and married Gabriel, Nathan always hoped for Gabriel's demise," another Nazareth native added. "He never stopped dreaming of marrying Rebecca and becoming Daniel's heir. He craved Daniel's approval. In fact, Daniel accepted Nathan more than the rest of us. He felt compassion for Nathan's loneliness and anger. Look at how Nathan has repaid him!"

"Yes, look!" shouted another man.

"Get Nathan!"

"Kill him!"

"Villagers of Nazareth and fellow pilgrims," started Seth, "we must proceed carefully. Felix's Roman cavalry officer now holds Nathan. At least he hasn't escaped. This is an opportunity more than an obstacle. The question becomes, how do we take advantage of this opportunity to do justice?"

"We outnumber those three soldiers!" said one man.

"No," replied most of the rest in near unison.

"Procurator Felix stands behind them," said Seth, "and the entire Roman Empire stands behind him. What we need is unity. Not just among ourselves, but among all two thousand souls here in Nazareth, pilgrims and natives alike. When they wake up in the morning, we should have a plan ready. A few won't go along, but most will, if we do it right. We need all the pilgrims to show Centurion Matthias that justice must be carried out against Nathan."

"How do you know it was Nathan who set the fire?" Aaron asked. He had seen Nathan being walked away by Centurion Matthias, and he did not think Nathan spoke like a guilty man. It was a dangerous thing to speak against Nathan's presumed guilt to the mob that was ready to kill him. But Aaron felt like Seth had enough control over the mob, for now.

First the others whipped their heads toward Aaron and gasped. Among them Aaron recognized Michael from Caesarea who had briefly been Aaron's host.

Then the men started clamoring all at once, until Seth held up his held and motioned for silence. In a few instants, he had it.

"My dear Aaron," said Seth, "how can it *not* be Nathan? He had two motives – a longstanding grudge against Daniel's family, and the more recent disagreement about sharing Nazareth's limited wells with all of us pilgrims. Many people witnessed Nathan's violent anger this afternoon, next to Pharisee Gad."

"Of course Nathan's guilty!" added another.

"Guilty!"

"Enough of this nonsense!"

There was no room for debate with this crowd, Aaron realized.

"Seth of Caesarea," said one man, "you have overseen much of our pilgrimage encampment – the layout of pathways for more and more tents, the system of sewage ditches to the central trench, the penning and caring of our animals. Now that Daniel is gone, or nearly gone, we need a single leader here more than ever. Won't you be our leader?"

"Only if it's necessary," said Seth.

Aaron thought that Seth did not sound very reluctant. In fact, he sounded self-satisfied. Had Seth planned this all along? Was *he* the arsonist, or at least the man giving the orders?

While Elisha sat cross-legged and watched the embers of Daniel's house from across the path, most of the remaining onlookers went back to bed. Only one stranger remained, though Elisha wondered whether others might be lurking in the shadows of the tents behind him.

Then another boy about Elisha's age walked calmly but purposefully down the path from the city center, with sewage pails in both hands. He walked right up to Elisha, set the pails down a few feet away, and sat cross-legged beside Elisha, facing the flaming house in parallel. The boy looked at the remaining onlooker several feet away from them.

Elisha could smell the full pails and wished this boy had set them farther away. He could see that the boy was hesitating whether to talk.

The remaining man noticed, too, and he turned his back and walked away, leaving the boys in privacy.

"Are you Elisha?" the other boy whispered.

"I am," Elisha whispered back. "Who asks?"

"I am Ishmael, son of Seth by his second wife Rachel. As you might guess by my name, my mother is the least favorite of his three wives. Perhaps you could not see by tonight's lamplight, but she is pale white. Father almost never lets her outside, even in our courtyard, and she suffers even more to live so close to her beloved sea while rarely seeing it. It is my mother Rachel who sent me. My father does not know I came."

Elisha was intrigued. The rich man's own son had to carry the household's waste to the sewage trench? Elisha rotated so that he sat facing Ishmael for their whispered conversation.

"As soon as my mother saw that your father Aaron was in the meeting with that vengeful mob in our tent right now, she wanted to get a message to him. She thought you were the best way to do it.

"My father is an ambitious, selfish, and dishonest man. All of his servants fear him. A couple of the servants are very bad men, capable of anything. The other merchants in our port city of Caesarea fear my father, too, but Seth is rich and powerful, and they must deal with him."

"Why are you telling me all this?" Elisha asked.

"It's about Seth's entire purpose for coming to Nazareth in the first place," said Ishmael. "For years in Caesarea, ever since the crucifixion under Pilate, father has provided patronage and protection for the followers of Joshua of Nazareth. While the Sadducees and the conservative Pharisees in our city try to persecute them, father's money and influence holds them back. Father has also convinced the Roman procurator that this is good, to keep the Jews divided between themselves. As a result, the Romans keep giving father advantages in the port business. And father's network among the Jews grows and grows. Every time someone big or small has a grievance with the local priests, father summons them and sides with them against the religious authorities. It has been twenty years of divide-and-conquer. And it has worked.

"Many of us in his household, though, we see how cynical he is about it. He occasionally mocks the followers of Joshua as poor people just looking for vengeance against the rich. He calls them stupid. He says similar things about the priests as well, all the way up to the high priest of the Temple.

"For years," Ishmael continued, "my father Seth has been able to push aside certain emerging leaders of the congregations of Joshua followers whenever those leaders presented a challenge to him. Some of them argue against polygamy, which ensures father's forceful opposition – one such leader even disappeared, unheard from again, and we fear the worst. Everyone in Caesarea has heard the rumors that a number of women in our town claim children by my father Seth, though they are afraid to make those claims openly.

"Recently, this scheming has become more difficult for my father. Too many of Joshua's followers presume that all rich men are bad. Seth cannot control all of them. He has been losing control of the Joshua congregations in our city. When word reached us of this disciple Daniel of Nazareth and his writing about Joshua, Seth got angry . . . and scared. It was bad enough for him that Joshua's Jerusalem disciples and Joshua's own brother Jacob the Just were ranting against rich men. Their sympathizers in Caesarea would be even more emboldened if written words told the life and teachings of Joshua of Nazareth, next to scrolls of the older prophets. Father would have no authority against the written testimony of a disciple from Nazareth itself."

Elisha could hardly believe his ears. He wasn't sure about any of this story, but he perceived Ishmael's genuine hatred of his father Seth. If that anger was real, much of the story must be as well.

"That is why our family made this journey. Here in Nazareth, too, Seth poses as a sincere follower of Joshua's teachings of charity and forgiveness. He wanted to control the disciple Daniel like he used to control most of the Joshua followers in Caesarea until the past year or two. If he did, if Seth could change Daniel's Nazareth Scroll to match his tactics of control in Caesarea, then he might regain that control. He became even more ambitious – perhaps he could control Joshua congregations throughout Israel. One night after much wine, he explained the strategy of taking advantage of the arguments between Jacob the Just and Saul of Tarsus, and to use his money to slowly gain much more control, even in Jerusalem. This was divide-and-conquer again, moving into a split between Joshua's followers.

"And now Daniel and the Nazareth Scroll are gone – or nearly. I assure you that my father Seth is pleased beyond pleased. He is rushing into the leadership gap. I doubt that father thinks this Nathan is guilty, but he sees the crowd's anger as an opportunity."

"Do you think . . . ," Elisha's question trailed off unfinished.

"Is my father Seth responsible for the fire at Daniel's house? I don't know. Is he capable of ordering such a thing? Yes."

Elisha turned his head back toward the fire and thought about everything he had heard. "So your mother, Rachel, Seth's second wife, wants my father Aaron to know about your father Seth's plotting?"

"That's right."

"Aaron told me to call him out of that meeting soon anyway. I'll do it now. But what will you do? Does your father know you've come to talk to me?"

"No!" Ishmael almost forgot to whisper. "He must not know!"

"All right, certainly, we will keep your confidence," Elisha whispered. "How will you return to the tent – how did you get out? Won't it look suspicious if we both show up at the same time?"

"There is a back door from the men's quarters, and the shortest path to the sewage trench cuts through the camp, not here. He will not know I have come this way. If you go get

Aaron now, I'll cut back through the camp and return to my father's tent after you have left."

Both of the young adolescents stood up, tall for boys but not yet fully grown men.

"Thank you," Elisha whispered.

"Thank *you*," Ishmael replied. He retrieved his pails and walked farther down the path before turning left on one of the main paths that his father Seth had designed.

Elisha glanced back at Daniel's house fire. Soon it might be cool enough to explore for any traces of the Nazareth Scroll. Then he turned and walked up the path toward Seth's tent to get his father Aaron.

Just two rows of tents back from the path by Daniel's burning house, a man stood behind a corner with a woolen blanket covering and hiding most of his head. As the spy watched Elisha and Ishmael walk away, he pursed his lips, scowled, and nodded slightly to himself.

CHAPTER FOURTEEN

"Papa Aaron," Elisha called from the path outside, through the tent wall. He tried to sound just loud enough, but not too insistent. "Papa Aaron," he repeated.

"Excuse me, Seth, everyone, I must see what my son requires," said Aaron. He stood and exited the tent.

As soon as Aaron was out, Seth looked over the heads of the small crowd seated before him, directly at one of the men standing at the separation curtain in front of the men's tent chamber.

The man was Seth's oldest son Boaz, still called Bull for his quick temper as a child. The first born of the first wife, Boaz was now a man, and unlike his father or most men, he grew out his beard. He nodded to his father that he understood, and he exited to the men's chamber behind him. Boaz walked straight through and quietly exited the tent from the back.

"Friends of justice," Seth said, "under my leadership, we will punish Nathan. We outnumber the officer and two soldiers from Felix's guard. Be careful not to provoke them – there are more where they come from. But they must focus on their prisoner and on new arrivals to Nazareth passing their guard post. We can spread out to control the entire tent city, and we can raise the people so much against Nathan that Procurator Felix's centurion will have no choice but to surrender him. Nathan must pay the price for his assassination of Daniel and Daniel's family."

"Get him!" cheered the small crowd.

"Be careful not to awaken anyone else tonight. The most important thing is to get into position to control movement and information in our tent city. When this meeting is over, everyone move to your positions at the path intersections in the camp, as we discussed earlier. I designed the camp to enable this purpose, since I feared things could get out of control and dangerous. Try to stay awake. If you fall asleep, so be it, but stay put in order to wake up in position with the morning's first risers. When morning comes, remember you have three purposes. First, make sure everyone understands that Nathan has attacked Daniel's family and must be punished. Second, recruit helpers and send them to me. Make sure they understand this is to do justice for the attack on Daniel. Third, note anything unusual and report it to me after I send someone to relieve you at your post."

Elisha and Aaron walked down the path to Daniel's house.

"Are you sure it's cooled off enough to look for the scroll?" asked Aaron.

"No, actually, it's not," said Elisha. "And I haven't seen anything suspicious out here, just a number of people who lingered to watch the burning house for awhile."

"Then you must have some interesting news." Aaron stopped and stood in front of the embers of Daniel's house. He looked down at his son's concerned face.

"I do." Elisha told Aaron everything he had learned from Ishmael.

Two rows of tents away, Boaz approached the spy at his post and tapped him on the shoulder.

The spy whipped around to see who had found him. When he saw Boaz, he partly relaxed. The spy was one of Seth's servants. He motioned for Seth's son to follow him farther from Daniel's house, where their whispered conversation would not be overheard.

Following the side path of Seth's design, they reached a point where they were certainly out of Aaron's earshot. The servant spy pulled the taller Boaz's head down so that they were mouth to ear.

"Your younger half-brother snuck out of the tent for a conversation with Aaron's son," whispered the servant.

Boaz pulled his head back to look at the servant's face by the dim light of the waning house fire. "Ishmael?"

The servant nodded.

"That traitor! No wonder he volunteered to take out the waste pails. Usually that's just his punishment for something. I thought he was working up to ask father for a favor. That little schemer! I ought to wring his neck." In his anger, Seth's oldest son Boaz whispered almost too loudly. He bent back down to the servant's ear. "Could you hear what they discussed?"

"None of it," replied the servant. "Whatever it was, though, it was very deliberate and one-sided. Ishmael sat right next to Aaron's son on the path and whispered very quietly. He went on and on while the other boy just listened. Then they stood up together, and Aaron's son went straight to get his father. They came right back there to Daniel's house. Now it is Aaron's son doing the talking and Aaron doing the listening."

"So it was a message for that Pharisee Aaron, delivered through his son. Ishmael's mother Rachel put him up to this, I'm sure of it. And it's something against my father Seth. Go back to your post and see if Aaron and his son are still by Daniel's house."

The servant did as he was told. Once in position, he carefully moved his head forward just enough to look for the two silhouettes in front of Daniel's house embers. Then he turned back to Boaz and nodded.

Boaz motioned for the servant spy to remain at his post and then returned to his father's tent.

Elisha told Aaron what Ishmael had said. Seth was completely dishonest and insincere – he sided with the followers of Joshua of Nazareth precisely to ingratiate himself with the Romans and to earn more trading rights at the port of Caesarea. Now he was scheming to take over Nazareth. He might even be the murderer responsible for Daniel's looming death. Elisha was alternately agitated and sleepy, and he kept yawning. It was past midnight, and they had risen before dawn for the walk from the Sea of Galilee to Nazareth.

Could Aaron trust the story of the thirteen-year-old Ishmael? Could he trust the motives of Ishmael's mother, the unfavored second wife of Seth? After everything else Aaron had witnessed, especially Seth's late-night meeting with the murderous mob, Aaron thought this latest news made sense. Moreover, Aaron had already seen enough that it didn't matter. Seth was willing to steer a crowd to kill Nathan, who was probably innocent, and to use the occasion to assume power over Nazareth's encampment and its two thousand pilgrims. Aaron had seen more than enough.

"What do we do, Papa?" Elisha asked.

"The Scroll is probably lost forever," said Aaron. "Its author is about to die. Gabriel the scribe is dead. Daniel's daughter Rebecca is now a widow with two little girls."

"I'm tired, Papa." Elisha yawned again. "Can't we just give it up, Papa? You'll never convince Martha to change her belief that Joshua was an Anointed One, a Messiah. You two will never get married. I'll never have another mother." Elisha started to sob.

"Oh, Elisha, I'm so sorry." Aaron held his son tight. "All these fires are awful for you, I'm sure. I'll take over. My whole Hillel school of Pharisees sent me here and expects that I do everything possible. I must not fail them. This isn't about me. Or if it partially was, it isn't any longer."

"I can't take it anymore." Elisha kept weeping.

"Go get some sleep, son. I'm so sorry."

Elisha turned to walk up the path, but there appeared several men walking down toward them. These were the men from the mob that had chased Nathan and then met with Seth. Father and son looked back at Daniel's house embers.

"Their meeting has ended," Aaron whispered.

Elisha walked past the men up to his bed in Seth's tent. He just wanted to sleep and forget about the Nazareth Scroll.

When Elisha entered Seth's tent, he found most of the oil lamps relit from the recent meeting. Except one guard, though, the center chamber of Seth's tent was now empty. There were no sounds from the women's and children's tent chamber on the left, and just a few from the men's on the right.

Elisha proceeded to the right, where a few men and older boys were settling into their beds of blankets on the ground. Their conversation stopped when Elisha entered, and an awkward silence ensued. Several servants and sons of Seth were missing – including Ishmael. Why wasn't he back from the sewage trench? Elisha was worried. He involuntarily looked to Seth's separate compartment on the side of the men's chamber. He couldn't see whether Seth was there or out with the others.

In their silence, the other men extinguished the remaining oil lamps except one in the main chamber next door. Only the dimmest outlines remained visible for Elisha to finish his way to bed.

Elisha's thoughts turned first to that night's fire at Daniel's house, and then to the memories of the fire that had killed his family six years earlier. As those thoughts evolved into dreams and nightmares, Elisha fell into a troubled sleep.

Aaron sat cross-legged in the middle of the path in front of the dying fires of Daniel's house. Just ten feet away stood one of the men from the mob against Nathan that had also met in Seth's tent afterward. So purposeful was the man's guard of Daniel's house that Aaron was certain it was part of a coordinated plan from Seth's meeting. Seth was after the Nazareth Scroll, too, it seemed. If Ishmael's story was right, his father Seth would probably welcome the Scroll's destruction. This thought helped Aaron stay awake and maintain his vigil.

At first, Aaron tried to hold Seth's new guard in his peripheral vision. But every time Aaron rotated to face a little away from the fire, the man retreated that much more, beyond Aaron's field of vision on his right. After a few failed attempts of this subtle two-way maneuvering, Aaron gave up.

For two hours Aaron sat there, sleepy and cold, sad and angry and perplexed about the attack on Daniel's family. And what about the fire in Michael's tent earlier that day? That had followed not long after Aaron and Elisha had settled their belongings there for the night. Were both fires arson, and if so, were they related? Did they target Daniel's Nazareth Scroll?

And who was behind it all? Aaron had little doubt that Daniel's fire was arson, after Elisha had observed traces of pitch painted into the mortar gap by the house's rafters. Nazareth native Nathan had seemed innocent to Aaron during his midnight arrest, but Nathan had resented Daniel and his family for years, and he was still suspect. Aaron's estranged brother Benjamin had been with Centurion Matthias at the start of Daniel's fire, which probably ruled him out, but not certainly, with all of Ben's servants doing his bidding. The conservative Pharisee Gad had screamed denunciations of Daniel that afternoon, and he had three followers at his disposal. The rich man Seth now appeared to be a fraud, a professed admirer of Daniel who was actually an enemy. He had plenty of servants and sons, and an unfolding record of plotting. And what about Centurion Matthias from Procurator Felix's cavalry? Felix wanted Daniel out of the way. And except Nathan, all of these suspect men had servants or followers or soldiers under their command, any one of whom might follow the hatred of the master to the point of taking the murderous initiative himself. And some of them could be watching Daniel's house – and Aaron – right now.

Aaron recalled, too, what his brother had said about Ruth. She had renounced her betrothal to Aaron in favor of the younger brother and loyal heir Benjamin. The more Aaron thought about it, the more he thought Ben must be telling the truth about Ruth. It was just like Ruth to stand up for herself and to demand good manners of those around her. Aaron had been anything but mannerly in his tunic-sundering denunciation of his inheritance, his family, and the entire Sadducee party.

Ruth was right. There was no need for that drama and disrespect, even if Aaron was going to leave his family anyway. He had never told Ruth, or even fully admitted to himself, that he planned such an insulting departure from his family. But deep within him, he had planned it. He lacked the courage for a calm conversation, to leave his father the initiative of a scathing response and an attempt to stop Aaron from joining the Pharisees. Aaron had not trusted himself to hold steady in the face of family pressure to change his mind. So he made it impossible for them by announcing his departure with such conflict and insult that he could never go back. In his heart, Aaron had always known this was wrong. But until tonight, he had never confronted himself with the reason he had done it that way: his own cowardice. Ruth had believed in him and his decision for the Pharisees more than he himself had. Yet the way he handled the break lost him his betrothed and beloved. Precisely Ruth's strength and resolve were a main reason why Aaron had always liked her, these characteristics more common among laborers and artisans than among the daughters of the aristocracy.

Staring into the ruins of Daniel's house, Aaron realized that Daniel's daughter Rebecca reminded him of Ruth. In his focus that afternoon on meeting Daniel and learning about the Nazareth Scroll, Aaron hadn't paid her much attention. Now his thoughts turned to the woman who had lost her husband and probably her father to the arson attack. Though a peasant woman, she had clearly learned much about the outside world from her father's days as a disciple of Joshua, and from her husband's wide reading of the Greeks. Perhaps Aaron could return to Nazareth some time after her mourning, even if she had no interest in recreating the parts of the Nazareth Scroll that she could remember. Aaron displeased himself, and stopped thinking this way about the new widow.

About halfway between midnight and dawn, Aaron's thoughts shifted from analyzing what had happened to imagining what would happen next. He had to keep reminding himself that the old today was merging into the new today. Daniel's house was nearly cool enough to explore, at least parts of it. Would the stranger lingering behind Aaron race him into the house or even try to stop Aaron? What about the morning and the rest of the day? Procurator Felix's cavalry was coming for Daniel and the Nazareth Scroll, and to disband Nazareth's tent city of pilgrims. If the Nazareth Scroll was indeed lost, what should Aaron do?

Could he help Nathan get an honest hearing? Could the true arsonist and murderer be found and brought to justice? Could Aaron do anything to lessen the danger of an armed cavalry, or at least to protect Daniel's daughter and granddaughters from any attack?

Aaron's questions then merged into answers. He envisioned the stranger following him into the embers of Daniel's house and dragging Aaron into a wrestling match. Next Aaron saw the Jerusalem fire that had killed Elisha's family, except this time, Daniel and his family were the victims.

Aaron caught his head falling forward and jerked it upright. He had fallen asleep, with his eyes open, for no more than a minute or two. He glanced back to his right and saw Seth's nighttime recruit still in place.

Although the house fire was now limited to large hot coals and small flames, its glow against the night's cloud cover seemed to brighten slightly, like clouds before the slowly rising sun. But it was much too early for that. Aaron looked up and observed that the cloud cover was now pure white, reflecting the exact color of the fire, with no visible texture in the clouds. That could mean only one thing. Within moments, Aaron saw and felt snowflakes, wet and in fast-falling clumps. He stood up to avoid accumulating a lap full of snow, and he pulled one edge of his woolen blanket into a hood. His unknown, silent companion barely flinched.

The snow started falling harder, and it sizzled against the large bed of coals and the remaining flames of Daniel's house. Much more of this, Aaron realized, and the flames would yield to dying coals.

Aaron did not have an oil lamp with him, and he would need remnants of the fire to show him the way through Daniel's house. The moment to enter the house was now. The snow had probably cooled things just enough, but it had not yet doused the glowing coals to guide Aaron's way.

Aaron stepped toward the front doorway. The clouds poured forth wet snow such as Aaron had never seen, almost like grain from a sack. The house fire sizzled and steamed, and its light rapidly diminished. Soon it would be too dark for Aaron to see anything.

Two tents away from the path, Seth's spy could barely see through the snow to Aaron's silhouette against the fading firelight. He saw what he needed, though. This was the moment. He retreated between the tents to go tell Boaz about Aaron's move.

CHAPTER FIFTEEN

Seth lit another oil lamp in his tent's central chamber, among the many already burning. Four of his male servants and his two oldest sons gathered quietly around him.

"Rachel's son Ishmael has betrayed us," Seth told them. "Tell them, Boaz."

Seth's oldest son Boaz explained. "Our spy by Daniel's house fire saw Ishmael having a long conversation with that Pharisee's boy, Elisha. When Ishmael returned here, he lied and said he had been nowhere except to the sewage trench and back. He accused our spy of lying instead. I told Ishmael to be careful in his sleep tonight." Boaz grinned maliciously. "That was a couple of hours ago."

Behind the curtain separating the men's quarters, Ishmael lay wide awake in terror. He could hear the gathered men whispering in the next chamber, but he couldn't understand them. It was about halfway between midnight and dawn, and Ishmael could not wait for the night to end. He heard Elisha tossing and turning, too, but he dared not speak across the fifteen feet that separated them. They were both supposed to be asleep.

Elisha lay awake and worried about the constant coming and going. Two or three hours earlier, he had witnessed the end of Boaz's conversation with Ishmael. It sounded threatening. From then on, movement continued in and out of Seth's tent, including several from the crowd that had accused Nathan of starting Daniel's fire. Elisha was alone in the large servants' bed on the floor, because they all had been doing errands and other tasks for hours in the night. He thought he could hear Ishmael tossing and turning, too, but he was afraid speak.

Minute by minute, Elisha's mind raced between scenes of fires and different emotions. Although he often told people about his family's demise in the fire that only he survived, he almost never revisited that night in his mind. Tonight's inferno at Daniel's house changed that. No matter what else he tried to think about, Elisha could not stop seeing the fire from that night in Jerusalem's poor district when he was seven years old, and he could not stop hearing his mother calling to him to go to the roof. Elisha involuntarily curled himself under the blankets in Seth's tent, just as he had on the street that night where Aaron first found him. Each time Elisha noticed that his knees were nearly to his shoulders, he straightened out again. But soon he was clutching his legs to chest again. He tried hard, very hard, not to weep. Tears streamed down his face and through his nose, as Elisha forced himself into silence, but he was constantly sniffing.

The only thing that sometimes stopped Elisha's tears was the anger. Why did his parents and siblings have to die? Why couldn't Aaron and Martha just agree to disagree and get married, so that Elisha could have a mother again? There were no easy answers, and tonight, Elisha had no patience for hard answers. For the first time in six years, he was more mad than sad at the loss of his family in the fire. But he had no target for that wrath. So he turned himself to Daniel's house fire from tonight. The man and his family had been kind to Elisha and Aaron that afternoon, as newly arrived strangers. And someone had burned their house, killing Gabriel and certainly Daniel in the days to come. Papa Aaron had deduced the evidence, burnt pitch smeared by a rafter. Who did it? Not Nathan, Elisha was convinced. Nathan looked shocked, even more shocked than his accusers. Had this rich man Seth ordered the murder of Daniel and his household? Had he? Who else could it be? Seth's own son Ishmael all but accused Seth of murder back in Caesarea. He seemed capable of it. He wanted Daniel stopped. Part of Elisha's mind told him that he could not be sure it was Seth, not yet. Mostly, Elisha thought and felt that Seth was guilty. He was determined to see justice done against Seth. Maybe no one could be found guilty for his childhood fire in Jerusalem, but by heaven above, Seth would pay for what he'd done tonight!

The two thirteen-year-olds tossed and turned some more, Ishmael and Elisha, sensing each other across the tent chamber, maintaining silence – Ishmael in fear of his family's anger, Elisha back and forth between agonized sorrow and boiling rage.

Suddenly, two servants whipped aside the curtain that separated the men's quarters from the central tent chamber. They went straight for Ishmael and pulled him to his feet.

"Silence!" whispered one servant. "Complete silence!"

Ishmael rose and walked to the central chamber with one man on each arm.

Seth sat on his high cushion while the others stood in front of him.

"Son," Seth spoke in a calm voice, "your brother Boaz claims you are holding news from us." He took a bite from a date and started chewing it, but still spoke clearly. "Is it something your mother put you up to?"

Ishmael glared at his father. He hated his father for the way he disrespected Ishmael's mother Rachel and her younger children, too. Seth esteemed his first and third wives. But the second wife Rachel, the most beautiful of all, Seth constantly insulted. He treated her like a heifer, serving the purpose of enlarging his household and reputation by producing another baby every year or two. Seth forced her and her sons and daughters to perform menial tasks, unlike the children of his other wives. And he was already planning to marry off their oldest daughter into an alliance of commerce, before she was ready.

Ishmael refused to answer his father's question.

"You know, Ishmael, your mother would prefer that you answer."

Ishmael thought he understood a threat. He still said nothing.

"Very well," said Seth. He turned to his right and nodded to someone behind the curtain to the women's quarters.

Ishmael's mother Rachel appeared, flailing her arms and legs, held tight and remorselessly from behind by Seth's strongest servant. As she struggled, she grunted under the hand that covered her mouth.

When she saw her son Ishmael, she suddenly went still.

Ishmael's half-brother Boaz pulled out a knife and pressed it to the bottom side of Ishmael's jaw bone, ready to slice downward through the boy's neck. In the light of many oil lamps, Ishmael's eyes glistened at his mother, and the knife sparkled.

From the next chamber, Elisha listened to Seth's threats and the sounds of struggle. Each time someone spoke or struggled, Elisha made another small movement, first to remove his covers in the cold night, then to take small steps across the men's chamber toward the separation curtain.

Seth watched his second wife Rachel with amusement and grinned at the scene he had created. "Ready to talk?"

Ishmael said nothing.

Seth nodded to Boaz.

Boaz jabbed the knife tip under Ishmael's jaw.

A drop of blood appeared and began to grow on Ishmael's neck.

"Oww!" shouted the guard holding Rachel.

All heads turned, and it was clear she had bitten the hand that muzzled her.

"Noooooo!" Her scream was short but loud enough to awaken everyone in nearby tents.

Another servant stuffed a cloth napkin into Rachel's mouth. The strong servant then grabbed her jaw from the bottom and pressed it up into her skull.

Rachel's eyes bulged as she gagged and gasped for air through her nostrils. She still focused on her son Ishmael and his bleeding neck.

Seth narrowed his glare at his wife Rachel. Then he turned back toward Ishmael. "Cut him again, Boaz," he growled, the false calm gone from his voice.

Boaz pricked the skin under Ishmael's other jawbone, and a little trickle of blood sprang forth.

"Ishmael!" Elisha roared as he leapt from behind the curtain and tackled Seth off his high cushion. In the same move, before anyone could react, he smashed a ceramic cup against Seth's skull. Elisha sat on Seth's back to pin him to the ground, and his legs pinned Seth's arms to his own body. Elisha's mouth winced, and he instantly switched the cup's largest shard from his bleeding hand into the other. The bleeding hand then seized Seth's collar from behind and smashed Seth's face into the ground. Elisha drew the pottery shard to Seth's neck, and pressed it in until Seth gagged.

"Let him go!" Elisha shouted in a deep man's voice for Boaz to release Ishmael. He sat astride Seth and glared and panted clouds of breath into the cold moist air.

An awakened baby cried in the chamber behind the curtain.

Everyone else froze in paralyzed silence.

Aaron stood in the front doorway to Daniel's house. The charred fragments of the door itself lay before him, sizzling as the wet snow hit their coal remains. Three hours earlier, Aaron had crossed this threshold, and the inferno's heat alone had lit his hair and chafed his face. He looked inside. There lay Gabriel's charred body, fallen half out of the main room's doorway, even less recognizable than earlier, in the dim glow of the coals on the patio. Since Gabriel's wife Rebecca survived mostly unscathed, Aaron wanted to leave the body for proper attention after dawn.

He stepped forward onto the patio. As he did, he looked back to the path, where Seth's deputy remained in place. At least Aaron did not have to compete to explore the house.

Aaron knew that no scroll could have survived this fire out in the open. Even in a cupboard or a covered hole in the wall, it would have burned to a crisp from the sheer heat, without the outside flames even touching it. The only possibility was a cellar. Did Daniel have one? With the rocky hillside rising at the back of the house, Aaron doubted it. Besides looking for a cellar entrance, Aaron could tap each part of the stone floors hard and listen for any hollow spots.

He bent over, picked up one of large stones from the threshold, and cradled it in his right arm. The first doorway to the right seemed like the main bedroom, Gabriel's and Rebecca's. Aaron stepped inside, and snow fell through the burned-out roof. From the looks of the walls and the patterns of burned beams criss-crossing the room, Aaron guessed that the two little girls had shared a loft above their parents' bed. The floor was covered in debris. The patterns of shadows and dimming orange light made it impossible to see much of the floor stones. Aaron did not know where he might start looking for an open or secret cellar. He decided to move to the other large room, where he had met with Daniel and his family.

From the patio Aaron entered the second door on the right to the house's main room. It was destroyed. The side walls were higher than Aaron had noticed that afternoon – the short second floor above it had burned out. Tiny bedrooms had been tucked above the main room. Only three feet high, two or four little bedrooms had housed Daniel and perhaps his scroll. Those rooms were gone, their only remains a mess of black logs burnt to sticks and sizzling in the snow from the open sky above.

"Nooooooo!"

Aaron heard a blood-chilling woman's scream in the distance, choked off at the end. He ran back out to the path and saw the other man glancing uphill toward Seth's tent. The two men looked at each other, barely visible in the black night as wet snow poured around them. They stood still, not sure how to react. Something was very wrong.

Then Aaron's mouth dropped at the sight. There was an orange glow in the snow ahead – another tent was burning on the far side of Nazareth! Aaron thought the scream had sounded closer than that, but he started jogging toward the fire.

"Ishmael!"

Was that Elisha's voice? It sounded much lower, like he was suddenly a year older. Elisha sounded both anguished and furious. Aaron sprinted up the path. His heart pounded. The cold air invigorated his lungs until Aaron inhaled several snowflakes. They did not slow him down. Elisha was in trouble! What did he and Ishmael have to do with the woman's scream?

"Let him go!" Again it was, yet was not, Elisha's voice, much older-sounding, overwhelming even. Something was terribly wrong for Ishmael, the son that Seth disliked.

The man who had stood behind Aaron for two hours at Daniel's house ran up the path behind him. Aaron didn't know if having a member of Seth's angry mob trailing him was good or bad.

No more sounds came from Seth's tent, and this worried Aaron. He was almost there.

When Aaron threw open the entrance to the tent, he could not believe the scene before him. More than ten individuals were all but frozen still in the light of many oil lamps, which flickered when Aaron burst in. Everyone focused on the pair on the opposite side, and only a few of them pulled their eyes away for the instant it took to identify Aaron.

There sat Elisha on Seth's back, on the rug, clutching the rich man's collar with one hand and pressing a piece of broken pottery into Seth's neck with the other. The crying baby behind the curtain accentuated the silence of everyone else.

"I said, call him off!" Elisha pressed the pottery shard even harder, and Seth gagged again.

Aaron had never seen Elisha so enraged. He looked to the right. A boy about Elisha's age – it had to be Ishmael – was held tight from behind by a man, and one of the man's hands covered Ishmael's mouth. Another man stood to the side with a shining knife blade one Ishmael's throat. Two streams of blood trickled from his lower jaw down his neck, one on either side.

Aaron saw that Ishmael's eyes looked not in his father's direction but rather to the left side of the tent chamber. Aaron turned and saw Ishmael's mother Rachel, restrained and gagged with a rag in her mouth. She wept uncontrollably and screamed muffled screams. Tears streamed down her cheeks, and she gasped to breathe through her nostrils, choking desperately on tears and her running nose.

"Aa—" Seth started to call Aaron.

"No talking!" Elisha ordered, and he pressed Seth's head harder into the carpet and the hard ground beneath it.

Seth winced and kept quiet.

Aaron furrowed his entire face to make sense of Elisha's involvement in this. How would Elisha ever escape from this? Seth had deputies all over the tent city and bags full of money to buy almost any allegiance he wanted. Only the higher authority of Procurator Felix's officer could protect Elisha from Seth. But that new fire would keep Centurion Matthias away from here for some time, even if he wanted to come investigate the screams.

"I'm sorry, Papa." Elisha spoke without removing his eyes from Ishmael's throat. He was ready to kill Seth if Ishmael received any more cuts. "This evil rich man sat on his cushion like a king while his eldest son was about to kill the younger one."

"It was just to get him to tell the truth!" The oldest son Boaz spoke while still holding the knife at Ishmael's throat.

"I said no talking!" Elisha shouted and pressed Seth's face into the ground again, bringing another grimace of pain on the rich man's face.

"The fire, Papa. The fire." Elisha's voice started to shake.

Now Aaron understood. Elisha was still reliving the fire that had killed his family six years earlier in the nighttime street in Jerusalem.

Elisha eased his grip on the pottery shard at Seth's neck.

Seth's eyes darted inquisitively at the relaxation. He looked to his loyal son Boaz for guidance.

Boaz nodded and watched Elisha closely.

Elisha noticed Boaz's gaze and reasserted his control over Seth. He pressed the pottery shard even harder into Seth's neck and rattled it against his flesh in sheer anger.

Seth's eyes bulged and he gagged, much like his second wife was gagging on the rag in her mouth across the tent chamber.

"Tell them to stop choking Ishmael's mother," Elisha ordered.

"Do what he says," Seth ordered in the brief moment when Elisha partly withdrew the shard from his neck.

The servant reached to Rachel's mouth and removed the rag.

Rachel gasped for air and collapsed into the arms of her captor, no longer standing on her own, exhausted from near suffocation.

"You are done for, son of Aaron," said Boaz.

"No talking!" Elisha again pressed Seth's head harder into the ground.

"Or else what, boy?" asked Boaz. "If you kill him now, you are the murderer."

Elisha fully processed that fact for the first time.

"I've got all night," Boaz told Elisha. "We are many. You are one."

"Three," said Aaron. He began walking to the far corner of the tent chamber, between Rachel and where she had been dragged in from the women's and children's quarters behind the separation curtain. "Rachel and I cannot overpower you. But we will witness your harm to Ishmael, and it will only be worse for you if you harm him more, not to mention the two of us. More than three, really. Do you think every servant of your family will lie to protect you and your father, when Procurator Felix's soldiers press them about the harm to your brother Ishmael? What about all the women and children listening right now from behind the curtain?"

In one swift movement with the knife he always carried, Aaron sliced the end of the cord that held the heavy separation curtain. It fell swiftly to the ground. Half of the women and older girls were not wearing their head scarves. All of them stood or sat in their bedding listening, as did most of the younger children, Seth's family and servants alike. The women without scarves raised to cover their heads. All the others, except the youngest, sat wide-eyed, unsure how to react.

Boaz looked at Aaron. "You will pay for this. Your son will pay for this."

"He already has, Boaz. He must live forever with the memory of your evil tonight. Elisha, no more harm will come to Ishmael here. There are too many witnesses, and I daresay some are emboldened enough to testify against their master and his eldest son, should they do any more harm. Wouldn't you agree, Boaz?"

Boaz glared at Aaron.

Elisha was unwilling to release Seth while Boaz still held his knife to Ishmael's throat.

"Boaz?" Aaron repeated.

Boaz slowly lowered his knife and spat on the floor in insult to Aaron.

Aaron turned to the back center of the chamber. "Elisha, your turn."

Elisha didn't budge.

"Elisha?"

Elisha looked at Ishmael's bleeding neck and still did not move.

Suddenly everyone heard pounding footsteps approaching the front of Seth's tent, and they turned to see who it was.

"Seth of Caesarea, Centurion Matt—" Procurator Felix's soldier spoke as he stormed inside in a swirl of snow. Just as quickly, he stopped and gasped at the scene, from Elisha pinning Seth to the ground with a pottery shard to his neck, to Ishmael's bleeding neck, to the exhausted woman Rachel. The soldier's mouth dropped when he looked over the fallen separation curtain straight into the women's chamber.

"Seth of Caesarea."

"Yes?" he spoke from under Elisha, looking at the soldier with tired, defeated eyes.

Elisha made no effort to stop Seth from speaking. Nor did he yet loosen his grip on Seth's collar or on the pottery shard at Seth's neck.

"Centurion Matthias is commandeering your quarters here. Someone lit our own tent on fire, so we require a place to stay.

We will occupy this central chamber, exclusively. You and your household will use the back entrances, including to get from one side chamber to the other. You will repair this separation curtain immediately, by the way. Only five of us will stay in this chamber – Centurion Matthias, the two of us soldiers, and our two prisoners."

"Two?" asked Boaz. "You mean another one besides Nathan?"

"Actually, we released Nathan. He was with us when the latest fire started, so he's not the culprit. One of the new prisoners is the man I caught fleeing our tent's fire. The other is his master – Seth of Caesarea. You are under arrest."

CHAPTER SIXTEEN

The entire company in Seth's tent gasped. Seth was under arrest? The master of the house, the husband of three wives and father of many children, the wealthiest man in Caesarea, the architect and new elder of Nazareth's tent city – under arrest?

At that moment, Centurion Matthias himself stormed into the tent, accompanied by his second soldier and their prisoner, Seth's servant. They brought another burst of wet snow and cold air with them through the tent's entrance. All the oil lamps flickered again, and dim little clouds of exhalation danced around everyone's mouths.

"Seth of Caesarea, Roman justice against you will be swift! What the devil?" Matthias took in the scene: A young man with blood trickling down his hairless throat. Another young man on top of Seth and ready to slice open *his* throat. And the entire women's quarters exposed.

"Aren't you the new Pharisee's boy?" Centurion Matthias asked Elisha. "Should I arrest you for the attempted murder of Seth? Or are you simply administering justice that he deserves? Speak, boy!"

Elisha looked down at Seth and pulled the pottery shard away from his neck. He was nervous and did not know where to start, and he kept looking downward.

"Speak!" bellowed Centurion Matthias.

Elisha looked up at Matthias. "Seth and his oldest son Boaz threatened to murder the younger son Ishmael," said Elisha.

"Why?"

"You'll have to ask *them*."

"Which one is Boaz?" Matthias asked.

"I am." The large man stood tall, his hair very short and his beard less than a day old. He held the bloody knife by his side.

"You cut your own brother's throat?"

"Half-brother. We— I wasn't going to kill him. I just wanted to scare him."

Although Ishmael had lost little blood, he was pale with fear and shock, even in the dim light of small oil lamp flames.

"It looks like it worked," said Matthias. "Did he think you might kill him?"

"I don't know," answered Boaz.

"Of course he did," interrupted Elisha. "That was the point. I too thought they would kill him, with the father Seth perched on his little throne there, overseeing the whole thing." Elisha spoke in his new, deep voice of a man. His nervousness was set aside, for he knew he was in the right, and he could see that Centurion Matthias would not be fooled by Seth and Boaz. Elisha's speech carried palpable rage against their wicked deeds.

"I scarcely have chains enough for this household," said Matthias. "Boaz, you too are under arrest."

"But—" started Boaz.

"Silence." Matthias did not even shout. His authority and resolve were clear.

"And let me say this to the entire household of Seth of Caesarea. I am not blind to the fact that you outnumber the three of us from Procurator Felix's guard. I am also aware, Seth, from your own mouth, that you are an official citizen of Rome, in the good graces of Roman Procurator Cumanus in Samaria. But here in Galilee you are beyond his authority. And remember this: Procurator Felix is better connected in the court of Emperor Claudius in Rome, as is well known. Felix's star is rising. If anyone from this household or otherwise should act against us tonight or tomorrow, you will surely suffer a gruesome punishment. I bluff you not. Tomorrow the cavalry of Procurator Felix comes to Nazareth, under Tribune Philip."

Aaron guessed that Seth had not known this before now. He watched Seth's and Boaz's reactions to Matthias' revelation. They both looked shocked, especially Seth. All of Seth's scheming during the night to take control of the crowd and to take command of Nazareth's tent city – it was all for naught anyway, with the scheduled arrival of Felix's cavalry.

"And as an extra security," continued Matthias, "I have placed identical written notes in the hands of three unrelated men among the tents out there. They are to deliver their messages to Tribune Philip tomorrow, and they will be well rewarded, as the message instructs, whatever happens. If something happens to me, the message states, the commander is to understand that Seth and his household are to blame. . . . Have I made myself clear?"

"Yes," Seth exhaled in resignation where he lay on his stomach, still bearing Elisha's weight on top of him.

"Boaz?" asked Matthias.

"Yes, Centurion." Boaz appeared halfway between despair and fury, and undecided about which attitude to adopt.

"I had nothing to do with any fires," said Seth.

"Quiet, man," said Matthias. "I did not ask for more lies. The rest of you in Seth's household, you are not in trouble – but repair this curtain immediately." Matthias motioned to the cut line above the women's quarters. "Soldiers, chain each of the three prisoners to different tent poles – Seth and the servant at the corners by the women's quarters, Boaz in the middle. Then prepare our beds. If anyone else interrupts my sleep tonight, woe unto you!"

The crying baby in the women's chamber paused, and then recommenced.

Centurion Matthias sighed.

Suddenly they all heard a thump on the tent fabric from outside. Then another. Then many.

"Great," said Matthias. "Something else to keep that baby awake."

After the thumps, a steady torrent of rain hit the tent. A new wind howled between nearby tents and overhead.

A flash of light lit up everything like the noonday sun, and as the flash stuttered in second and third bursts, the women with uncovered heads raised their arms to cover them.

Everyone held their breath.

A tremendous clap of winter thunder rattled everything in the tent, and then crackled its last force into the distance, as the new wind ushered in the downpouring rain. Babies and small children wailed in Seth's tent and all around Nazareth's tent city.

Centurion Matthias almost had to shout to be heard over the wailing children and the cascade of rain: "Seth of Caesarea, you did not cause the storm, but your scheming disrupted Nazareth's night until now. You will feel my sleep-deprived anger in the hours to come."

Elisha rose from his seat on Seth's back and walked to his father Aaron, and the two entered a tight embrace.

Seth's servant released Ishmael, and he ran to the arms of his mother Rachel, who still knelt on the ground as she recovered from the gagging cloth.

Fifty-year-old Seth seemed fifteen years older, and more so every minute, after his arrest and the sleepless night.

Boaz was adjusting to the turn of events, and he settled into a new anger. He glared at Ishmael and Elisha, the focus of his rage.

Seth's servants repaired the curtain line and raised the women's chamber curtain back in place.

Matthias' soldiers bound their three prisoners in chains to their separate tent poles.

As Elisha and Aaron embraced, the father whispered to the son, "You now have an ally here in Ishmael. Get some sleep, if you can. I will keep watch until things settle down. There won't be any search for the Nazareth Scroll either until daylight or until the rain stops to allow lamplight outside." Then Aaron kissed Elisha's cheek and turned his son to face Ishmael.

Ishmael and his mother were watching Elisha together, waiting for him to come speak with them. Ishmael held out his arm to pull Elisha into their conversation. "Thank you, Elisha." Ishmael tried not to cry. "When you had no idea of success or even survival, you risked your life for mine. Thank you."

"You saved my boy!" Rachel exclaimed. "You saved my Ishmael! Without you, the soldiers would have been too late!

Thank you! Thank you!" Rachel threw herself at Elisha's feet and around his ankles.

Elisha squatted and lifted Rachel back up. The two of them and Ishmael all stood at about the same height. "Ishmael is my friend," Elisha told her.

Ishmael and Elisha smiled at each other and then held each other in a tight embrace. Their new friendship was sealed by the risk of death that they had just shared.

Boaz glared, his arms chained behind him the center tent pole that he leaned against on the tent floor.

"Go back to my brothers and sisters, Mama," said Ishmael. "I will be fine."

Rachel kissed and embraced her son, then turned and retreated to the women's tent behind the curtain.

The pouring rain was loud but steady on the tent's roof. No more children cried from the thunder, and the baby was either asleep or being suckled behind the repaired curtain.

"Everyone, to your quarters," Centurion Matthias ordered. "Daylight will come soon enough."

Seth's family, servants, and guests did as commanded.

Aaron wondered whether any more of Seth's servants posed a threat. He motioned for Ishmael's attention and then whispered in his ear. "After the servant who was arrested, are any of these others bad men?"

"They are mixed, but no, that one was the worst," replied Ishmael. "They will not risk anything now, with my father's fate uncertain."

"Then let's get some sleep," said Aaron. His blood was still racing after the mortal standoff between Seth and Boaz and Ishmael and Elisha. Aaron could feel his tired eyes, and he could see the same in others.

Tiberius City

An hour before dawn, the rain tapered off, and the clouds parted. The cavalry stables of Procurator Felix were bustling with activity. Each of one hundred men saddled a horse by the light of his own oil lamp flame suspended over the straw-strewn floors. Each man carried two black pitch-smothered torches in a shoulder sack and a sheathed sword on his side.

The stables' main door suddenly slammed open. Tribune Philip walked in and stood next to his own horse, already saddled by his footman.

"Good news!" Philip announced. "The stars have come out. We ride to Nazareth! Our horses will walk until the sky turns gray. Then a fast trot, all the way to Nazareth."

Philip leapt into his saddle. "Swords and torches at the ready! Even before we dismount in Nazareth, you will need them! Joshua's followers will pay for what he did to my family." Philip laughed in wicked eagerness, showed the back of his horse, and led the way out.

CHAPTER SEVENTEEN

Nazareth

"Papa," Elisha whispered into Aaron's ear and shook him from his sleep in Seth's tent. "Wake up, Papa." They had both been sleeping on the large, shared servants' bed on the carpeted ground.

It was still well before dawn, and Aaron was in a deep sleep after spending most of the night awake. He rolled his head toward Elisha and opened his eyes. He barely saw Elisha's face in the faint lamplight from the next tent chamber.

"The rain stopped," Elisha still whispered. He didn't want any attention from Procurator Felix's soldiers or their prisoners in the main tent chamber next door.

Aaron absorbed the news. The rain had stopped . . . Daniel's house . . . the Nazareth Scroll. . . . Aaron bolted upright and gathered his woolen blanket in his arms as he stood, having slept fully clothed, including his boots. "I'll go," he whispered. "You stay here."

Before Elisha could say anything, Aaron was slipping quietly out the back door of the tent.

Elisha wondered if Felix's soldiers had heard anything. Their lamplight started flickering – someone was moving the oil lamp. Elisha rested his head and kept his blanket tight against the cold. He closed his eyes and breathed slowly to feign sleep.

The soldier on watch looked behind the curtain into the men's quarters, saw nothing strange, and returned to his post in the main tent chamber.

Aaron was cold outside, even with the blanket around him. By the starlight from above, he followed the path down to the left and tried to see puddles and avoid them. But twice he soaked his right foot in ice-cold rainwater.

Aaron saw no sign of anyone at the blackened shell of Daniel's burned-out house. Rainwater trickled out the front door. Aaron approached the entry and looked at the patio inside. Nothing appeared to have moved since Aaron's last visit in the snowfall a few hours earlier. For the third time since the fire started, Aaron stepped through the doorway onto Daniel's patio. The son-in-law Gabriel's charred, soaked body still lay unclaimed. Aaron was increasingly hopeless that the Nazareth Scroll could have survived the fire, even in a cellar, if there was one. In any case, he would not be making any discoveries by starlight. In the hour until daylight, Aaron decided to stand and keep vigil over Gabriel's body. He propped his foot on a fallen stone and waited.

Elisha awoke to the sounds of horse hooves walking and splashing and knocking into the rocky path only thirty feet from his bed inside Seth's tent. He lifted his head and looked through a crack in the back door flap to see the faint light in the western sky of the new day. Then he turned to Ishmael ten feet away, and saw him sitting up at the noise, too. They looked at each other in silence. Having slept in their clothes and boots, they were ready to move.

"Who dares ride my horse?" Centurion Matthias called out from the main tent chamber next to the men's quarters. "Who goes there? Halt, in the name of Procurator Antonius Felix!"

The horse hooves stopped.

"We ride our own horses, man," called a deep and calm voice from outside. "I am Isaac of Zippori, here with my servant. We saw the fire in last night's clouds, and we come in concern for the inhabitants of Nazareth."

Elisha heard the tent entry flaps ruffle as Matthias exited to meet the riders. Everyone would be awake now. He and Ishmael both jumped up and scurried out the back entrance to see for themselves.

As Elisha and Ishmael ducked under the tent guideline near the path, they beheld Nazareth's new arrivals. Two freshly shaved men with cropped gray hair sat astride beautiful white horses, and a third horse walked riderless behind them. Behind them shone a dark blue and orange sky in the east, and the sunrise had nearly broken over the horizon. In the cold, wet air, the horses billowed breath from their nostrils, and the two men floated gentle clouds from their mouths. The men's clothes were new and clean, in matching patterns of gray, light brown, and white, like a wealthy family's uniform.

Centurion Matthias looked up at the two men on horseback and was about to speak when he paused to observe Elisha and Ishmael twenty feet to his left. Then he faced Isaac again. "You speak with Centurion Matthias of the Roman cavalry, and I am in command in Nazareth. What exactly do you seek?"

"We come to offer help to any victims, and we seek a meeting with my friend Daniel of Nazareth."

"Then you seek only one man. Daniel will not long survive his burns from the fire in his house, if he has even lived through the night."

The blood drained from Isaac's face, his jaw went slack, and he breathed quick shallow breaths.

"Isaac!" Daniel's daughter Rebecca cried as she opened a house door across the path from Seth's tent.

Isaac slid down from his horse.

The two embraced and Rebecca sobbed into Isaac's chest.

"So it's true," Isaac mumbled to himself, in shock.

"It's awful, Isaac! Gabriel is g—" Rebecca wept. "G—gone."

"No! And the girls?"

"They are unhurt. Come see Papa," Rebecca said. "Come." She took Isaac's hand and led him into the house of Daniel's sister.

Isaac closed the door behind them, and his servant remained on the path next to the horses.

Centurion Matthias stepped forward to Isaac's servant. "How do Isaac and Daniel know each other?"

"They became friends when whiskers barely grew on their lips," answered the servant. "When Daniel was a very young man, he worked in Zippori on a new house that Isaac's father was having built. Isaac wanted to learn the trades of his father's craftsmen, so he worked side by side with Daniel, for almost two years. For some of that time, Joseph of Nazareth worked with them in carpentry, and he brought along his son Joshua. All three of them were the same age, Isaac, Daniel, and Joshua. They developed profound friendships with each other. It has long been said in Zippori that Isaac's father was the only rich man that Joshua of Nazareth ever liked." The servant nodded his head at a memory. "Joshua liked to talk about rich men and their camels. As it happens, Isaac's father and his favorite camel often won the annual race of three laps between the main city gate and the small after-hours gate – the eye of the needle, which a crawling camel can barely enter. We used the same water clock every year, so he raced against his old times as well. Joshua loved those races.

"When Joshua later became a wandering preacher, he remembered Isaac's father as the rare example of an honest and exceedingly generous rich man. Indeed, I can tell you, Centurion Matthias, Isaac's father gave jobs to hundreds of the destitute in Zippori. To this day, his son and heir Isaac tries to do the same, always inventing tasks to employ the poorest in ways that help other poor men and women, in the fields, in the city, or anywhere that makes sense.

"After Joshua was crucified under Pontius Pilate, his Zippori disciples returned home, including Isaac and Daniel. Daniel returned to his native Nazareth, which is four miles from Zippori. He has visited Isaac about once a week all these twenty years. Occasionally, Isaac has come to visit Daniel in Nazareth, especially at harvest time. We were here just two months ago, before all this started." Isaac's servant waved his arm toward the hundreds of tents downhill from the village center where they stood. "Nazareth was always so tiny, so unimportant."

"I see," said Centurion Matthias. He paused for several moments. "What would you say if I told you Daniel's fire was set deliberately?"

Isaac's servant just nodded his head as if he'd expected as much.

Aaron still stood guard over Gabriel's body in Daniel's burned-out house. The sun chased the stars from the sky, but it did not yet break the horizon, and the cold wet air lingered. Aaron held the woolen blanket tight around his shoulders.

As pilgrims awoke throughout the tent city, Aaron could hear the soft conversations of morning. Some of the curious and sorrowful started arriving to view the remains of Daniel's house. But even the most venturesome paused at the front door when they saw Aaron standing over Gabriel's body, and they stepped back to the path.

Then one figure remained in the doorway for a moment before stepping forward onto Daniel's small patio across from Aaron. It was Aaron's brother Ben.

Aaron no longer felt cold. For the first time in years, he felt jealous of Ben's marriage bed with Ruth, Aaron's long-ago betrothed. After Ben's revelations last night, Aaron also felt the shame of Ruth's scorn for his behavior, even though it was youthful self-righteousness seven years in the past. Aaron knew he had to forgive himself. Suddenly he was reliving the sorrow of losing her, and he had to overcome that, too.

"Is that Daniel's son-in-law, Gabriel?" asked Ben.

Aaron nodded and looked at Ben. He felt his profound fatigue from lack of sleep and the resulting emotional weakness. His thoughts repeated Ben's words from last night about Ruth's scorn. Aaron wanted to make peace with Ben, as he always had. But it no longer needed to be on Aaron's terms. He didn't require Ben to recognize any validity in his choices. Aaron felt tears start to fill his eyes, tears of sorrow for what he had lost, including his own seven years of isolated arrogance. But the tears were also for the joy and relief and letting it go, of finally moving beyond the moment of his rupture with his aristocratic family. Yes, Aaron had developed deep friendships and mutual respect in the community of the Pharisees and among his neighbors in the poor quarter of Jerusalem. But he always kept one foot in the door of self-justification for leaving his family with a temper tantrum. As Aaron looked at his brother through a swirl of tears, he pulled away from that part of his past and turned his back on it, forever. As he fully accepted himself and his Pharisee skin, he no longer needed to defend himself to his brother.

The tears began to wash Aaron's cheeks. He opened his mouth, but his voice failed him. Instead, he exhaled, voiceless, and dropped to his knees facing Ben. His sleeplessness made his epiphany and his release overwhelming. But Aaron thought, too, that perhaps it was his exhaustion and the stress of the night in Nazareth that finally pushed him to release his tensions from leaving his family and Ruth seven years earlier. For the first time, he felt real peace about the Pharisee's life he had chosen.

Aaron found his strength, yet remained on his knees. He wiped his tears with his left hand. "I'm sorry, brother. Not for what I did, leaving the family, but for how I did it. My present life was my calling. Treat me how you must. But I will no longer force my self-defense on you. When we have passed each other without speaking in the streets of Jerusalem, we have both felt it, this hostility we bore each other. I no longer bear mine. For what you told me last night about Ruth, thank you. She was right, of course. You are lucky to have her."

Aaron stood up and offered both hands palms down for Ben to take if he wished.

Ben long hesitated. Finally he stepped slowly toward Aaron.

Aaron stood in place, hands and arms outstretched.

When Ben was close enough, he took Aaron's hands without speaking.

Aaron took one small step toward embracing Ben, to allow his brother the choice to lean back and avoid it.

Ben stood still or maybe even leaned a bit toward Aaron.

Aaron wrapped his arms around his younger, slightly taller brother and squeezed him with all the strength of a man who lifted heavy amphoras of salt all day.

Ben gagged a little and chuckled at Aaron's strength. "Even the chief priests would be impressed with your strength, Aaron, greater than what we require for hours of sacrifices."

Aaron pulled back and smiled. "When I left, I thought I should find a profession that built on that strength."

Ben smiled back, but his eyes still looked guarded. "You certainly found it."

Then Ben stated the obvious. "We both know that the other wants the Nazareth Scroll, Aaron. And you know that I do not wish it well. But look around you. It's gone. There's no way it survived this fire."

"He's right," said a third voice from the front doorway.

On the road from the Sea of Galilee, Tribune Philip trotted at the head of his hundred-strong cavalry. He had often traveled to Zippori, and he knew they must be approaching the side path to Nazareth. Although he was eager for the horses to accelerate and canter the rest of the way, he had to hold back. They would need some reserve strength for what he planned to inflict on Nazareth's pilgrims.

Philip remembered the stories of a few years ago, when Roman forces had massacred a large pilgrimage near the River Jordan. What was it, about four hundred killed? Philip hoped for more than four hundred in Nazareth, and by the sound of Centurion Matthias' report, their numbers were far greater. After wiping out Nazareth, he would be famous. He glanced at Councilor Marcus riding next to him, sent by Procurator Felix to urge restraint. Philip had a plan to deal with him.

Rebecca and Isaac stood in the main room of the two-story house of Rebecca's aunt, Daniel's sister. Daniel lay unconscious in a makeshift bed on the floor, tended by his sister and Miriam the Samaritan. His clothes and hair were burnt and covered with soot. His face and hands and arms were charred black in some places, blistered and bleeding in others. His breathing was shallow and irregular.

"Oh Rebecca, I'm so sorry," Isaac said, and he hugged her again.

The two older women shifted on the floor to make room. Isaac and Rebecca both kneeled next to her father.

"He drifts in and out of sleep," whispered Miriam. "He mumbles things we can't understand, except one word he keeps repeating: 'Micah, Micah, Micah.'"

"Are any of Nazareth's new pilgrims named Micah?" Isaac asked Rebecca.

Rebecca shook her head. "Not that I've heard about."

Isaac smiled thinly. "Then it's our friendship scripture from the Prophet Micah, a favorite of Joshua, too: 'What does the Lord require of you but to do justice, and to love kindness, and to walk humbly with your God?'"

"The scroll is gone, too, Isaac," said Rebecca. "Both copies. There's no way they survived the fire." She looked at Miriam, but the family secret of the second copy didn't matter anymore.

"Is Gabriel here?" Isaac asked.

"He's still in Daniel's house," answered Miriam. "Rebecca says he saved her and the girls. When he first saw the fire, he had fallen asleep in the main room like most nights, with the scroll on the table. He had planned to finish it last night. When the smoke and flames awakened him, he ran to the family bedroom, awakened Rebecca, and pulled the girls down from the loft. Then he ran back for Daniel in his tiny bedroom above the main room. It took a while before Daniel staggered out. Gabriel never made it behind him."

"Your father knew from the first day that Gabriel was worthy of you, Rebecca," said Isaac.

"Rebecca," Miriam whispered.

Rebecca and Isaac both turned to Daniel. He wasn't breathing. Miriam held Daniel's hand to show that it was already stiffening into rigor mortis.

Then through his slightly parted lips, Daniel made a short and shallow breath out and in, then held it. Many seconds later, he did it again.

The family and Miriam and Isaac watched him together in reverent silence.

Daniel took another little breath. He held it a long time. Another quick and shallow exhalation and inhalation followed, and then another long pause. Finally, his last, slight, lifeless breath drifted from his mouth, like air from an opened wineskin.

Daniel's sister wept with her friend Miriam. Rebecca and her two girls sobbed in a heaving embrace. Isaac put one hand on Rebecca's shoulder and cried with them.

Outside the door, Centurion Matthias and Isaac's servant heard the lamentations.

Isaac emerged with tears streaming down his cheeks, and he closed the door behind him. "We need to retrieve Gabriel's body," he told his servant.

The two men led the three white horses down the path to Daniel's house. They were followed by Elisha and Ishmael, and by a growing crowd who had come out to admire Isaac's horses.

As they came around the curve, Isaac heaved a sigh at the shell of his friend's house, roofless and blackened from the inside. His tears were silent, but his jaw trembled in agonized sorrow. Many people were gathered on the path in front of the house, and they stood aside for Isaac's little entourage and horses. Isaac handed his reins to his servant, and he approached the remains of the house he had known for almost forty years.

When Isaac reached the front door, he looked inside and saw Aaron standing in the middle of the small patio. Ben stepped away from Aaron. Isaac stared in extended silence at Gabriel's body by Aaron's feet. Finally, he stepped through the doorway. "Who are you?" he asked.

"Aaron of Jerusalem, a Pharisee and a friend of the teachings of Joshua of Nazareth. Daniel and Gabriel were my new friends."

"Daniel visited me in Zippori five days ago, and he didn't mention you."

"You must be Isaac," replied Aaron.

"I am."

"I arrived yesterday."

Isaac stepped onto the patio, walked up to Aaron, and knelt to the body of his friend Gabriel.

Aaron knelt beside him. "Rebecca and the two girls survived."

"I know. I just saw Rebecca. Daniel is dead."

"No," Aaron whispered. But he knew it was due.

"The death of Socrates," said Isaac.

Aaron knew that story, but he had no idea what Isaac meant by it. He gave a puzzled look.

Isaac managed a brief, weak smile through his sadness. "When we were young men working with Joshua in Zippori, I told them the story of Socrates. Daniel and Joshua were both impressed that Socrates taught the best truths and questions that he could, even after he knew that he risked execution. Joshua admired Socrates' final choice for execution over self-censorship, but Daniel and I disagreed. We argued that Socrates should have accepted a muzzled life in order to continue supporting his young wife and children. But Joshua never wavered from his belief that Socrates had made the right choice.

"Years later, Joshua found himself in the very same position, and he made the very same choice. We loved him and we tried to talk him out of it, but you know how that ended.

"Now, another twenty years on, Daniel, too, has taken the path of Socrates, although he didn't realize this until after the pilgrimage started. Dangerous opponents started taking an interest. Yet by then, the Nazareth Scroll was almost complete. He consulted Gabriel and Rebecca, and they all agreed, they would take the risk, which was never as certain as Joshua's had been." Isaac bent his head and sobbed. "But in the end," he stammered, "it was just as deadly." He buried his face in Gabriel's rain-soaked, charred chest and wept.

Aaron sat aside and let him mourn.

Finally Isaac lifted his reddened face and looked pitifully at Aaron.

"It isn't over yet," said Aaron.

"What do you mean?" asked Isaac.

"Did Rebecca tell you about Procurator Felix's cavalry?" Aaron asked.

"What?" replied Isaac.

"They are coming to Nazareth, today, probably before noon," said Aaron.

CHAPTER EIGHTEEN

"The Roman cavalry?" Isaac asked. "And you're certain these are the forces of Felix in Tiberius?"

"As I learned two days ago in Tiberius, Felix wants – wanted – to destroy the Nazareth Scroll," said Aaron.

"Well, that work is now done," said Isaac.

"Is there any way the scroll could have survived the fire?" Aaron asked. "A stone cellar or something?"

"I'm afraid not," replied Isaac. "Rebecca is convinced that both copies are destroyed. So am I."

"Both?"

"Gabriel copied each evening's work after Daniel went to bed. They usually kept one copy in the main room and one in a tiny spare bedroom upstairs, near Daniel." Isaac turned his head toward the main room behind Gabriel. Blackened stone walls surrounded criss-crossed burnt rafters on the floor, all open to the morning's blue sky. The upstairs bedrooms were gone. "Nothing survived in there. Nothing."

In shock at the loss, Aaron put one hand over his mouth. The Nazareth Scroll was gone, beyond a doubt.

Isaac glanced over his shoulder to the front doorway and the crowd outside. He gave Aaron a serious look and whispered, "Do you think Procurator Felix's Centurion Matthias did this?"

"Not sure, but I don't think so," Aaron whispered. "There were two other fires last night, and the last one was at Matthias' own guard tent."

"Where the path enters Nazareth's tent city?" asked Isaac.

"Exactly," answered Aaron.

"I saw that on the way in. Interesting. Are there any suspects?" Isaac asked.

"There were three different suspects during the night. It looks like this man Seth ordered the last fire by one of his servants. The servant was caught fleeing Centurion Matthias' burning tent. Seth is the richest man in Nazareth's pilgrimage, here with three wives and their children and servants."

"Why would Seth do that? What was his motive?" asked Isaac.

"Control of the ports and churches in Caesarea, it seems," said Aaron. "When news of this disciple Daniel reached Caesarea, Seth started losing control of his workers who were followers of Joshua of Nazareth."

"Who else here disliked what Daniel was up to?" asked Isaac.

"The first suspect was Nathan, a native of Nazareth," said Aaron.

"Oh, dear," said Isaac.

"So you know that Nathan already disliked Daniel," said Aaron.

Isaac nodded.

"He also disapproved of sharing Nazareth's spring waters with of all us pilgrims," said Aaron. "After Daniel's fire, a mob cornered him, and Centurion Matthias arrested him – and saved him in the process. Nathan was Matthias' prisoner when the third fire broke out, so they released him, and he's back home with his old mother.

"Another suspect is a conservative Pharisee named Gad," continued Aaron. "He openly opposed Daniel about Joshua, and then again just last night about how to light the Hanukkah menorah. Finally is a Sadducee from Jerusalem by the name of Benjamin. He happens to be my younger brother, but he was Matthias' prisoner when the second fire broke out, so he was released."

"You traveled together with your brother?" asked Isaac.

"We came unknown to each other until he passed me on the road a few miles before Nazareth," said Aaron. "For seven years he refused to speak to me, until last night."

Isaac lifted his chin and scrutinized Aaron in silence.

"Centurion Matthias," started Isaac. "The Sadducee Benjamin. The Nazarene Nathan. The rich man Seth. The Pharisee Gad. And Seth looks guilty. But has anyone seen Gad this morning?"

"I asked myself the same thing," answered Aaron. "It's early, but no, I haven't, not here."

"Who can be sent to find him?" asked Isaac.

"My son Elisha. He's right outside on the path. Will you see to Gabriel's body?"

"Of course," said Isaac.

Aaron walked across the patio to the doorway and motioned for Elisha to approach.

"Yes, Papa?" Thirteen-year-old Elisha retained his new, lower voice. A few hours' sleep and the new day's sunshine had soothed some of Elisha's frustration and anger from the night.

"This man is Isaac of Zippori, Daniel's best friend, as we learned yesterday. He wants to speak with the Pharisee Gad. Go find his tent and bring him here."

"Yes, Papa."

Isaac appeared at the doorway next to Aaron. "Will you help me carry Gabriel to my horse?"

"Of course," replied Aaron.

Isaac started for Gabriel's shoulders, but Aaron was half his age and a manual worker, and he scooped up the entire burned corpse as if it were a child's. He brought Gabriel out of the house and laid him over Isaac's empty horse. The crowd stood by in solemn silence. Then Isaac and his servant turned their three horses around and started the walk back uphill to the village center, where Gabriel's widow Rebecca tended to her dying father Daniel.

"Help! Help!" Men and women and children suddenly began screaming somewhere up the path.

Aaron looked up the path and saw smoke starting to rise – from the back of Seth's tent.

"Fire! Help! Help! That woman!" That was Seth's voice.

Rachel? Aaron wondered. Was the mistreated second wife exacting revenge on her torturer husband Seth?

Women and children poured onto the path from Seth's tent, and smoke billowed up from its backside.

Just as Aaron rounded the bend in the path, he saw Ishmael dash off between tents to the right.

Aaron ran past the slower pilgrims who also trotted up the path to see the commotion.

"Help! Help! Unlock our chains!" screamed Seth from inside the burning tent.

One of the chained prisoners inside the tent screamed in excruciating pain and fear. Aaron thought this was Seth's oldest son Boaz.

"Hurry! Help!" called Seth again.

Matthias fumbled at his keys, found the right one, and pointed his two men into position before he ran inside the tent.

As he opened the tent flap, smoke billowed out the top of the opening. The flames were now shooting above the back roof of the tent and piercing through the roof in two places, where the thick curtains inside separated the main chamber from the women's and men's chambers to either side.

Matthias ran back out, and flames started to pour out the front entry as he exited. "I can't make it. Olive oil is spilled and burning everywhere."

The screams continued nonstop.

Matthias darted to the side of the tent where the women's chambers met the center tent. "We can save one of them, the prisoner servant tied to the pole right here." Matthias pulled out his sword, stabbed the tent level with his eyes, and sliced the tent to the ground. He lifted the bottom of the tent side out of the sand and rocks, sliced it all the way through the bottom seam, and pulled the two new flaps apart.

Seth's servant who stood chained to the pole was the only prisoner not covered with oil, but flames were climbing up his pants. His face was terror-stricken. "Hurry! Please! I didn't do anything wrong!" He twirled around the pole to bring the lock in front of Matthias.

Matthias fell on his knees, fumbled for the key, and then quickly unlocked Seth's servant.

The servant dove out of the tent and onto the rocky path. He found a puddle to his right and rolled through it, then splashed water all over his burned, blistering legs. He was about to stand up and run away as far as he could get when Isaac's servant pushed him back down.

"Not so fast," said Isaac's servant. "We're not sure about you yet."

Seth still screamed between desperate coughs.

Boaz could be heard wheezing between his weakening yelps.

The tent was now an inferno, sucking wind into itself and spewing flames and smoke into the morning sky. The smell of burning camel-hair tent fabric was acrid, and it crackled as it shredded into ashes.

Everyone standing outside winced at the disappearing sounds of the two choking men.

Aaron looked for Ishmael's mother Rachel among the refugees from Seth's tent, but he did not see her there.

The burning men's choking stopped. Still the fire raged.

Dozens of Nazareth's pilgrims grimaced at the horror, while their eyes were wide with their own fright that the fire might spread to their adjacent tents. If not for the previous night's rain, the tent city would have been doomed. It was still in danger. Men and women stood with blankets and small shovels, ready to swat away any sparks or drifting flaming tent fabric. Occasionally something landed on a nearby tent, but the tenters descended on it like a swarm of locusts, snuffed it out, and returned to their attentive vigil.

Isaac of Zippori emerged from the house across the path and shut the door behind him. He, too, frowned and winced at the sight and smells. "If the fires weren't ordered by the rich man Seth, who did it?"

"Let me go, you scoundrels!" A woman screamed as Ishmael and Elisha dragged her into the path. All three were covered in filth.

Everyone turned to the right and saw the woman twenty yards away, with Elisha and Ishmael each holding one of her arms. Elisha held a coal pan in his free hand hand, while Ishmael carried a crude torch.

"Let go!" shouted the woman.

"Naomi," Aaron muttered in shock. "Michael's wife Naomi."

"I saw her running away with this torch still on fire and that hot coal pan in her other hand," said Ishmael. "She tried to light us, too, but we tackled her, in the sewage ditch."

The two panting young men looked pleased with themselves, but at the same time disgusted at their own filth and horrified of the inferno of Seth's tent.

"Elisha, do you recognize this woman?" Aaron asked.

"Yes, Papa, it's Naomi."

Aaron stepped closer. "Centurion Matthias, this is Naomi of Caesarea, wife of Michael. They were to be our hosts until theirs was the first tent to burn yesterday evening." Aaron looked at Naomi while he spoke to Matthias.

"You burned down your own tent?" Matthias asked her.

"Of course not! I don't know who did, or if it was an accident. I don't know anything about the other fires. It was that wretched man Seth I was after. Seth never recognized me, but he wouldn't. That was long ago, and I was only a child. My family served in his father's house in Caesarea. One night when Seth was a young man and drunk, he— he—," Naomi started crying. "He attacked my mother and killed her. My brother tried to help, but Seth crushed his skull and made an idiot out of him. My poor, simple brother. He just died this past harvest season."

She refocused her anger through her tears. "We appealed to Seth's father for justice, and got nothing. The Roman procurator – nothing. Our local priest, a Sadducee – nothing. The representative of King Herod Antipas – nothing. The merchant rivals of Seth's family – nothing. Everyone in Caesarea knew that Seth had killed my mother, yet no one in power did anything about it. I quit my work in his house before Seth could even know my face, and I swore my revenge. When I learned that Seth was coming to this pilgrimage, I saw my opportunity – a chaotic mess of tents and people unknown to each other. Finally, more than twenty years later, Seth has received justice! He's dead, isn't he?"

Naomi smiled through her tears as she watched Seth's tent collapse in flames. Seth and his son Boaz were both dead. "It was worth whatever fate awaits me." Naomi looked to the sky above, "Mother, brother, justice is finally done to that wicked man!"

Aaron stared at Naomi. "How do you explain the other fires?"

"I told you," she answered, "I don't know anything more about them than you do."

Aaron was almost certain that Naomi knew all about them.

Tribune Philip hoped this was the last ridge before reaching Nazareth.

"Yes!" he smiled to himself as he observed the tent city below. The hundred-strong cavalry continued behind him, fifty pairs of horses riding side by side. The morning sun lit up Nazareth below and all the pilgrims scurrying around like ants. Philip observed a small crowd around some horses at the village center of stone houses to the right, upslope from the tents.

"Something is not right." Councilor Marcus looked the part of an elegant Roman advisor. He was well educated and worldly from his upbringing in Rome. He spoke Aramaic in broken grammar, with a thick Latin accent of soft, haughty-sounding vowels and "z" sounds in place of "th's." "Why little crowds this early in the morning? And those horses? Centurion Matthias is supposed to greet us at edge of Nazareth. But I see only small gatherings, and a black stain on the earth."

"What's not right is all these people worshipping the false prophet Joshua of Nazareth, and this man Daniel encouraging them!" replied Philip. "We must arrest Daniel and occupy his house at once, before anyone can react."

Marcus glared at Philip but held his tongue.

"That big tent is on fire!" shouted one of the cavalrymen behind them.

Tribune Philip squinted, and as the fire grew, it became obvious. He scowled, "No! It is for me to decide what happens here!" He smacked his horse and led the cavalry down the path to Nazareth.

CHAPTER NINETEEN

Between Seth's burning tent and the cluster of stone houses, Aaron lifted Gabriel's body from the horse that carried it.

Suddenly someone cried, "Look! Felix's Roman cavalry! Coming down the path!"

Centurion Matthias looked, too. "Tribune Philip," he said to himself. "It's about time." He turned to Ishmael standing nearby. "Boy, go down to the animal yard and fetch my three horses. Find someone to help you. Bring them to my guard post, where my tent stood until it burned last night. Fast!"

"Yes, sir," replied Ishmael, and he dashed off.

Isaac looked and saw the cavalry with his own eyes. He motioned for his servant and held a finger to his lips for silence. Then he moved behind the head and neck of his white horse, out of Matthias' view.

Isaac's servant stepped forward and placed his chin at Isaac's shoulder and his ear by Isaac's mouth.

Isaac whispered, "Do you remember the back path out of Nazareth, downhill from here?"

"Yes," answered the servant.

"Take my horse. Go, now, as fast as you can, back to Zippori. Don't let Felix's men catch you. Find the Roman Governor Quadratus and his general who are visiting Galilee from Syria. I sent word to them this morning that there might be trouble in Nazareth. Quadratus has come south to investigate the Jewish-Samaritan fighting, and he will be outraged at the threat of more violence here. Bring Quadratus with his general to outrank the tribune, as quickly as you can!"

Isaac pulled his head away and made eye contact with his servant. The servant gave one small nod. They understood each other.

The servant calmly mounted Isaac's horse and casually pointed it downhill toward Daniel's burned house and beyond. Before Centurion Matthias or anyone else could notice, the servant gave the command, and the horse trotted down the path to the far side of the tent city. "Make way! Make way!" the servant cried, to clear the path of people and goats.

"Halt! Halt!" cried Matthias.

The servant paid him no heed and rode on.

"You will pay for this, Isaac of Zippori," said Matthias. "No one plays games with Tribune Philip."

"I am a free man, Centurion Matthias, and an official citizen of Rome. There is no law restricting where I tell my servants to go."

"Tell that to the tribune," replied Matthias.

Tribune Philip was halfway down from the last ridge to Nazareth when he spotted the man on horseback riding away. He stopped and turned to the cavalry's trumpeter. "Sound a warning!"

The trumpeter stopped his horse, lifted the trumpet to his mouth, and blew a long clarion call across the plateau.

In the tent city, every human froze in place and looked toward the trumpeter uphill, while every animal tried to run in the opposite direction. Isaac's servant on horseback did not pause from his trot into the hills beyond Nazareth.

Philip pursed his lips. Without looking behind he gave an order. "Two of you, go back to path to Zippori, where it forks off up at the ridge. You'll have a straighter journey than the rider who flees us. Beat him to Zippori and arrest him. Do whatever it takes."

The first pair of cavalrymen looked at each other. One of them answered, "Yes, Tribune Philip," and the pair turned around and rode past the rest of the cavalry back uphill.

Tribune Philip resumed the cavalry's descent into Nazareth.

As they neared the edge of the tent city, more people stopped what they were doing to stare at the cavalry's uniformed might. Strong horses carried men in white and black shirts. The subdued atmosphere of Nazareth's tent city grew quieter still.

When they were fifty yards from the first tents, Philip turned to Councilor Marcus. "Wait here. I will advance alone in search of Centurion Matthias."

He came to the edge of the camp and saw the burned-out remains of one tent. Centurion Matthias was nowhere to be seen. "Inhabitants of Nazareth," said Philip, "what is the meaning of this burned-down tent? Tribune Philip of Procurator Felix's cavalry wants to know."

One man stepped forward. "This was the tent of Centurion Matthias, until it burned late last night, the third of three fires during the night. Centurion Matthias finished the night in a large tent by the old village center."

Philip turned to a second man present. "Is it true what this man reports?"

"That is what we have heard, yes sir," the man trembled.

Philip turned back to the first man. "Tell me about the other two fires," said Philip.

"Just after sunset, the smallest of tents burned," said the man. "Everyone thought it was just an accident, and maybe it was. I heard the occupants were a simple husband and wife, old beyond child-bearing years."

Philip turned his forehead downward to stare and squint at the man in an attempt to judge his honesty.

"Then around midnight came the big fire, in the old stone house of Daniel, downhill past the village center."

Philip's heart raced at the mention of Daniel's name. "Was anyone hurt?"

"Daniel's son-in-law was killed, and they say that Daniel will not long survive his burns."

Philip was angry at this turn of events. Daniel, the man at the center of his mission, the basis for Philip's planned massacre, was already out of the way. "Where is Daniel now?"

"At his sister's house in the village center," replied the man.

"Man, come with me," ordered Philip, who directed his horse twenty yards back up the path away from the tents and people before turning around to face the man.

The crowd at the edge of the tent city grew as morning onlookers came to see the spectacle of so many uniformed men on horseback. They whispered to each other in nervous anticipation of what might come next. The tent city behind them seemed to come to a halt, focused on Tribune Philip.

Philip angled his horse so that Councilor Marcus up the path could not see. He reached into a saddle bag and pulled an object barely into view and shook it. "Do you hear what that is?"

"Coins," answered the man, both impressed and frightened.

"Lots of coins," said Philip. "They are yours if you carry out one simple task."

The man stood still with a questioning look.

"You see the decorated man at the head of the cavalry behind me? The procurator's councilor?" asked Philip.

"Yes, sir."

"He's not one of my men. We don't need him. We do not *want* him. He's no fighter. If you pull him from his horse as the cavalry walks by, this purse of coins is yours."

The man stood paralyzed by the offer to attack a Roman official riding with a hundred-strong cavalry.

"Well?" insisted Philip. "That man is our enemy, disliked by everyone in the cavalry."

"I— I don't know," stammered the man.

"So be it!" Philip glared at the man. "Be with me or against me – your choice!" Philip was infuriated that his plan was not working. If only he could get one of the pilgrims to attack Marcus or any of the cavalrymen, he could rain a torrent of violence on the entire camp before Marcus or anyone else could stop him. He was determined to see fighting today, and to make these pilgrims pay for the father whom Joshua had taken away from Philip's childhood.

As Philip raged against the pilgrim's refusal, the man's eyes bulged, and he ran away from the tribune, past the other pilgrims and into the tent city.

Philip gave his horse a command, and the stallion reared up on its hind legs and kicked his front legs high into the air, asserting his dominance over the people and animals just downhill. He held the position for moments on end and screamed an incredibly long neigh, forcing one long column of breath vapor upward, where the sun lit it in a brilliant yellow-orange.

Philip gripped the saddle with one hand and laughed, and he lifted his sword from its sheath high into the air.

The men and women at the edge of the tent city widened their eyes at the display of raw animal power and armed force before them.

Tribune Philip waved his sword for the cavalry to advance steadily from behind him. He rode his own horse to the first tents by the path and turned around to meet the advancing cavalry. "Break ranks and gather around!" he ordered.

The pairs of horses pulled off the path and crushed forward into a controlled mob focused on the point where Tribune Philip sat on his stallion at the path's entry into the tent city.

"Cavalrymen, remove your first torch!" As Philip spoke, he removed his own torch from his saddle bag.

Philip turned his head to the pilgrims on the ground behind him. There stood Centurion Matthias.

"Centurion, where have you been? Where are your men and your horses?"

"My horses are on the way. My two soldiers are guarding a prisoner in the village center, after my tent was burned here late last night." Matthias gestured to the burnt remains on the ground. "Two other prisoners just died in that fire." Matthias pointed to the smoke still rising from the dying fire that had consumed Seth's tent.

Tribune Philip pointed to the remains of Matthias' tent beneath him. "Who did this?"

"We thought it was a servant of the richest man here, Seth of Caesarea. But the woman we caught who just burned Seth and *his* tent has confessed to burning mine."

"And the other fires that I just learned about?" asked Philip.

"It must be the same woman, though she denies it," answered Matthias.

"Why did you suspect this rich man Seth?"

"We caught his servant fleeing our fire. From what I understand, Seth wanted control of the pilgrims in Nazareth, just like he has patronized and controlled the church of Joshua in Caesarea. So he tried to remove the obstacles – Procurator Felix's forces, and the man Daniel at the center of the Nazareth pilgrimage."

"And where is Daniel now?" asked Philip.

"In one of the old village houses, breathing his last. I doubt he will live till sunset."

"And the Nazareth Scroll?"

"Destroyed in the fire," answered Matthias.

"What about that horseman we just saw fleeing into the hills on the far side of Nazareth?" demanded Philip.

"An inhabitant of the nearby city of Zippori, sir."

Philip laughed. "Our appearance scared him, did it?"

"I'm afraid it's not that simple, sir," replied Matthias. "He is the servant of Isaac, a rich man from Zippori who arrived this morning only shortly before you did. When your cavalry appeared, Isaac sent him away immediately and on the longer path, to avoid you."

Philip frowned. "Time is short," he mumbled to himself. "Make sure this man Isaac remains here in Nazareth," he ordered Matthias.

"Yes, sir."

Philip pondered the changes in Nazareth. The main reasons for his mission were gone, the Nazareth Scroll incinerated and its author dying. Yet Philip was also charged with disbanding Nazareth's tent city of pilgrims. He held out his torch.

"Light my torch, Centurion Matthias."

Matthias took Philip's torch to the nearest cooking fire and touched it to the coals.

The pitch torch lit up with a small burst of air and burned strong.

Tribune Philip grinned as Matthias lifted the burning torch back to him. He sheathed his sword and took the torch.

"Tribune Philip," interjected Procurator Felix's advisor Marcus in his Latin accent, "this is not necessary."

"*Advisor* Marcus," replied Philip, "I am the tribune, and you are not. Stand aside."

"Beware, Philip," said the councilor. "Even Emperor Claudius in Rome will learn of any great misdeed done here today, and Antonius Felix will have to answer to him."

"Not if the pilgrims provoke us first." Philip grinned again.

"If you endanger my friend Felix's chances of promotion, he will punish you in severest form, to prove himself to the emperor."

"Shut up, Marcus," seethed Philip.

The gathered cavalrymen stared in awe at the momentous debate before them. Some of them scowled and clutched their unlit torches in front of them, clearly eager to join Philip in action against Nazareth's pilgrims and their tent city. Other cavalrymen frowned with worry and dangled their torches at their sides.

By now, the closest pilgrims were backing away. Their nervousness spread across the tent city as its inhabitants sensed the cavalry's ill intent.

"Cavalrymen!" shouted Philip. "Stand by and await my orders! Six of you here in the front, follow me into the village center. We will find this Daniel."

Tribune Philip extended his flaming torch and lit the torches of the six who were to follow him into Nazareth. Then he turned his horse around and led them down the path. Marcus rode right behind them.

"Papa!" Elisha walked up the path. "I finally found Pharisee Gad's tent." Elisha dragged a younger boy by the wrist.

When they reached Aaron at Nazareth's center, Elisha told the boy, "Tell him what you told me."

The boy looked like he was about ten. He wore old, tattered clothes, and tears ran down his trembling cheeks. "What's happening?"

Aaron knelt on one knee, put a hand on the boy's shoulder, and looked at him with reassurance. "New soldiers have arrived, boy, and they have more fire."

The boy lifted his hands to his eyes and cried harder.

"I will try to protect you," Aaron promised him. "Who are you?"

Elisha started to answer for the boy, but Aaron shook his head.

"My name is David. I am an orphan and a student of Master Gad. We walked here from Jerusalem about a month ago."

"Gad dresses you in these rags?" asked Aaron.

The boy nodded.

Aaron sighed. "What news do you have for us? Where is Gad now?"

"We don't know."

"We?" asked Aaron.

"The two of us left here, his younger students. When I woke up this morning, Gad and his oldest student were gone. They took the camel and two oil lamps, too."

Aaron looked up at Elisha and then back to the boy. "When was the last time you saw him? How late in the night?"

"Bed time, sir. We both slept through the night. For the first time ever, Gad gave us wine to drink, at our Hanukkah supper. The other boy is still sleeping. I couldn't wake him up. But Gad and the older one, they didn't drink any."

"Thank you for your honesty, David."

"What's going to happen to me?"

"You're not in any trouble, all right? My son Elisha and I will take care of both of you."

The ten-year-old David nodded and burst into tears.

Aaron reached forward from where he knelt and embraced David. Then he turned to Elisha. "Take David and bring the other boy here. Drag him half-asleep if you have to. Don't leave him in that tent."

"Yes, Papa." Elisha turned and led David away gently by the hand.

Isaac had witnessed the whole exchange and stepped toward Aaron. "You are a kind man, Aaron. I can help those two orphans. It will be easy for me." He made no mention of Aaron's apparent modest means.

"That might be best for them," said Aaron.

Tribune Philip and his half-dozen men approached on their horses, flaming torches in hand. Councilor Marcus and Centurion Matthias rode just behind them.

From where Aaron stood, the bright rising sun was behind the cavalrymen to the right. He and Isaac both raised their hands to shield the sun while they looked up at Tribune Philip.

Philip looked down at Isaac and Aaron. Isaac had the nicer, newer clothes and the freshly shaven beard. Philip asked him, "Who is responsible for all these fires?"

Isaac gestured to Aaron. "My friend here would know better."

Philip shifted his glare to Aaron.

"We just caught one culprit a few minutes ago, tribune," said Aaron. "There beside you, the woman restrained by your own cavalryman. Naomi of Caesarea says she had an old score to settle."

"She burned Centurion Matthias' tent? My cavalry's tent?"

"She denies that one," replied Aaron. "It's only this smoldering fire right here that she claims."

"Bring her here," ordered Tribune Philip.

"No," said Marcus, as he pulled his horse forward. "She has already been arrested, so she is now under my jurisdiction, not the cavalry's. Keep her where she is, soldier. She is my prisoner, and I will deliver her to Procurator Felix."

Philip growled with rage. He started to reach for his sword but stopped himself. Marcus and Felix were childhood friends, and there was nothing Philip could do on that score. "We'll settle that later, Marcus." Philip looked back at the men on the path. "Whose two white horses are these?"

"Mine," answered Isaac.

"And the third one that just left Nazareth by a back route, that was yours, too?"

"Yes, sir," replied Isaac firmly, standing straight and tall.

Tribune Philip whipped his flaming torch back and forth in a frothy sound of fire-wind. Then he leaned forward and brought the torch close enough to Isaac's face to make him sweat from the heat.

"Don't wear your pride with me, man. Why did you send him?"

Isaac faced the flame and did not flinch. "He went to summon Governor Quadratus and his general who are visiting Zippori. They should return in less than an hour."

"The governor? With his general? Damn! Damn, damn, damn!" Tribune Philip threw his torch in aimless anger, down the path.

Aaron held his breath while the torch spun and arced past the goat-hair tents that were steaming as the morning sun dried last night's rain. The spinning torch was crossing the path, into the line of tents on the left. It looked like it was going to hit the roof of one tent, but it disappeared between that tent and the next.

It hit the next tent with a thud. Aaron tensed to race and put out a fire. Then he heard the hissing sound of a flame doused in water. He ran forward to be sure, and he found it extinguished in a puddle of rainwater next to Nazareth's central stream and sewage ditch. The torch had bounced off a tent and rolled down the steep incline into the ditch. Aaron inspected the tent, and found only a smudge of pitch on the dark gray woven goat hair, no flame or sparks. He returned empty-handed to the gathering by Seth's tent.

"It landed in the sewage ditch, sir," said Aaron.

Marcus burst out laughing from just behind Tribune Philip.

Philip's face filled with red rage. He pulled his horse forward, drew his sword, and put it to Isaac's neck.

CHAPTER TWENTY

"I am an official citizen of Rome," said Isaac. As his throat moved to speak, it scraped against the point of Tribune Philip's sword. Isaac felt it, and a drop of blood began to form. Without moving his arms, he slowly lifted one foot and took a step backward, away from the sword.

"Citizen this! Governor that!" shouted Tribune Philip from his mount on the stallion. "How is the Roman cavalry supposed to get anything done?"

"Properly, that's how!" Councilor Marcus shouted back, almost in Philip's face. "Your command here is suspended, Tribune Philip."

"Our orders are to disband this camp by sunset!" insisted Philip.

"And so we shall," said Marcus. The procurator's advisor lowered his voice, but spoke firmly. "They can start soon. But all of these torches are dangerous and unnecessary. Tell your men to douse them, Tribune Philip."

"I'll do no such thing, *Councilor* Marcus," said Philip.

The tribune and the procurator's councilor glared at each other.

Marcus turned to the six cavalrymen behind them. "Douse your torches!"

Philip said nothing.

The six soldiers looked at one another. Then one of them spotted a pail of water, slid down from his horse, and extinguished his torch. The others followed.

"You'll answer for this," sneered Tribune Philip.

"I'll answer to Procurator Antonius Felix." For the moment, as long as the cavalrymen held back at his command –

and as long as none of the pilgrims provoked them – the procurator's man trumped the tribune.

Marcus climbed down from his horse and approached Aaron and Isaac. "We heard what happened to your man Daniel. Is he in one of these houses?"

"He just died," answered Aaron.

"Oh." Marcus looked around for any family members. "Sorry," he said to Aaron.

Philip sneered. He turned his horse around and started to ride back to the rest of the cavalry. "Follow me," he ordered his six cavalrymen.

They paused and looked to Councilor Marcus.

"Stay," he ordered.

Philip turned away and galloped dangerously up the path, forcing people to jump aside for their lives.

Down the path toward Daniel's burned house, about twenty yards away, Elisha and ten-year-old David appeared with Gad's other young student. "We've got him," called Elisha. He and David each had one of the other boy's arms around his neck. The boy staggered half-asleep between them, still drunk from Pharisee Gad's wine.

Aaron shook his head. "Very good. Set him down against the wall here."

Elisha and David put the other boy on the ground, where he immediately lay sideways and fell back asleep.

"What's this?" asked Councilor Marcus.

"Their master gave them wine last night. A Pharisee named Gad. David here says that Gad fled in the night with his camel and his oldest student."

"What is so important about Gad?" asked Marcus.

"We suspect him in the first fire," answered Aaron. "It was at sunset, against this woman Naomi's own tent, and perhaps against me and my sympathy to Daniel and the Nazareth Scroll."

"Complicated," said Marcus. "When was the big fire, the one in Daniel's house?"

"Midnight," Aaron replied.

"And why did you think it was arson?"

"A half-full pot of pitch yesterday evening was emptied some time before the fire – and fresh pitch was spread under an exposed rafter on the side wall."

"Show me," said Marcus.

Aaron led everyone down the path to Daniel's burned-out house. On the near side, perpendicular to the path, was the wall with burnt pitch stains, which Aaron showed to Councilor Marcus, along with the empty pitch pot on the ground.

"Why was this pitch here?" Marcus asked.

"Giant Hanukkah torches," Aaron replied. "For safety, we tipped the poles into the house during the fire."

"Any witnesses to arson against Daniel's house?" asked Marcus.

"None that we know of," said Aaron.

"Did anyone keep a night watch in this tent city?"

"That's a problem. The dead merchant Seth kept watchmen in shifts through the night, but he's the only one – wait! There is another – a native of Nazareth, a slow and simple man named Solomon who lives with his mother. I heard that he wanders around for much of every night."

Councilor Marcus turned to the gathered crowd. "Who here knows where Solomon lives?"

"It's far down there, by the cliff over the valley," answered one man in his forties.

"Here, ride with these two soldiers and bring him to us," said Marcus. "Be as quick as you can."

The man bowed his head to accept the order. One of the soldiers lifted him onto his horse, and they trotted down the path.

Back up the path above the village center came a shout. "What are you doing to my wife?" A man began to run down toward the crowd around Aaron and Marcus. "Naomi! What are they doing with you?"

Naomi looked up from where she kneeled under the heavy hand of Centurion Matthias' soldier.

"Not so fast," one of the other soldiers warned Michael. "Is this your wife?"

"Of course it's my wife!" Michael turned and stared at the dying fire where Seth's tent used to stand. He looked very disoriented. "What's the meaning of all this?"

"I burned Seth's tent, Michael," confessed Naomi. "You know he killed my mother. I finally got justice! But they caught me running away with the fire still in my hands."

"What? I thought Seth's men lit all the fires," he said.

"No, Michael. Except our own tent, I lit them all. Every man of power and wealth, they should all die!" screamed Naomi. She spat at Isaac.

"You killed Daniel?" Isaac screamed. He stared wide-eyed, perplexed and furious, on top of his grief for Daniel.

Michael looked like he was in shock.

Down the path, the two cavalrymen trotted back uphill. Their guide rode with one of them, but Solomon was still missing.

"Is Solomon not at home?" asked Aaron. "He usually sleeps during the day, right?"

"He does," answered the forty-something native Nazarene. Tears ran down his cheeks. "Solomon has been murdered, slit in the throat. His mother, too."

"Nooooo!" screamed Naomi. "Michael, you murderer! You lying scoundrel! You promised you would leave him alone after he saw us ignite Matthias' tent! Solomon never would have told – he was so fond of me. Michael, you horrible excuse for a man!"

"What are you talking about, Naomi?" asked Michael.

Naomi turned to Aaron and looked up from where she kneeled. "I take it back, the part about the other fires. All I did was Seth's tent. I didn't do the rest – they were all Michael's doing. Daniel deserved it, though, from everything Michael told me from years ago in Zippori. Michael and I promised each other, if either of us were caught, that one would take the blame for all the fires and let the other go free."

She looked back at her husband. "You demon, Michael! You burned our own tent, too, didn't you? Give me my punishment, sirs, but do not let this cold-blooded murderer escape. Find Gad – he can tell you. Gad saw Michael when Michael was about to set Daniel's house aflame." Naomi cried some more. "Oh, Solomon! Tender, pure Solomon, just like my brother! Nooo!" Naomi bent her face to the ground and heaved sobs for Solomon, while Centurion Matthias' man held her arms tight.

Isaac of Zippori turned from Naomi to Michael. He stepped slowly toward Michael. He lifted his chin, squinted, and scrutinized the man.

"Daniel never lifted a hand against anyone," Isaac said to Michael. He turned around and called to Naomi. "What was his grudge against Daniel, exactly?"

She lifted her tear-stained face from the ground. "He said that Daniel killed his first wife."

Isaac furrowed his face as his thoughts raced far back through his memory. Suddenly he gasped and snapped his head back to Michael.

Even the pilgrims fending sparks off their nearby tents heard his gasp over the sounds of the ebbing fire of Seth's tent.

Isaac's jaw dropped, and he took a few steps toward Michael.

Michael's face transformed, no longer looking shocked by the charges against Naomi and himself. For a moment, he looked stern and defensive. Then he re-masked himself in a look of confusion.

Isaac stared at Michael, bending his head one way and then another. It had been more than twenty years. Would he even be able to recognize the man? Isaac walked around Michael and the two soldiers who held him, and viewed Michael from all angles.

"His name is not Michael," declared Isaac for all to hear. "It is Uriel. He should have a scar across the palm of his hand."

"Michael has that scar!" shouted Naomi. "He said he barely escaped Daniel's knife."

"That's not how it happened, Naomi," said Isaac. "Is it, Uriel?"

Michael-Uriel stared back. "I don't know what you're talking about."

"Show everyone your hands," said Isaac.

Michael-Uriel did not budge.

"Show us!"

Michael-Uriel lifted his palms for everyone to see. A thick white scar with thin brown edges ran straight across his right palm.

Everyone gasped.

"I know the whole story from Daniel," Isaac began. "All of Zippori learned the story. Uriel here grew up in our city. As he entered his manhood, he fell in love with Daniel's cousin, Rebecca. But she did not love him, and her father very much disliked him. Instead, Rebecca liked Daniel. But Daniel was happily betrothed to his family's choice back in Nazareth – who died far, far too young herself. But this was before all that. Daniel was kind to his cousin Rebecca, but he was true to his betrothed, and he thought Rebecca too young for marriage anyway.

"One day, my father's carpenter – Joseph of Nazareth, the father of Joshua – sent Daniel to buy a new handsaw from the blacksmith shop where Uriel apprenticed. Unknown to Daniel, his admirer Rebecca followed him to the shop and hid behind the back door while he entered the front. Uriel started an argument with Daniel about something trivial, but it built upon Uriel's fundamental anger about Rebecca's rejection of him in favor of Daniel. Uriel hated Daniel. In the heat of the argument, before Daniel knew it, Uriel took one of his master's knives and lunged at Daniel. Standing by the back door, Daniel flung it open and leapt out of the way. But there stood Rebecca. As Uriel fell forward, the knife plunged into Rebecca's belly. She fell over backward, and bled to death.

"Uriel trembled at what he had done. He pulled the knife out of Rebecca while she lost consciousness, and he held it in both hands. Daniel leapt up and grabbed the knife handle to run away with it. Uriel tried to hold onto it, but all he got was the blade, which sliced across his palm. Daniel tried to tackle Uriel, but Uriel dodged him and started running into the alleys of Zippori. He was gone in an instant. We searched for him all day and all night and all the next day. No one ever saw him again . . . until now.

"No wonder you grew a beard, Uriel, posing as a poor man when it suits you," said Isaac. "You almost escaped us again."

"You wretched man! You demon!" Naomi screamed at Uriel. "For twenty years I thought I was married to someone named Michael. It was your idea to come to Nazareth's pilgrimage. You said that this famous Daniel of Nazareth had killed your first wife. If we came to Nazareth, you said, we could both do justice – you on Daniel, Rebecca's alleged murderer, and me on Seth, the murderer of my mother. You deceitful killer! She wasn't your wife, and Daniel didn't kill her – you did! No wonder you always told me I wasn't as good a wife as Rebecca. You never even had another wife – just your imagination about a girl who died before she married anyone."

"I don't know what everyone is talking about. My name is Michael. I was married to a woman named Rebecca in Zippori, and after she was murdered, I moved to work in the port of Caesarea. I can explain my scar. . . ."

"Three nights in a row you tried to set fire to Daniel's house," said Naomi. "The third night it finally it worked, because of all the new pitch he had."

"She's inventing all this," growled Uriel. "So is this man," he pointed at Isaac. "All I know is that Naomi kept going out at night with the coal pan."

Naomi searched the crowd behind Uriel. "There you are – Tabitha, tell them! How I was asleep in your tent when people starting screaming about Daniel's house on fire. Tell them!"

Tabitha reluctantly stepped forward. She fearfully moved her eyes between Naomi and Isaac.

Aaron stood beside them. He thought Tabitha looked afraid of Naomi and uncertain about Isaac.

"Is it true what Naomi says about last night?" Aaron asked Tabitha.

"I don't know if she was asleep," Tabitha replied. "But yes, she was in our tent when the screaming started. I was asleep before that, but my bed on the ground was next to hers. I don't think she could have come and gone without awakening me. She did not start Daniel's fire."

"See!" shouted Naomi.

Tabitha continued, "Also, yes, Michael – or Uriel – he was out when Daniel's fire started, and he did not come back all night. Around dawn, Naomi got up and quietly left, before the rest of us were out of bed. Everything she says seems to be true."

Aaron turned to Uriel. "Who else knew you in Zippori? Who can witness that you were married to a woman named Rebecca, as you claim?"

"They all moved away," Uriel replied. "There's no one left to testify for me."

"It's all lies," said Isaac. "I recognize him. He has the same wicked eyes he ever had, and the same small ears. After he fled Zippori, Daniel testified to us all against him."

"That's enough," said the Councilor Marcus. "Naomi and Uriel, you are both under arrest. You will have to endure each other's company a few days' longer, while we transport you to Procurator Felix in Tiberius."

Marcus turned to everyone else. "Antonius Felix gave orders for the arrest of Daniel and the seizure of the Nazareth Scroll. Both are now gone. There was a third order. This pilgrimage to Nazareth is to be disbanded immediately. Every tent must be struck down before sunset."

Marcus looked to the hills where Isaac's servant had fled. "When the winter sun disappears behind those hills, no tent shall remain standing in Nazareth. Everyone is to pack up and leave Nazareth by sunset."

Tribune Philip reappeared riding his horse down the path with at least a dozen cavalrymen on horseback behind him. Half of them held flaming torches, and the other half all brandished swords. "Any tent still standing at sunset will be burned to the ground!"

From out of nowhere, a pilgrim man ran along the front of the houses up to Councilor Marcus, and swiftly pulled out a knife and stabbed his side.

Marcus collapsed to the ground with a distant look of shock in his face. A blood stain appeared immediately on his tunic. Marcus clutched his side and winced.

Aaron ran to Marcus' side to help.

The assassin dropped his knife and ran back along the front of the houses and then up the path.

None of the cavalrymen tried to stop him. None of them even looked at the assassin, especially not Philip.

"Soldiers, we are under attack!" shouted Philip. "Light the tents!"

The half-dozen men with flaming torches approached various tents by the path, lit them, and then threw their torches into the tent city to try to light others.

Hundreds of pilgrims screamed in unison and ran to the inflamed tents.

All of Philip's cavalrymen now held swords ready, and they started slashing at any pilgrims that approached the flaming tents from the path side where the cavalry was.

Several pilgrims fell into bleeding heaps, and the others ran screaming to the far side of the tents.

"Attack! Attack!" Philip shouted. He held his sword aloft, turned his horse around, and watched his forces his left as they cut down the pilgrims. His eyes were inflamed with excitement, and he grinned from ear to ear.

Without warning, Centurion Matthias reached up to Philip's exposed right side, pulled him off his horse, and dragged his own knife through Philip's abdomen.

As Philip fell to the ground, he did not even attempt to look at his killer. His face turned as white as fine salt, and he clutched at his belly as he slumped to the rocky ground. A second later, bright red blood gushed from his mouth. His body was still, and his open eyes were instantly lifeless.

It was so quick and quiet that the cavalrymen did not notice right away.

Then one of them shouted in wide-eyed shock, "By the River Styx!"

The remaining cavalrymen ceased their attack and looked back toward Philip's riderless horse.

Centurion Matthias held its reigns and pushed it backward until the men could see Philip's body and bleeding mouth on the ground.

Hundreds of pilgrims paid no attention while the camp started to go up in flames, as they screamed advice and orders to each other.

In both boldness and fear, standing alone, Matthias stared at the dozen armed cavalrymen above him on their horses.

"Councilor Marcus, can you hear me!" He kept staring at the cavalrymen.

"Yes," Marcus coughed.

"Order these men to stand down."

Marcus looked confused.

Aaron nudged Marcus. "Do it."

"Stand— down," Marcus managed. Then he continued his shallow coughing.

Aaron looked down at Marcus. The procurator's councilor was in bad shape, but he wasn't bleeding very much. Then he looked up at Matthias in his battle of wills with the leaderless cavalry. Matthias was sweating like crazy and very scared. The cavalrymen could obviously see it. If any one of them chose to face down Matthias, the centurion was done for.

"He said, 'Stand down'!" shouted Matthias. "As do I! As centurion of the Roman cavalry, I command you, sheathe your swords!"

One of the cavalrymen looked furious. He glanced between Centurion Matthias and Councilor Marcus, and he kept his bloody sword ready at his side.

One by one, though, the remaining cavalrymen sheathed their swords. Matthias had carried the moment of decision unchallenged. The cavalry would now obey him. The lone holdout finally sheathed his sword, too.

Isaac leaped onto one of his remaining white horses, lifted his own sword, and shouted to the cavalrymen and frenzied pilgrims alike. "Pull the tents uphill across the path! Let them burn alone on the uphill side!"

Not all the pilgrims could hear him over the screams, but the nearest ones did. They started to do as he suggested. The cavalrymen slowly moved their horses out of the way. Two or three of them even dismounted to help. More and more pilgrims understood the plan, and soon a wave of hundreds of men and women surged up the tent city's slope to pull all the burning tents from the ground and from their poles, and to drag them away. They even tore down unburned tents that stood between burning ones. Like a swarm of locusts, half or more of Nazareth's pilgrims stripped the upper end of the tents from the earth and heaved them into a bonfire on the upper side of the path. The shouting continued, but it was increasingly victorious, and even some screams of burning pain sounded triumphant.

Beyond the immediate pilgrims, the entire encampment raised a single cheer of solidarity, more joyful than militant, unlike anything Aaron had ever heard or imagined. Even Isaac cheered and smiled before bursting into tears again for his deceased friends.

Strangers hugged and even kissed.

Most of the cavalrymen looked relieved, and most of the pilgrims looked ready to forgive them, although scowls of resentment lingered on both sides.

Then someone pointed toward the ridge above Nazareth. Little by little others noticed and turned their heads and pointed to.

The camp fell into a hush of murmurs.

To the piercing sounds of two trumpets, a dozen men on horseback crested the ridge wearing blazons of red and carrying a red flag above them, and they descended the path to Nazareth.

"Governor Quadratus!" shouted Matthias.

"Hooray! Hooray!" Relieved pilgrims lifted their voices in one surge after another of powerful, jubilant cheering.

CHAPTER TWENTY-ONE

Governor Quadratus looked worried as he passed the first tents and led his modest force down the path, past ongoing swells of cheering. Dozens of Felix's cavalrymen stood outside the camp in confusion, and a bonfire of tents burned ahead on the right. The first cavalrymen on the path inside the camp seemed shocked, and some had blood on their swords. Then Quadratus saw several bodies on the ground at the village center – two of them in Roman uniforms.

"Who is in charge here?" he asked. As he looked around, he saw Naomi and Michael restrained on the ground.

The closer pilgrims quickly silenced themselves to listen, while cheering continued in the distance.

"Centurion Matthias, sir." Matthias stepped forward and bowed his head.

"What is going on here?"

"In summary, sir, Tribune Philip attacked first the procurator's councilor and then the pilgrims. We killed him and stopped it."

Quadratus looked at the bloody dagger in Matthias' hand, where he stood over Philip's corpse. "You killed him?"

"Yes, sir."

Quadratus look down at Marcus to the right. "Is he still alive?"

Marcus lifted one forearm off the ground.

"Councilor, can you confirm the centurion's report?"

Against the backdrop of much shouting in the distance, everyone nearby silently awaited Marcus' response.

Marcus tried to speak but coughed instead. "Yes," he finally whispered.

"All of you, prepare to follow us back to Zippori for an investigation."

"Greeting, Quadratus." Isaac stepped forward. "May the native families remain? The only ones implicated were the family of Daniel, who was attacked and killed last night, along with his son-in-law Gabriel."

"On your word, Citizen Isaac?"

"Of course."

"Very well, then," said the governor.

"One more item for your immediate attention," said Isaac.

"Yes?"

"Procurator Antonius Felix has ordered this encampment to be dispersed by sunset tonight. Councilor Marcus here can confirm that. That is the current standing order to the two thousand pilgrims gathered here. What say you?"

Quadratus twisted his mouth to consider this. He looked like he didn't like Felix's order. "Very well, then. I won't remand it. All pilgrims are to depart by sunset."

Word spread through the camp like fire through a field of dry summer wheat. There was no more cheering.

Governor Quadratus dismounted his horse and embraced Isaac in a formal greeting of mutual respect.

Isaac gestured for Quadratus to walk down the path with him alone.

Aaron knew that many of Nazareth's pilgrims would struggle to leave so quickly. Taking down the tents was easy. But no one had planned for food or money or water for the journey of several days back to their respective hometowns. Some had enough, and others did not. After the fires that had spilled Aaron's amphoras of salt, he was among those who did not.

Isaac's servant stepped forward and addressed the pilgrims who remained around their nearby tents. "Pilgrims of Nazareth, many of you have traveled here the distance of more than one afternoon's journey. You cannot possibly make it home by tonight. You are all welcome to tent tonight outside the walls of Zippori. If your tent has survived the fires, you are urged to share shelter with others. After one night, you must journey homeward. Please spread the word."

Elisha and Ishmael looked at each other in awkward sadness. Their bond of friendship from the traumatic night faced immediate separation.

Aaron wondered how he could keep Elisha and Ishmael in touch. He would give this some more thought during their evening together in Zippori.

While Nazareth's pilgrims lowered their tents in the late morning sun, a dozen horse riders appeared on the ridge above. Aaron recognized Isaac's white horse, and he knew this must be the Roman general that Isaac had sent for. Although things were now proceeding calmly in Nazareth, Aaron was glad to see them. The threat of their arrival had helped to sideline the dangerous Tribune Philip in the first place.

The first pilgrims to pack up began their ascent from the Nazareth plateau toward Zippori. After an hour or two, the trickle of departing pilgrims turned into a steady stream. Two thousand pilgrims with their livestock and belongings were anxious to leave in time for the short winter daylight to guide their hour's travel to Zippori.

Aaron and Elisha were among the last to leave, along with Ishmael, Ishmael's mother Rachel, and all five of her younger children.

On their walk to Zippori, Rachel would not stop thanking Elisha and Aaron for all they had done during the night and morning. She invited them to come visit her and her family in Caesarea. With the deaths of both Seth and Boaz, her son Ishmael was the oldest surviving son, and he would inherit a large share of the Seth's vast property and interests. Although Seth had refused Ishmael access to his businesses, Ishmael had observed them carefully. He knew how they operated, including which parts were honest, not based upon bribes and threats.

Aaron thought it would be nice for him and Elisha to visit Rachel and Ishmael and her other children. He would love to visit the Great Sea again, finally after all these years. Perhaps he could expand his business to wealthier clients in Jerusalem and sell them salt from Caesarea by the Great Sea. As long as he could keep serving the poor with cheap rock salt from the Salt Sea cliffs, he might try it.

When Aaron reached the ridge above Nazareth, he turned back for one last view of the place. His thoughts turned to Daniel's daughter Rebecca. She wasn't worldly like Ruth or Martha or even Rachel, but she was smart like Ruth, or even smarter, and pretty and kind. Aaron had no doubt she would observe a full year of mourning. She had livestock and farmland to tend to, minus the two men who had led the work, although other villagers would help, and her father's friend Isaac would look in on her. Perhaps Aaron might see Rebecca again one day as well.

Although Daniel and the Nazareth Scroll were lost, Aaron had learned new things and had met old northerners who knew things about Joshua that were unknown in Jerusalem. Maybe one of them could still help him prove to Martha, the woman he loved, that Saul of Tarsus was wrong – that although Joshua was an inspired teacher, he was not the anointed heir of David and would-be king of the Jews. Aaron had also hoped to use the scroll to confirm that Joshua never claimed to be the gatekeeper of heaven (if there were a heaven), as Saul claimed more emphatically with each passing year. Could Isaac or even Rebecca help him address that claim?

Four miles away, outside Zippori, Isaac sat on his horse and welcomed everyone to camp by the one spring outside Zippori's gates. Moreover, he invited all of Nazareth's fire survivors to spend the night in his vast house in Zippori, including everyone who had lost a tent in the large final fire.

It was the most unusual rich man's house that Aaron had ever seen. As Isaac explained, the fifty-year-old house was under continuous expansion ever since his grandfather had purchased a one-room house as its start. As Samaritans, their family was able to lend money with interest more easily than most, because of the rules against Jews charging interest to other Jews. Isaac and his forefathers kept their rates low, allowed temporary defaults, and rarely pursued debts from heirs. When they turned much of the proceeds back into projects employing the poor, they became the most popular money lenders that anyone could remember. As they purchased surrounding houses and land, they maintained most of the warren of previously separate lodgings for their guests and some tenants, with minor adjustments to integrate them all. When they constructed large gathering rooms, they kept them relatively modest, with low ceilings, simple furnishings, and almost no seat cushions to be found.

After a somber dinner for dozens of guests in Isaac's largest dining hall, Isaac invited Aaron for a private conversation in one of the odd small rooms preserved from previous owners. They entered the windowless room, and Isaac closed the door behind them. A fire already burned in the fireplace, with ample spare wood beside it, and water and wine on a very short table. Both men sat cross-legged on the stone floor, across from each other in front of the fire. Isaac poured two cups of water and two cups and wine.

"To the memory of Daniel and Gabriel of Nazareth." Isaac lifted his cup, met Aaron's eyes with his own, and took a drink. He put his cup on the floor and stared at it, as he silently reflected on all the years and decades of his friendship with Daniel.

"To Daniel and Gabriel of Nazareth," Aaron repeated. He drank from his cup and then held it in his hands.

"Before we left Nazareth, Rebecca told me some about your visit," said Isaac. "How you were sent by the golden-rule Pharisees of Hillel to meet Daniel and to read his Nazareth Scroll, even to copy it for circulation if you could. She said you were particularly interested in whether Joshua of Nazareth ever thought of himself as the next Anointed One, a Messiah and heir to King David."

"That is correct," said Aaron.

"No one will ever be able to replace the Nazareth Scroll, Aaron."

Aaron sighed so hard that his breath rippled the surface of his cup of wine.

"But there is much that I can tell you about the second half of his life, after he started working in Zippori. I traveled with him that last year after he left Zippori for the Sea of Galilee and his final Passover in Jerusalem. For the first half of Joshua's life, two women back in Nazareth can tell you much. One is the old Samaritan woman Miriam, who knew Joshua from the moment she delivered him and heard his first cry, in the very same room in Nazareth where Daniel just died, where Joshua's brothers and sisters were born, too.

"The other woman is Rebecca. She spoke to me before I left this afternoon, and she asked me to tell you that you are welcome to return to Nazareth to continue your quest to learn about Joshua. His youngest brother Simon has agreed to house you, should you ever visit Nazareth again."

Aaron was entranced.

Isaac continued. "For my part, tonight I will speak only briefly. You are welcome to stay in my household as many nights as our conversations last. From the sound of it, your son Elisha hopes to stay here in Zippori anyway, to learn masonry."

Aaron was saddened by this fact. He knew that Elisha was old enough to make this choice, but he preferred that they both return to Jerusalem instead. There Aaron could keep raising Elisha and teaching him the scriptures in the ways of Teacher Hillel, and Elisha could learn stone masonry there, if he wanted. But he knew that was less exciting than all the building projects in Zippori.

"Daniel and I knew Joshua of Nazareth before he was much of a teacher. Yet from the first day, even my father saw that Joshua was extraordinary. He knew the scriptures and had no patience for the patterns that most Pharisees needed to attain such learning. He always understood right from wrong, and he recognized dilemmas where there was no perfect right."

Isaac laughed at one memory. "When Joshua met his cousin John the Essene, also known as John the Baptizer, he was surprised. Before Joshua even had time to shave that morning,

John pulled him out of bed and down to the head of the River Jordan for baptism. All day long after that, John kept staring at Joshua as I have never seen a man stare, before or since. While Joshua talked with friends and strangers and gave his judgments on all sorts of local conflicts there in Philoteria, John just stared into Joshua's eyes in complete silence.

"Some time after the evening meal, John suddenly spoke, silencing all conversation around him. 'You're the one, Joshua. You're the one. We Essenes have been waiting for the leader who will recover Israel from the gentiles, expel the Romans, return the Jews to religious purity, and destroy the Herod family and all other Jews who refuse the strictest laws of Moses. You're the one! Look at how everyone listens to you. You can be our next Moses, our next David and Solomon, the prophet-king to deliver Israel from all corruption and rule it wisely. You are the next Anointed One, the next Messiah!'

"Never did I see Joshua so taken aback as at that moment. His mouth hung open, and he furrowed his eyebrows. Many men and women witnessed John's speech, and they will all tell you, Joshua was stunned. Everyone was speechless. Joshua soon collected himself. It was getting dark. John kept staring at Joshua. For a very long time, at least an hour, Joshua stared back at John, each scrutinizing the other without speaking. Soon everyone went home. We disciples went to our beds and slept. When we awoke at dawn, Joshua was sleeping where we'd left him, but John was gone. We never saw him again."

"After that day, Joshua almost never talked about what John had said. But it seemed to weigh on him. From then on, he joked with us much less, and he seemed to age quickly. He continued teaching and preaching and healing as before, and now and again, he smiled or laughed like before. But as people around Galilee and even Jerusalem asked him about what John had predicted, Joshua retreated into himself and told us he didn't want to talk about it.

"Aaron, Joshua knew he was no king. He wasn't going to drive the Romans from Israel, or the Herod family from their throne, or unfaithful Jews to their deaths. Joshua wanted to remind them of the one-hundred-fifth Psalm, that the entire nation of Abraham, all Jews are the Lord's chosen Anointed Ones, Messiahs. But Joshua also knew that John had set something in motion that could not be stopped. It was already tough for Joshua teaching Jews that the rulers and priests of our times were often wrong. When more and more Jews repeated John's prediction, the authorities only got angrier. Joshua could have stopped it all and returned to a quiet life in Zippori or even Nazareth, but he never changed what he was doing. He knew that what he was preaching was right, at least mostly. Sometimes he thought new thoughts out loud and later continued those thoughts to different conclusions. But mostly, he was on the mark and revered for it. It was his doom, and he knew it – just like the choice of Socrates."

Aaron was fascinated, and he was thrilled to be learning so much more about Joshua than anyone in Jerusalem could imagine. He knew he had to share this news.

When Isaac's servant finally led Aaron to his room for the night, Aaron found Elisha sound asleep after the long night before. As soon as Aaron lay down, he drifted into intense dreams of everything they had just experienced, which blended into all the people and places he had ever known, and ended with the master mason he and Elisha had met at Isaac's dinner.

The next morning Aaron awoke from such dreams to Elisha's excitement about visiting the stone mason's workshop.

"It's finally time, Papa! I finally get to try my hand at stone cutting. Aren't you excited for me?"

Aaron smiled at Elisha's happiness. He knew it was right for Elisha, and he was happy for him. "Very much, son." He was still exhausted from the events in Nazareth, from Isaac's testimony of Joshua, and from the whirlwind of Elisha's potential masonry apprenticeship. As he observed his son's joy, Aaron smiled even more broadly.

After breakfast, Aaron took a long, hot bath in Isaac's house. When he was done, he sat down at Isaac's own writing desk to begin the long letter reporting everything to his golden-rule Pharisee friends in Jerusalem. He had good news: He had confirmed that they were right, and Saul was wrong. Joshua of Nazareth had lived a prophet's life, making no claims about expelling or killing gentiles or lapsed Jews or anyone else, nor about reclaiming David's throne. Joshua had insisted instead that people of all nations love and challenge one another as he had loved and challenged them, and as he had invited them to love and challenge him. In the coming days, Aaron was going to learn more from Isaac and others, and he promised to write again soon.

HISTORICAL NOTES

Year 51 Current Era (CE) and Background

Roman Emperor Claudius, in power from 41 to 54 CE, reigned over the lands of the Jews. From 50 to 60, **Governor Quadratus** was the top provincial political authority for Jewish lands, which he oversaw from the Syrian capital of Antioch to the north. The more local Roman authority over the Jews was **Procurator Cumanus**, based in the port city of Caesarea Maritima in Samaria. It is possible that in the year 51, Cumanus' eventual successor **Antonius Felix** was already deputy procurator or co-procurator for Galilee (historical sources are in conflict). (In 52 CE, Felix replaced Cumanus as procurator for all of Galilee, Samaria, Judea, and Idumea; see Acts 24.)

King Herod Agrippa II, great-grandson of Herod the Great, had direct authority in parts of Syria, north of Galilee. His father Herod Agrippa I had been close friends with Claudius, and the son was personally close to the emperor as well, having spent much of his childhood in Rome; Agrippa was a Roman name. In 51 CE, the twenty-four-year-old Agrippa was lobbying Claudius to expand his authority southward into the former domains of his father.

Jewish priests were those male-line descendants of Moses' brother Aaron who exercised their religious-legal right to the priesthood, numbering about twenty thousand. They could marry and have families. The high priest and the other chief priests supervised the daily affairs of the Temple. The vast majority of the priests were based outside Jerusalem and rotated through the Temple only one week every six months, plus the three annual crowded pilgrimage holidays (for example, Passover), where their duties focused mostly on expert butchering of sacrificial animals, from which they retained a part. The rest of their time, these priests tended to their own affairs and livelihoods, such as supervising their lands and property. Some priests also taught scripture, served as legal scribes and judges, or conducted synagogue services, although these functions were also performed by laymen. Priesthood was defined by worship leadership rotations in the Temple in Jerusalem itself, not by local worship or ministry. Many of the priests were also Sadducees. A few of them were also Pharisees.

(After the Roman destruction of the Temple in 70 CE and the institution of direct Roman rule, the Jewish priesthood quickly dissolved, without its exclusive function of ongoing Temple sacrifices and national religious leadership, although the bloodlines remained recognized. Thereafter, worship in synagogues was led by rabbis, who included many former Pharisees and perhaps many former priests and sons of priests. The Hebrew word "rabbi," which originally meant "my master," was used to mean "teacher" or "master teacher" in the first century. Only after 70 CE did "rabbi" come to mean a Jewish cleric.)

The Sadducees were Jewish traditionalists of disproportionate wealth and aristocratic background who also dominated the priesthood, especially its uppermost ranks in the Temple in Jerusalem. The Sadducees' numbers are nearly impossible to estimate, for lack of historical sources. Their theology was conservative insofar as they recognized only the most ancient religious textual authority – the five books of Moses, to the exclusion of later prophets and writings. The Sadducees did not believe in resurrection (life after death) of the body or the soul, a belief that was a later addition to ancient Judaism from Babylonian and Persian influences, not part of the five books of Moses.

The Pharisees were mostly part-time scholars and teachers and commentators on Jewish laws and practices. As reformers and advocates for equality under religious law, the Pharisees enjoyed widespread popularity (often more so than the wealthy establishment Sadducees, who nonetheless were also widely respected). Most Pharisees practiced other, regular trades and occupations for their livelihoods. They numbered perhaps around six thousand, but they were not a single organized group. Unlike Sadducees, Pharisees believed in resurrection, and they believed in the scriptural authority of many later Jewish writings (prophets, histories, commentaries, etc.), in which ideas of resurrection had first been introduced into Jewish scripture (from Babylonian and Persian influences starting around the 500s BCE). The Pharisees emphasized detailed, pious observance of scriptural laws, including those in later scriptures. In this way, they tried to hold the Sadducees accountable to all the same laws and regulations as applied to the whole of the Jewish people.

Pharisees often self-identified in sub-groupings according to their teachers and their teachers' teachers, and they formed two loose factions. Conservative Pharisees in the tradition of Rabbi Shammai (50 BCE – 30 CE) were the most punctilious about observing all possible points of piety and the law, as they saw them. Comparatively progressive Pharisees in the tradition of Rabbi Hillel (died at an old age in 10 CE) were more likely to recognize the uncertainties of some legal points and were sometimes open to new ideas. Some of the progressive Pharisees were sympathetic to some of the teachings of Jesus/Joshua of Nazareth. (See also "Jewish priests" above.)

The Essenes were radical, ascetic, pietist Jews, numbering perhaps around four thousand. As a group, they were not very influential, but the individual John the Baptist might have been an Essene, and some parallels can be found between the teachings of the Essenes and those later ascribed to Jesus/Joshua. A few hundred Essene men lived in a monastery at Qumran (of the Dead Sea Scrolls). The remainder of this strict sect were distributed across Jewish towns and villages. Among many other rules, Essenes argued for the prohibition of sexual intercourse from the city of Jerusalem. Some Essene writings predicted and prescribed the military expulsion of all gentiles from Israel, and the destruction of all impure Jews who refused to accept the strict rules of the Essenes.

Early Christians in Jewish lands did not call themselves "Christians." (The word "christ" is Greek – see "Names and Translations" below.) For several decades after the crucifixion of Jesus/Joshua around 30 CE, until at least the 50s or 60s CE, most Christians in Jewish lands were also practicing Jews, unlike the non-Jewish Christian converts of Saul/Paul abroad.

Starting around the mid-40s, following the prodding of Paul/Saul of Tarsus, Christian leaders became bitterly divided over whether to remain purely Jewish or to accept willing gentiles as baptized members of their congregations, even when those gentiles refused circumcision and other points of Jewish law. James/Jacob the Just, who was a brother of Jesus/Joshua, together with the disciple Simon Peter/Cephas, initially argued for exclusive Jewishness. Paul/Saul argued for admission of gentiles to Christian churches. His opponents eventually accepted gentiles, in part because of the desires of gentile converts themselves (Acts 11). (See also Matthew 10:5, against gentiles, a proscription that is lacking in the corresponding narratives in Mark 6 and Luke 9.)

Another difference between these two factions was in emphasis of self-definition and of the requirements for eternal salvation. James/Jacob the Just, the brother of Jesus/Joshua, emphasized works to help the poor and needy (Letter of James). Paul/Saul emphasized belief in the divine intervention of Jesus/Joshua (e.g., Philippians 2:6, Galatians 2:15, Colossians 1:15-20).

We know almost nothing about early Christians in the northern region of Galilee where Jesus/Joshua practiced most of his ministry, including Nazareth and Zippori.

The Samaritans were a Hebrew people who worshipped the same Lord and followed the same laws of Moses as did the Jews, but with a different capital, a different temple, and a different high priest. The Samaritan-Jewish rivalry dates perhaps to the era of the two kingdoms or earlier (Isaiah 11:13) The Samaritan-Jewish schism as such was essentially about whose high priest and temple were the legitimate authority for the Hebrew religion. In geography, theology, and written Hebrew script, first-century Samaritans appear to have been closer to Biblical Hebrew origins than were the Jews.

First-century Samaritans numbered in the hundreds of thousands, in the range of 10 percent to 30 percent of the population of Palestine. Like their first-century Jewish neighbors, the Samaritans spoke Aramaic. They lived mostly in their own towns and villages and on farms in the region of Samaria, in the mountains and valleys midway between Jerusalem and Nazareth/Zippori, but some Samaritans settled elsewhere. Their historical capital was Shechem (near modern Nablus). The respective Samaritan and Jewish books of Moses were the same in almost all important aspects, with otherwise minor differences. Like the Jewish Sadducees (in contrast to Pharisees and to much of the Jewish population), the Samaritans did not believe in resurrection (a foreign import), and like the Sadducees, they regarded the five books of Moses as the sole authoritative scripture.

The ancient Samaritans called themselves "Israelites," of the tribes of Ephraim and Manasseh. Their capital Shechem was the center of most or all Biblical Hebrew history from Abraham through Moses and Joshua and beyond. Probably Abraham's Mount Moriah (as Mount Moreh) and certainly Jacob's Well are very close to Shechem. The Lord's Commandments to Moses were initially to be housed in a temple on Mount Ebal, above Shechem (Deuteronomy 27:4).

The Samaritan-Jewish schism has been corroborated by genetic studies including today's very small Samaritan population (less than one thousand remaining). Most of the male lines of Jews versus Samaritans are genetically distinct, but more closely related to each other than to other long-term ethnic neighbors. The respective Jewish and Samaritan male priest lines are even more closely related.

In 51 CE, a Samaritan-Jewish guerilla war was being waged in border areas, the result of escalating vendetta murders and village massacres.

The crucifixion of Jesus/Joshua took place around the year 30 Current Era / A.D.

First-century Nazareth was tiny, barely a village, limited to about three dozen somewhat scattered houses.

Palestine is an ancient name for the lands from the Mediterranean Sea to the Jordan River and somewhat beyond. The word origin of "Palestine" is from the Philistines and Philistia, the non-Jewish people and land in the Old Testament along the east-southeast coast of the Mediterranean. References to this much smaller territory predate written Hebrew, as found in ancient Egyptian "Peleset" and Assyrian "Pilistu." By the 400s BCE, the ancient Greeks were applying the term Palestine to the broader area, for example by Herodotus, and a century later by Aristotle. In the first century, though, the lands of Palestine were usually referred to by specific province names, not as a whole. The modern country of Israel does not correspond to the ancient geographical concept of Israel, which was the Old Testament northern kingdom (including much of today's Palestinian West Bank), separate from Judah in the south. (See also notes on Samaritans-Israelites versus Jews-Judahites, above.)

We do not know when the first Biblical gospels were written. The oldest surviving copies date from about one century after Jesus/Joshua, or later, roughly the same amount of time as from the First World War to the present 2013. Scholars are divided over whether any parts of any surviving gospel might have been written as early as 51 CE. Most scholars think that none of the surviving gospels were written, or at least completed, before 70 CE.

Jesus/Joshua had almost one hundred disciples, if not more. Each of the four gospels names twelve disciples. However, the four gospels do not agree on their names, and a total of fourteen disciples are named in the combined lists of the twelve. The Gospel of Luke discusses a further seventy disciples, although it does not name them (Luke 10). *Witness*'s disciple Daniel and his Nazareth Scroll gospel are plausible and fictitious.

Saul/Paul of Tarsus never met Joshua/Jesus. The fictitious letter by Saul/Paul in *Witness* is modeled on, and partially taken from, the first few verses of Saul's/Paul's letter to the Galatians, including chapter 1, verse 9: "if anyone proclaims to you a gospel contrary to what you received [from me], let that one be accursed!"

Sources include:

Bart D. Ehrman. *The New Testament: A Historical Introduction.* New York: Oxford University Press (various editions).

Everett Ferguson. *Backgrounds of Early Christianity.* Grand Rapids, Mich.: Wm. B. Eerdmans (various editions).

Clayton Lehmann. "Palestine: People and Places," incl. map, http://sunburst.usd.edu/~clehmann/erp/Palestine/people&p.htm, accessed 9 July 2013.

Megan Bishop Moore and Brad E. Kelle. *Biblical History and Israel's Past.* Grand Rapids, Mich.: Wm. B. Eerdmans, 2011.

E. P. Sanders. *Judaism: Practice and Belief, 63 BCE – 66 CE.* London: SCM Press, 1992.

Peidong Shen, et al., "Reconstruction of Patrilineages and Matrilineages of Samaritans and Other Israeli Populations From Y-Chromosome and Mitochondrial DNA Sequence Variation," in *Human Mutation* 24:248-260 (2004).

NAMES AND TRANSLATIONS

Jesus of Nazareth was known during his life as Yeshua, his Hebrew-Aramaic name, the same original name as some of those called Joshua in English translations of the Old Testament. In *Witness*, he is called **Joshua of Nazareth**, the closest modern English equivalent to his actual Hebrew-Aramaic name.

The letter J was invented only around the year 1300 CE, and it was gradually substituted as the first letter in many English names over the next three hundred years. Before that, no one in England or anywhere else was named "Jack" or "John" or "Joshua" or anything including the letter J. For example, King "John" of Robin Hood lore and the Magna Carta in 1215, was called "Ion" (something like yohn or yahn) in the medieval Middle English of his times.

Saul/Paul of Tarsus answered to both of his names both before and after his conversion (Acts 13:9), according to whether the speaker used Aramaic (Shaul/Saul), as in Nazareth and Jerusalem, or Greek (Paulos/Paul). (He did not "change" his name after Damascus.)

Joshua/Jesus of Nazareth is one of many "Christs" in the Bible. The Greek word "Christ" means "the Anointed (One)," as does the Hebrew word "Messiah." The Bible uses the same term, the Anointed = Messiah = Christ, to refer to many different people, including eight specific individuals in addition to Joshua/Jesus. The Bible states very clearly that there are multiple Messiahs/Christs in Jewish-Christian history. *Neither the Hebrew word nor the Greek word connotes deity.*

English translations of the Bible arbitrarily translate only some instances of "the Anointed" into English, while leaving others untranslated in the original Hebrew "Messiah" or Greek "Christ." By contrast, the Greek translation of the Old Testament uses the Greek word "Christ" for "the Anointed" in all Old Testament instances of the original Hebrew word "Messiah." The Christs of the Old Testament include even the non-Jewish Persian King Cyrus Christ = King Cyrus the Messiah = King Cyrus the Anointed.

Old Testament Christs = Messiahs = "the Anointed"	**Bible Verse(s)**
Abraham Christ, **Isaac** Christ, and **Jacob** Christ	Psalm 105:15
possible reference to all Prophets as Christs	Psalm 105:15
all Jewish Priests as Christs	Leviticus 4:3, 16:32
King **Saul** Christ	1 Samuel 24:6
King **David** Christ*	Psalm 132:17
King **Solomon** Christ	1 Kings 1:39
King **Zedekiah** Christ	Lamentations 4:20
possible references to all Davidic Kings as Christs	Psalm 20:7, Habakkuk 3:13
King **Cyrus** Christ (Persian, not Jewish)**	Isaiah 45:1
a predicted "Prince Christ" in the future	Daniel 9:25-26***
possible reference to all Jews as Christs	Psalm 105:15

* According to the Psalms and their attributed author King David, he too was a son of God (Psalm 2:7).

** King Cyrus was the beneficent ruler who defeated the Babylonians, liberated the captive Jews, and allowed them autonomous rule back in their homeland.

*** Some English translations maintain the untranslated Hebrew word "Messiah" in Daniel.

Names in Biblical Times and Changes in Later Translations

original Hebrew	first translation Ancient Greek	Modern English
Yeshua	Iesous	Joshua (Old Testament), Jesus (New Testament)
Yaakov	Iakobos	Jacob (Old Testament), James (New Testament)
Yochanan	Iohannes	John
Miriam	Maria	Miriam (Old Testament), Mary (New Testament)
Kefa	Cephas, Petros	Cephas, Peter
Yehuda	Ioudas	Judah (both Testaments), Judas, Jude (New Testament)
Shaul	Paulos	Saul, Paul
Shimon	Simon	Simon
mashiach	christos	messiah, christ, anointed (one)
Pelesheth*	Palaistine	Philistia, Palestine
Tzippori	Sepphoris	Zippori,** Tzippori, Sepphoris

* Pelesheth/Philistia was specifically only the area of the Old Testament Philistines, a small fraction of the subsequent Greek-Roman designation of Palestine.

** Zippori was the city just four miles from Nazareth. Its population in 51 CE was around 30,000 or more, probably the second-largest city in first-century Palestine after Jerusalem.

Author Jeffrey Vanke holds a Ph.D. in history from Harvard University. He lives in Roanoke, Virginia.

coming soon: the first sequel to *Witness*

also by Vanke: *The Berlin Deception*

31736586R00124

Made in the USA
Lexington, KY
23 April 2014